DEVOURING
DARKNESS

By

Martyn Rhys Vaughan

Print ISBN 978-1-8384289-5-2

Published by
Llyfrau Cambria Books, Wales, United Kingdom.
*Cambria Books is a division of
Cambria Publishing.*
Discover our other books at: www.cambriabooks.co.uk

Cover design by Terry C. Evans (www.terry-evans.com)

The cover photo-montage includes images
from www.dreamstime.com by © Dirk Ercken. Candle image
courtesy of Anugrah Lohiya

REVIEWS
Other books by Martyn Rhys Vaughan

The Cave of Shadows

'Martyn Rhys Vaughan's book is shot through with big ideas and big questions, and in that sense it's a bold and brave undertaking. The book picks up pace and is never less than entertaining, but the fact that the speculation is set squarely within the realms of possibility means that the book which at first seems like science fiction melding with fantasy might actually be a guidebook, a guidebook to chaotic times ahead.'
J. Gower, review in Nation Cymru.

Hideous Night

'The storyline hums along at a cracking pace' spreading mayhem in all directions. And the title is a quotation from Shakespeare. What more could you ask?'
Chris Green – RFOH, review from Amazon.

'Reading this brilliant novel was just like riding a scary roller coaster! I found myself hanging on with an enjoyable sense of dread throughout the many thrilling plot twists and turns, as I the reader was propelled along with each new page to what seemed like an unavoidably hideous climax.'
Wayne Edwards, review from Amazon.

Doom of Stars

'In this brilliant novel, Vaughan imagines a futuristic world engulfed in chaos and devastation as climate change wreaks havoc on the planet... Meticulously crafted, fast-paced, and richly imaginative, the novel makes for a necessary read for both lovers of YA and adult dystopian fiction.'
LitandCoffee, review from Goodreads.

'Greetings! Dear readers. I recently came across this marvellous science fiction by Martyn Rhys Vaughan, and I must say that this is really fantastic in every way. The storyline is just so gripping and the plot is perfectly created...Turn the pages to witness the dystopian situation, an era of great apocalypse.'
Jessica_bookreviews, from Instagram.

Martyn Rhys Vaughan is an intrepidly bold adventurer in the realms of speculative fiction, who can take the reader along with him to extraordinary places, offering glimpses of a what-might-be future of ruined metropolises and a climate out of kilter and of an earth doomed to hear the sounds of humanity's sand-timer running swiftly out of so much as a grain of hope.
Jon Gower Nation.Cymru

Author's Foreword

This is my second book of short stories, following on from my debut collection *Domains of Darkness*.

In this one, I have experimented with a variety of formats; mainly to do with the length of the stories.

Opinions differ as to the word counts which define the various categories, but by the most usual definitions *Cycle of Thanatos* qualifies as a novella, or at least a novelette.

On the other hand, *Keeping Pets Is Fun!* and *It Happened On The Stroke Of Midnight* are Flash Fiction.

Regarding the subject matter, the stories follow the template set by *Domains*, in which happy endings are not guaranteed. Indeed, the tales herein definitely lean to the noir side of the spectrum, without, I hope, being gratuitously unpleasant.

That said, I did essay a few attempts at humour.

Whether or not I succeeded, I leave to you, my reader.

If you enjoy this collection, try out my recent novels:

Quantum Exile: A man finds himself swept from reality to reality in the Quantum Multiverse; getting further and further from his home. But he gradually becomes aware that malign forces are following him, eager to take a secret from him that he doesn't even know he possesses.

The Cave of Shadows: There comes a day when Jon realises that there is something wrong with the Universe. At the same time Shana reaches the same conclusion. Both warriors must face terrible dangers before they meet and together decide to face the dread ruler of their world, the fearsome Korok.

Hideous Night: A laboratory accident allows Marius Larsen to become aware that the human race is being preyed upon by parasites from another dimension, which hide in the shadows. How can he convince a sceptical world of his terrible discovery? Is there an ally who can aid him in his quest to free the world of these monsters?

Doom of Stars: The world is ending. It has been prophesied many times but this is the reality. For young Kalli, the pain is doubled for everyone believes it was one of her own family that has brought destruction upon humanity. But Kalli has in her possession a mysterious sphere that tells a completely different story. But can it help Kalli and her lover escape the Doom of Stars?

Check them out at:
www.martynvaughan.co.uk

'Time, devourer of everything, and you hateful old age, you destroy everything and bit by bit you consume all those things which have been mangled by the teeth of passing age.'

- From 'Time the Devourer' by Ovid.

'O, Thou unreplenished lamp! Whose narrow fire
Is shaken by the wind, and on whose edge
Devouring darkness hovers! Thou small flame,
Which, as a dying pulse rises and falls,
Still flickerest up and down, how very soon,
Did I not feed thee, wouldst thou fail and be
As thou hadst never been!'

- From 'The Cenci' by Percy Bysshe Shelley.

CONTENTS

KEEPING PETS IS FUN!

'Aren't they cute!' she said, leaning over above their box and watching them scurry away into the corners at her sudden appearance. 'So soft and tiny and cuddly!'

'And quite intelligent, too,' her friend said, 'see how they've built themselves a little group of dwellings in that corner. I gave them some straw and mud and they made it all by themselves.'

'How about those baby ones you were going to give me?' the first one pressed.

'Oh yes,' her friend replied, 'they've had some new ones recently.'

She leaned over and picked up some of the tiny babies. 'Look at the mother,' she cooed, 'trying to get them back. She can't understand that we won't hurt them.'

She placed them in one of the cups of her friend's third anterior tentacle.

'And to think,' she wondered, raising herself to her full height of seventy-five metres, 'that when we first came to this planet, evolution had stopped at these little things. Remember how they shot at us with their silly weapons?'

'Yes,' her friend breathed, staring in wonder at the wriggling babies, 'humans really are cute!'

IT HAPPENED JUST AS THE CLOCK
STRUCK MIDNIGHT

They weren't going!—I couldn't stand these people anymore. How dare they come into my house like this—as if they actually owned the place?

I stared at them one by one: the fat middle–aged bloke with the comb–over; the bottle-blond woman who'd definitely had one too many facelifts (which had left her looking permanently surprised); the obnoxious twins who had spent all evening running around, shrieking and trying to make the other cry—all too successfully, unfortunately. It was all very depressing.

What was the world coming to, I wondered. How was it such an unprepossessing lot could have amassed enough money to think they could move into an area like mine?

I looked again at the man as he drank yet another glass of wine. I watched his jowls quiver as he slurped the stuff down. He looked like the type who would be happier with a pint of wallop down at the "Dog and Duck", where he would spend all evening giving everyone his opinions on where the Prime Minister had gone wrong or how the local football team had been robbed of promotion.

The screaming twins ran past me and collided violently with the dining room table. The glasses on it quivered violently, and I was certain that one was going to fall onto the plush carpet.

I directed a silent frown at them but only the cat noticed and uttered a kind of strangulated noise, which made the woman turn to look at it and give it a consoling pat.

I tried walking up to them and remonstrating in their faces, but they looked straight through me.

I gave up – how dispiriting to be haunting your own house when only the cat can see you.

CRIMSON CLOUDS

The clouds are always crimson these days. I liked them at first because they were so colourful. I'm not very good at colour names so I'm not sure whether all the clouds are crimson. I suppose some might be scarlet and some might be vermillion. I know that the clouds aren't always the same colour. Sometimes I can see two clouds side by side and it's obvious they're not the same. But, as I mentioned, I'm not very good with colour names. I say crimson clouds, but they might all be scarlet clouds or vermillion clouds. I suppose in the end it doesn't matter with all the other things I've got to worry about.

The clouds are still there at night but, of course, then they don't have any particular colour, except a kind of dull grey. Far more interesting at night are those wonderful auroras we have these days, with so many differing hues mixing and multiplying. It makes you wish that the skies weren't quite as cloudy as they are, but, as I said before, there are lots of things more important to worry about.

For one thing, I wish the clouds would drop rain once in a while. That store of bottled water I dug up out of the ruins won't last forever, especially as some of the women are now pregnant.

We are also running short of wood to burn now that everything's so damned cold. I really don't know how we'll cope now that all the trees have gone.

That damned incident between America and Iran—who could have known that in four short weeks it would lead to nuclear war? I suppose we should be grateful that at least when all the radioactive dust was put into the air it gave us all these pretty clouds.

But sometimes I find myself wishing for white clouds on a blue sky.

And a bit of rain occasionally.

SHAME THE DEVIL

'What's that?' I asked my wife, staring at the complicated apparatus on the table. It had lots of coloured lights that were flashing rapidly and it was giving off an unusual purring noise like a large cat.

'It's the latest portable lie detector,' she replied, fixing me with a cold accusatory stare.

'A portable lie detector!' I said, trying to laugh the whole thing off, 'why do you want that?'

Her stare became colder and I began to feel slightly alarmed.

'I need one because I want the truth out of you, once and for all. It costs £100 an hour to hire this, so let's make it quick.'

I spread my arms wide and tried to look innocent. 'Would I lie to you?' I said.

'Yes is the simple answer to that,' she replied, 'I've caught you out in lies before.'

'But I've told you everything!' I protested, 'what more proof can I give?'

'You are a slippery customer,' was her only comment, 'you're so crooked you could hide behind a corkscrew. You wouldn't know the truth if it came up and bit you in the bollocks.'

I wagged a finger at her. 'Now, now, there's no need for language like that. What is it that you so desperately want to know?'

Her gaze seems to go right through me and come out the other side, taking my vital organs with it. 'I want to know if you've started seeing Annette again.'

I showed my annoyance. 'I've already told you a hundred times—I have NOT started seeing Annette again.'

For reply she pointed to the purring, flashing thing.

'Sit there and take the test please. The machine is infallible. I'll finally know if you're a liar.'

I tried glaring at her. 'If I do this, I want a fulsome apology from you.'

She shrugged. 'If the machine clears you—you'll get one.'

I sat at the table and she put what seemed to be a headphone set on my head and then pressed a few buttons. I felt a warmth start at the level of my ears and then work inwards to meet in the centre of my brain.

I stared at a row of three LEDs on the machine, all of which were cold and black at the moment.

In the manner of a Grand Inquisitor, she said, 'Have you started seeing Annette again?'

With a voice as dry as sandpaper, I heard myself say, 'No, I have not started seeing Annette again.'

I watched the lights. One snapped on. Green.

Then the next. Green.

The last one seemed to take forever to come to life but finally it too flashed.

Green.

I tore the headphones off and stood up angrily.

'I think you owe me an apology!' I thundered.

She was all over me then, kissing me and smiling weakly.

'I'm sorry I doubted you, darling. It's all my fault! I'll make it up to you, I swear. Anything you want!'

'You'd better,' I growled, 'you don't know how upset I am. I'm going out for a walk and when I get back I expect you to be upstairs in that special lingerie I bought for you. Some chilled champagne will be a good idea, if you know what's best for you.'

She nodded meekly. 'Yes of course, whatever you want.'

I grabbed my raincoat and marched out, slamming the door so hard the hinges almost tore off.

I walked down the wet street and slowly a great smile spread across my face.

A liar, me! Me?

Of course, I was far too clever for that machine.

I was telling the exact truth when I said that I hadn't started seeing Annette again.

It was the exact, absolute truth.

Because I had never stopped seeing Annette!

THE POSTCARD

Felicity hesitated outside the entrance to the house. Should she go in? She twisted some strands of natural blond hair around a finger, twisting it back and forth in her indecision. She was displaying a wry smile as conflicting thoughts tumbled through her mind, because Felicity liked to think that she was a hard-headed young woman, not given to flights of fancy or any form of superstition.

She would gladly walk under a ladder, couldn't give two hoots about how many magpies she saw in the morning, and she absolutely adored black cats, whether or not they crossed her path.

But there are some things which are very close to a girl's heart; some things she absolutely has to be sure about.

And Dominic was one of those things. She had to be certain. But she could hear the scornful comments coming from her brain; hear it mocking her. What was it saying now? Ah yes: You are a silly little girl aren't you? And there's me thinking you were a clever, rational young lady who wasn't afraid of the dark, who didn't care what star sign her friends were, and here you are standing outside the house of a fortune-teller, afraid to go in, afraid to stay out. Shame on you girl, shame on you!

But she could also hear words of encouragement from her heart, words that she liked to hear, wanted to hear.

What was it saying now? Ah yes: *What harm will it do, Felicity? No-one will ever know—it's just a bit of fun, isn't it? And if there should be something in it...*

'I'll do it!' she said out loud in a strong, firm voice, which gave the young man who happened to be passing her at that moment quite a start.

There was a sign on the green-painted door which read: I'M MADAME MANFARIEL. IF THE DOOR IS AJAR, COME STRAIGHT IN!

The exclamation mark at the end of the words gave her a

kind of reassurance; it seemed so friendly!

So, in she went, blinking a bit in the dim hallway. There were several doors flanking the hallway, but the nearest bore a hand-written sign which read: YOU'VE COME THIS FAR SO COME RIGHT IN!

Once again, the sign seemed to indicate to Felicity that the writer was a kind, friendly person, so she obeyed the instruction and, after giving a slightly timid knock, she walked right in.

The room was even darker than the hallway and for a moment she wondered if this was some kind of trap and that she would soon be waking up in a distant harem as the Sultan's new favourite.

But then she heard a voice emanating from one of the larger shadows opposite.

'Don't be afraid dear,' said the voice. Felicity judged by its timbre that its owner must be a woman of somewhat advanced years, so all nervousness departed from her thoughts.

'It's a bit dark in here,' she said, moving into the room, moving very slowly in case she banged her shins.

'So sorry, dear,' the woman said, and Felicity could just make out a hand tugging at a pair of lace curtains that had been drawn over a window behind the large shadow.

As the afternoon sun entered, Felicity could see that the woman was indeed of advanced years (or rather, years that seemed advanced to someone like Felicity, who had only just entered into the springtime of womanhood.)

As she stood there in the gloom, Felicity desperately tried to remember the name on the door of this house.

'Ah, it's—it's Madame Mandrake, isn't it?'

'Madame Manfariel,' the other said with a gentle, slightly amused intonation. 'Please sit down dear. I assure you that I don't bite.'

Felicity obeyed. Now that her eyes had adjusted to the gloom, she could see that Madame Manfariel was a small, rather corpulent woman whose wrists were covered in gold-coloured bangles and whose head was crowned with some kind of turban from which a few grey strands had escaped. On the table between them, Felicity could see what appeared to be a large spherical object, but as it had a cloth over it, she could not identify it.

'How can I help?' Madam Manfariel enquired, her face wrinkling in a pleasant manner with her great smile.

Felicity was suddenly struck dumb. It seemed ridiculous, even infra dignatum, to discuss her feelings with a stranger. Her mouth opened slightly but no words emerged.

Manfariel's smile achieved what had seemed impossible and became even broader. 'It's about—shall we say, "affairs of the heart", isn't it?'

Felicity's open mouth opened even wider as her jaw dropped.

'Yes, but, but—how did you know?'

'My dear, when an attractive lady, who is as young as you quite obviously are, comes to me, what else could it possibly be?'

Felicity blushed, hoping that her reaction would go unnoticed in the gloom.

'Yes, you're right, of course. It's, it's about...' She gathered up her strength, 'it's about Dominic.'

Madame Manfariel leaned back in her vast armchair.

'Tell me all about him, my dear.'

Now that she had said his wonderful name, Felicity felt that a dam had burst in her emotions.

'Oh, Madame, he's absolutely wonderful! He's tall, handsome as—as' (she could not think of a worthy comparison) 'as the most handsome man in the world! And his Daddy's very, very rich. Something to do with Private Equity—I don't understand it, you know. And he's going to take me all over the world in his Daddy's yacht while he's waiting to inherit, and...'

'My dear,' Manfariel said, raising a chubby finger to slow the outpourings of emotion, 'He sounds wonderful. So wonderful that I can't help but wonder why you're not with him instead of me.'

Felicity took a deep breath. This was the moment of truth.

'Well, Mummy doesn't like him very much. In fact, she doesn't like him at all.'

'And why would that be?'

'Well, Dominic's got a bit of a reputation with, with…'

She couldn't bring herself to say it, and sat motionless, frozen into silence.

'Everything said here is in the strictest confidence, my dear.'

'Well, Mummy says he's got a bad reputation with women. She says he picks them up, takes his pleasure with them, gets his fun, if you know what I mean, and then dumps them. Cuts them off completely. Has nothing to do with them.'

'And is there any truth in this?'

Felicity felt herself flushing again, but this time in righteous anger. 'No, he's not like that. Well, he used to be like that, but he's changed now. That's all in the past. He says I'm the only girl for him, that he loves me with all his heart!'

'That's excellent,' Manfariel purred, 'so if you're so sure of him why are you here?'

'Because he wants to take me away for a long weekend to a place he loves down on the South Coast, near some place called Durdle Door. He's just bought a lovely little village down there, and he wants us to have the whole place to ourselves, just him and me.'

'And?'

'Well, I know what he wants to do and I truly want to give my heart to him; to show Mummy that he's capable of True Love. True Love with me! As soon as I'm back home with my little cat I'm going to send her a postcard telling her how wrong she is!'

'And what do you want with me? Am I invited?'

Felicity laughed. 'No, no, of course not! But you can see the future, can't you? I want to know that everything will be wonderful! Look into the future and tell me!'

Madame Manfariel stared at her young customer for a moment.

'It is a little dangerous to know too much.'

'Please Madame Manfariel,' Felicity said. She leaned forward and held the other woman's hands. 'I must know.'

Manfariel nodded. 'I understand. But I will tell you only what I think is best for you. There's an old saying that I remind people of at times like this: One must suffer the laws of things, not merely observe them. I will decide what is best for you at this delicate stage of your emotional development.'

And without any further conversation, she removed the cloth from the spherical object, revealing it to be a large crystal ball. She looked into it, her large, red-nailed hands making strange movements over it. Her eyes flickered from side to side as if she was watching events unfolding before her eyes in the crystalline depths.

Then she said, 'It is done,' and leaned back.

Felicity squeezed her hands together and said in almost breathless voice, 'Yes? Yes? What did you see?'

Madame Manfariel said, 'I have seen your postcard.'

'Yes? Yes?'

The older woman leaned closer. 'My dear, it is important that you go. You will learn many things that are necessary for your emotional development, your development as a woman.'

Felicity clapped her slim hands. 'That sounds wonderful! I can't wait.' She reached for her purse. 'How much do I owe you?'

Madame Manfariel waved dismissively. 'Don't worry about that, my dear. This one's on the house. Your growth as a mature woman is my reward. Off you go.'

'Thanks for everything!' Felicity said, 'I'm so glad I had the courage to come in!'

Madame Manfariel watched as the girl left the room and she smiled a small, sad smile.

She had indeed seen the postcard.

And, of course, it was blank.

A ROOM WITH A VIEW

Norton was staring at his wall video when they came for him.

It was a lovely scene showing a waterfall dropping from a high granite cliff into a wide, blue-green plunge pool, half-hidden by tumultuous vegetation.

Norton had heard the soporific white noise murmurs of the waterfall while he leaned back in his armchair with eyes half-closed. He had known that if he stood up and approached the wall so close that his nose was almost touching the image of tumbling white water, the noise would become a distant thunder.

But he liked the sound of the waterfall to be just this pleasant, restful, distant murmur.

 Occasionally as he sat there, he could hear the plaintive cries of birds as they flew past the waterfall; some he knew were so brave that they nested behind the tremendous cascading curtains of water and spray.

He loved the waterfall video but occasionally he would change the scene so that sometimes he could watch the sunset colours fluctuate over the ribbed surface of Uluru or watch the archer fish shooting down their insect prey when those creatures dropped too close to the swirling green currents of the Amazon.

The sudden opening of his door was not entirely a surprise to Norton: he suspected that perhaps he had gone too far in his recent blog criticisms of the Council. No doubt they had tired of his continual demands for more democracy; after all, it had happened before. He could not complain that he hadn't been warned that the next time that he transgressed his punishment would be more severe. Still, was it necessary for them to come in so violently that the door crashed against the wall with a force that must have damaged the hinges?

'Norton!' the nearest of the two security guards roared, 'Up! The Council Leader wants to see you!'

Norton looked the two over. As usual, they were big burly men; obviously chosen for muscle rather than brains or tact.

11

He got up slowly, almost lazily, knowing that it would infuriate them.

'Couldn't he have sent a message on the communicator?' he asked sweetly, giving the small TV monitor on the desk a casual glance, 'you two must have something better to do. Like learning to read, perhaps?'

The nearest guard took a step towards Norton, raising a fist as he did so but was held back by the one behind him.

'Better not,' his companion said, 'the Leader doesn't like people taking the law into their own hands.'

The first guard glanced back as the other, then back to Norton and then nodded.

'You're right,' he said and then added, with a wolfish grin, 'I don't think Mr Norton here knows exactly what he's let himself in for this time.'

Norton shrugged, switched the wall video off and left his room with both guards walking directly behind him.

The corridor was well lit, and pleasant woodland scents were being wafted from invisible vents so all three men were aware of gentle breezes blowing softly in their faces, bringing the fragrances of deep, black loam, of gently trembling green leaves and the nodding heads of flowers. This scenario was familiar to them, and so they marched on, with the guards occasionally prodding Norton in the small of the back if they decided his progress was too slow.

Suddenly the fragrances changed and became totally different; instead of the sounds and scents of a woodland glade there came the sharp tang of a marine environment; they could smell the salt in the air; hear the cries of the gulls and the rhythmic pulse of the waves.

This was a rare treat, and all three stopped instantly, waiting for the next phase.

It was not long coming: the walls of the corridor changed from their pleasant, creamy-white opacity to display a marvellous vista of a mighty ocean showing great waves rising and falling in aquamarine ridges topped with crests of sparkling ivory.

Wandering albatross sailed serenely above them in the sparkling azure dome of the sky, high above the raucous gulls. And then they saw it: in the blue distance a great humpback whale breached the surface, raising its colossal body high above the swell before plunging back in a great cascade of spume.

The three men stood transfixed until, far too soon, the sea faded, and the curving white walls of the corridor returned.

'Wasn't that something!' the first guard breathed, turning to Norton. The wonder of that spectacle had momentarily wiped away the power relationship between them, and for a few moments, they were united in the warm embrace of remembered beauty.

It didn't last; no sooner had Norton begun to express his agreement when the expressions of the guards hardened and they resumed their distant, officious manner.

'On we go,' the first said, and added with what was almost a leer, 'we don't want to keep the Leader waiting, do we, Norton? That might make him even angrier with you than he is now.'

Norton said nothing, trying to hold on to the memory of what they had seen for a few moments longer.

But he could not because shortly they were standing in front of the Leader's door.

A red light above the door flashed for an instant, and Norton knew it was detecting his presence.

'Please come in Mr Norton,' a deep, powerful voice said, and then, presumably addressing the guards, 'Thank you, gentlemen, you can resume your normal duties now.'

The door opened automatically and Norton entered the Leader's sanctum.

It was plain and functional, with only a few chairs in front of a large desk. One wall was hidden behind a bookcase, whose shelves were buckling under the weight of the books piled upon them. And behind the desk in a large, undecorated chair sat the Leader.

He was a man whose physique matched his voice: large, powerful, commanding.

13

He stood and indicated one of the chairs.

'Please sit down, Mr Norton. It is regrettable that we meet under these circumstances—again.'

Norton accepted the invitation and he and the Leader sat down simultaneously.

'I agree,' he said, 'all you have to do is accept my suggestions and we can never meet again.'

The Leader smiled humourlessly. 'I see that you still haven't grown up, Mr Norton. This is very tiresome.'

'Democracy is tiresome, Leader? I fail to see how.'

'How do you think we got to be in this situation, Mr Norton? Through people disagreeing, squabbling, arguing—each one thinking he alone has the right way, the only way. And when others disagree, finding that the only way to silence them is through violence.'

'And your way?'

The Leader stared at Norton, and the latter felt his self-assurance, his certainty begin to ebb away.

'One man, Mr Norton. One man who decides and by the force of his being, the strength of his will, guides and controls the others so that there is no more in-fighting, no more factionalism.

'I am that man. And I will not let immature dreamers like you drag us back to the old ways. The ways that got us to where we are now.'

Norton did not speak—after all, what was the use? They had had this conversation before.

'And so,' the Leader continued, 'we come to the unpleasant topic of punishment. I have decided to give you a period of solitary confinement.'

Norton was unmoved: he had survived more than one episode of that punishment before. He was ready.

The Leader was about to say more when the wall on Norton's left suddenly burst into movement and colour.

A green hill appeared with a slightly cloud-spotted blue expanse behind. The field of view dipped down until a small

14

cluster of trees appeared. The view closed in on a single tree and in the branches they could see a jay feeding a brood of voracious chicks, which were frantically begging for food from their harassed parent. The view tracked to the right until a red squirrel appeared, hanging head-down on the trunk of the tree.

Both men watched, silently entranced, until the vision faded and was replaced by the blank wall.

'I have wondered whether I should increase the duration of those vignettes,' the Leader said softly, 'but then we'd never get any work done.'

He shook his head as if to throw off cobwebs and then returned his stare to Norton.

'Ah yes, your punishment. Solitary confinement. Two weeks. In a room with a view.'

Norton could not suppress a gasp. It felt as if a great cold hand had suddenly enveloped him and was crushing his life force. His hands began to tremble as he extended them towards the Leader.

'With a view? No, no, this can't be right! I haven't done anything that bad! Please, I would like time to think—maybe my opinions are a little too extreme, I...'

But the Leader was already turning away.

'Actions have consequences, Mr Norton. And this is your own, personal, consequence.'

***

Two hours later, Norton stood in the room. There was a chair, a table and a simple bed.

There was a lavatory in the centre of the room.

There was nothing else; no books, no monitors. Not even a vase with a flower in it.

Just the curving bare, white walls that enclosed him in a colourless, featureless dome.

And then the walls began to grow transparent as he had known that they would.

All around him, wherever he looked, images of what lay beyond the dome began to come into view.

And he could see it; in every direction—he could not escape it.

Everywhere he turned it was the same: the grey, twisted, shattered, blasted ruin of what had once been a verdant land and was now a lifeless, sterile desert; a desert that was both poisoned and poisonous—the horrific aftermath of the One Day War.

In the distance, he could see the broken stump of what once had been a great building, the windows long ago blown in, leaving just black holes like empty eye sockets.

Nearer in the cratered grey ash, still resolutely visible, were the remnants of burned human rib cages, sticking out of the ground like black twigs.

He slumped bonelessly onto the floor of his room, covering his eyes with shaking hands.

He knew he would never challenge the Leader again—even if he were to emerge a sane man from the Room With A View.

A NEW START

I don't know what made me follow them.

From a distance they looked like any other couple.

I was sitting with a carafe of Chateauneuf du Pape outside Andre's when I saw them on the other side of the street.

It was a sunny day and the sky was the rich, deep blue you only get in Provence. The smell of the market was in the air, tantalising with its messages of ripe fruit and fresh meat, mixing promiscuously with the salty tang of the nearby harbour.

I had no intention of doing anything that day; just sitting there outside the café with my carafe of wine, indulging in one of my favourite activities, namely people watching. And what better place to do that, than in Marseille? There you can see the whole gamut of people from around the great inland sea:— Italians, Arabs, Cypriots; even the occasional white-skinned Englishman, seeking refuge from his eternal drizzle in the dazzling sunlight of the Mediterranean.

But back to my couple. As I said, they looked like any other pairing from where I sat, so there was no reason whatsoever to leave my carafe and my fruits-de-mer and start following them.

And so I was puzzled with myself. Why was I doing this? Had I turned into some kind of stalker? And yet, despite those doubts, I felt compelled to follow.

They stopped outside various shops, gazing longingly through the windows, and even went into one.

I waited on the other side of the street until they came out, and then, as they moved off, fell in closely behind them.

Now that I was closer to them, I could see that they looked strangely familiar, especially the woman. Where could I have met them? How did I know them? I had not been in Marseille long and I was still building up my social circle.

Finally, they stopped outside a café not far from the harbour and ordered coffee. It was not long in arriving and I could see that the man had a tall Americano and the woman a cappuccino.

Now you may think that I was becoming a little obsessed with this couple, but those are exactly the coffees that my wife and I always order. Just a minor coincidence, you might say, but I felt a peculiar tension gradually take hold of me.

I had to get a better look at them.

Pretending to look at the various fishing nets and lobster pots that festooned the shop fronts, I gradually moved closer, exuding what I hoped was an air of complete indifference to everything but the sun-blessed scenery.

But as I passed them the warm Provencal air seemed to be replaced by an Arctic blast; one that sent a stiletto of ice into my heart.

For I did know the couple: one of them was my wife, laughing as she sipped her coffee and occasionally raising her hand to shield her eyes from the dazzling reflections off the slow, green swell in the harbour.

And the man? Yes, I knew him as well. Even better than the woman, you might say.

For it was I.

I was sitting there with my wife in that sunny street by the fishing boats.

I was rooted to the spot, almost standing over them, almost touching my wife's bare shoulders.

But for some reason they did not notice me or wonder who was the owner of the shadow that had fallen over them.

With a great effort I moved away, my heart hammering.

Was this insanity? Had I suffered some devastating breakdown that had destroyed my mind?

I turned the corner of the street; no longer wishing to see that weird couple.

I sat down outside a café on the very edge of the harbour, resting my head on my hands. Who was that man, and more importantly, why was my wife associating with him; laughing at the things he said, smiling at him; reaching out to gently touch his hands as if she was with me? I would have to go back and confront them!

'Monsieur?' a man said, very near to me. It must be the waiter.

I raised my head. And then jumped up, sending my chair flying.

For I knew the man who had spoken; the man standing next to me in his waiter's uniform, patiently waiting for my order.

The man was me.

I stared at him for a few moments and he stared back at me, apparently unperturbed by looking at himself. Puzzlement grew on his features.

'Monsieur?' he said again, pointing to the menu in the window.

I said nothing but moved quickly away, not knowing where I was going; not caring where I was going. Just away from the man.

But how could I escape from my madness?

One man who looked like me I could explain, even if it meant my wife was unfaithful. But two?

I walked along the seafront. Although the sun was beating down from near the zenith, I felt no warmth. It seemed I was alone on a great plain of ice and the raucous cries of the gulls had been replaced by the moans of a pitiless wind.

I was so lost in my thoughts that I was unaware of my surroundings. I could have walked into the water and not realised it.

But in fact I collided with a man walking briskly in the other direction.

I turned to him, ready to offer my apologies—but the words died in my throat.

The man I had walked into was—myself.

He glared at me but made no remarks on our apparent identity. 'Look where you're going, you idiot!' were his only words and then he marched away.

I watched him go; the last shreds of belief in my sanity marching with him.

There could be no doubt now. I was insane.

I knew not what to do; where to go; who to turn to for help. How could there be help for someone as mad as me?

As the day wore on, I saw myself, more and more frequently.

The men hauling boxes of fish off the boat. They were all me.

The man directing the traffic—it was me.

The man in the car, that I nearly stepped in front of, was me. He shook his fist at himself and then drove on.

The greasy beggar sitting on the pavement with his box of coins in front of him was me. He clutched at my trouser leg as I passed, begging for money, but did not recognise me.

I gave him nothing and walked on.

Eventually I just sat on the harbour wall and watched them all.

At first there were still a few men who were not me, but as the sun began to decline I could no longer see a single man who was not me.

I saw three policemen, who were all me, drag a protesting violent drunk, who was also me, into their car and drive away.

Then I stopped looking.

There was nothing I could do. How can one escape from oneself?

I would just wait for this madhouse to come to an end in its own good time.

As I sat there on the harbour wall, my head in my hands, shivering in the sweltering heat, I became aware of a change. Normally the harbour at Marseille is not the place one would choose for a quiet afternoon. Normally it is a cacophony of sound as the crowds go about their business; some activities legal, others definitely illegal.

But all that had stopped.

There was no noise.

None whatsoever.

I slowly raised my head from my hands and looked around.

Everywhere I looked I saw myself, carrying out every trade imaginable in a busy seaport.

Or at least they had been, for now every motion had ceased. They were all completely motionless, as if the pause button had been pressed on a video.

Feet were poised a few centimetres above the ground as the act of walking had not been completed; mouths were open in conversations but lips were not moving.

And it was not just the people. Two of me were in the act of throwing and receiving a large fish and there it was, motionless in the air, halfway between them. Above them, seagulls were somehow nailed to the sky, their beaks open soundlessly. Every wave in the harbour was still, forming a surface of corrugated green glass.

I looked at the weird diorama emotionlessly. This must be the end I thought.

So be it.

But then my peripheral vision caught a movement; a single movement amidst stillness.

I turned and saw myself walking towards me. I shrugged, and sat back down, turning to look at the still and silent water.

But he sat down beside me and gently touched my shoulder. I started and swivelled to face him.

He was looking at me with a gentle, but somehow sad, smile.

'Who are you?' I said, my throat so dry I could hardly speak, 'What has happened to me?'

He nodded and said, 'I'm afraid we owe you an apology. None of this should have happened.'

'And what has happened?' I said.

He looked around and I followed his gaze, hoping to see something of vast importance.

But he looked back at me and said, 'All of this. Marseille, the Mediterranean, Europe, your world—none of it is real.'

I stared at him and waited for him to continue.

'This world, your whole existence: it is a simulation running on our computers. Your world is not three billion years old; we started the simulation about three years ago and we've been monitoring it ever since. I'm sorry if that comes as a shock to

21

you. It must be unsettling to learn that you are simply lines of code. I thought that the least I could do is explain it to you in person.'

I stared at him. 'Then you are…'

'One of the programmers, yes I am,' he finished for me, 'I don't look anything like this, of course. The real world is nothing like the world you thought you grew up in. I can't explain it to you—we have no common points of reference.'

I stood up. 'Why did you do this! Why did you create thinking beings who believe that they are real but are nothing more than software? Why?'

'We have been a little thoughtless,' the other me said, 'I'm afraid we underestimated the ability of our emulations to become sentient beings. We run this simulation and many others purely for research; studies in social psychology, if you like. We create problems and see how our software beings deal with them. A few months ago, we created a pandemic to see how long it would take you to adjust to it. The next challenge would have been an asteroid collision. We never intended for anyone to actually suffer. I am sorry to learn that you do suffer. We hadn't foreseen that.'

I glared at him, feeling the desire to take him by the throat and shake him out of his god-like calm. But I knew it was pointless; he too must simply be an avatar; a software construct.

'And why all this duplication?' I snarled, waving at the silent surroundings, 'Why all these "me"s?'

'I'm afraid that there is a flaw in the software. It creates all the human beings that you see around you but for some reason it has started duplicating one particular model—you. Obviously, a society consisting of just one or two people is of no value for our studies, so we have to correct the flaw.'

'And how will you do that?'

'We will take the system down. I believe you are familiar with the method: you call it switching off and on. However, we will also take the opportunity to check the coding.'

'And will that restore things? Will I get my old life back, even though I am merely a simulation?'

His smile became sadder. 'I'm afraid we can't guarantee that. If we have to adjust the coding, we will probably start again. Which means that you won't be in the new version.'

'How long before you take it down?'

His eyes were filled with pity, pity for me, pity for a thing of shadows and moonbeams.

'In a few minutes' time. Once again, I'm sorry.'

But then something occurred to me.

'Thank you for your concern,' I said, 'But tell me one thing: how certain are you that you and your people, with all your cleverness, are not also simulations?'

His smile vanished.

THE WHEEL OF TIME

The wheels of the Heavy Goods Vehicle spun as it slowly inched its way up the hillside road. Rain was falling in a sheet of grey misery, making dull rainbows around the vehicle's headlights and turning the road into a glistening river in which those headlights were reflected in ribbons of wavering yellowish light.

The driver spun the wheel as the ponderous vehicle came to a turn in the road. He rubbed the back of his hand across his face and felt his coarse facial hairs prickle the flesh.

This was where all those accidents had occurred, he thought to himself. It looked like a normal enough road to him. Fifteen years in the business and not so much as a scratch on any vehicle he had driven in all those years; not so much as a dent.

He reached the brow of the hill and slowly descended the other side, the great weight of the steel bars pressing heavily down on the slowly revolving wheels.

The greengrocer's van swept along to the crossroads.

What a day! The driver thought, *I hope I can get home quick.*

As he approached the crossroads he realised that this was where all those accidents had happened.

He shrugged.

Accidents happen all the time. But not today.

The HGV had been gaining speed imperceptibly with every wheel revolution.

The driver automatically applied the brakes; slightly, expertly, with fifteen years of faultless driving behind every small muscle movement.

Yet he was worried. The heavily laden vehicle was travelling faster than it should be. He pressed more firmly on the brake pedal.

Nothing.

He tried again and heard the wheels screech in complaint

24

but the foot of the hill seemed to rush up to meet him as the massive vehicle hurtled on with ever-increasing speed.

This was serious!

He turned to the door, unclipping his safety belt as he did so and pulled the door handle.

Nothing.

It would not open.

He turned back to the windscreen just in time to see a small greengrocer's van appear in front of him.

The driver of the van became aware of the scream of tortured brakes a few seconds before he reached the crossroads. Then a huge vehicle seems to leap out of the curtains of swirling rain like a metal predator pouncing on its prey.

He jammed on the brakes.

Nothing.

The glare of the HGV's headlight filled his cabin. Then all was lost in an explosion of noise, the sound of rending and buckling metal.

And pain. There was pain.

The two vehicles had met.

The van was tossed as a tangled heap across the road, hurtling over and over in a whirlwind of flying metal shards.

The HGV spun around on two wheels, then crashed onto its side as the steel girders broke free from their fastenings and punched their way through the cabin. Then it toppled over and slid for a few metres along the shining road, the still spinning wheels flinging the rain back into the sodden air.

***

Richard Cross Ph. D. looked up from his glass of Nuits Saint Georges as a light shadow fell over him, cast by the warm glow of the log fire which flickered reassuringly in its vast inglenook fireplace.

He saw a tall young man standing near him bearing a

distinctly haggard expression. The white line of a recently healed scar was displayed sinuously on his left cheek.

Cross raised an eyebrow. 'Yes? I don't seem to know you and this is a Members-Only Club.'

The young man gave a nervous smile.

'I usually work in the kitchens but this is my day off.'

'And you chose to spend it in your place of employment. That seems a little eccentric.'

'I came in today because I knew this is the day you spend in the club. May I confirm that I have the honour of speaking to Richard Cross—the Psychic Investigator?'

Cross placed his glass on the table and waved at the armchair which faced him.

'You have that honour.' He smiled. 'Please sit down. You look as if you're about to fall down.'

The young man looked immediately gratified and accepted the offer.

As he sat down, he took a quick look at Cross, seeing a confident looking man in his late thirties; lean, angular, grey-eyed, bearing a clipped moustache and with raven-black hair showing the slightest hint of recession at the temples.

He suddenly realised that he must have been staring, as Cross leaned back, placed his fingers together, tip to tip, and said, 'Well, what can I do for you? And before you enlighten me, may I enquire as to your identity?'

'I'm Ralph Thomas, sous-chef here.'

'Indeed. I'm sure I must have enjoyed many of your dishes. My compliments to the sous-chef. But what can I do for you— in return, so to speak?'

Thomas looked hesitant for a few moments as if unsure of what he was about to say.

'I was cut-up pretty badly in an RTA some months back. On the Marlton crossroads. Do you know of the place and its history?'

Cross stroked his moustache absent-mindedly. It was a habit of his of which he was unaware. He tended to do it when the conversation was not of any interest.

'I believe it's an accident blackspot,' he said after a long pause, 'Quite a few bangs there I believe.'

'Twenty-eight bangs,' the younger man said, bristling slightly at Cross' obvious boredom, 'Ever since they built that new road. Twenty-eight bad bangs. Each one involving two fatalities.'

'That's very unfortunate. But I still don't understand why you're telling me this instead of the Local Authority.'

'Mr Cross, investigations show that every one of the vehicles involved was in perfect condition, and from witness evidence it is clear that there were no obvious driver errors. The vehicles involved appeared to accelerate towards each other. On several occasions, the drivers were seen trying to escape from their vehicles, as if they had lost all control.'

'I still don't understand why you have interrupted my post prandial reverie, Mr Thomas. I am not a traffic flow expert. Nor am I an M.O.T. Specialist.'

Thomas leaned forward, the flickering red glow of the fire seeming to light another fire in his gaze. Cross found himself held in that gaze, despite his earlier insouciance.

'Mr Cross, I was a witness at one of those accidents. I saw the two vehicles both accelerate towards each other even though the weather and road conditions were perfect. There was absolutely no reason for what happened. A flying shard of metal tore my face—a few centimetres higher and it would have blinded me. It was as if something had not wanted me to see the event but had not quite succeeded.'

'Somewhat melodramatic, Mr Thomas.'

'You think so? I've checked up. Every one of those smashes has occurred at 7:30 AM on a Monday. Every one. I'm not a road traffic analyst nor am I a statistician but what do you think the chances of such a pattern occurring naturally? Twenty-eight times?'

Despite himself, Cross found that a flicker of interest had begun to burn in his mind. He also leaned forward.

'Are you suggesting that there is something…' He paused,

as if weighing the consequences of his next utterance before committing himself, 'something—supernatural involved?'

Thomas showed the flash of a grateful smile for an instant.

'I am suggesting that. And I am certain that these accidents will go on, time after time, with a terrible slaughter unless someone can do something about it.'

Cross leaned back, taking his gaze off the younger man. Automatically, his hand reached for the wineglass and as he sipped the red liquid he ran through his engagements for the coming month.

Nothing that couldn't wait.

Instantly he decided.

'All right,' he said, returning his gaze to the expectant sous-chef, 'I'll see what I can do.'

***

'This is where the accidents occur?' he said, turning to Thomas.

'Yes. Always at the intersection.'

Cross looked up and down the roads. There was nothing unusual about them; the layout looked perfectly rational. One of the roads was on a slope, but not a particularly severe one. If this was an accident blackspot through bad design, then the carnage would be much worse at some other locations which had inferior layouts.

Except it wasn't.

'And always on a Monday at 7:30 AM?'

'Yes. Obviously not every Monday, but when they do happen it's always that day of the week and at that time.'

Cross nodded and Thomas saw that his expression had changed since they had arrived; the planes of his features had hardened into a display of flinty determination.

'I'm sorry I doubted you, Mr Thomas. This is not natural. It shouldn't be happening. Yet it is.' He looked around for a moment and then back at Thomas. 'Your place is not far from here, you say?'

Thomas nodded. 'Just five minutes away.'

'Good. I mustn't be too distant from this locus. Let's go.'

Just over five minutes later, the two men were in Thomas' flat. The blinds were closed and only a dim light penetrated to reveal Cross sitting in an armchair, with Thomas looking down at him with an expression which revealed that he was beginning to think he'd made a bad mistake in getting involved with this unusual companion.

'Sit yourself down, please,' Cross said, 'but kindly be absolutely silent when you have done so.'

Cross sat back and closed his eyes. His breathing began to alter slowly, becoming deeper and more regular.

'This is a perfect place, Mr Thomas,' he murmured, apparently drowsy. 'The air is alive with psychic energies—or, if you prefer pseudoscience, ESP influences. You see, when the mind receives a violent shock it emits a form of radiation, a radiation not to be found in the electromagnetic spectrum. This radiation does not travel through space and remains associated with the location of the event, but it is transmitted through time. It is a kind of memory of the trauma which generated it. When another mind encounters that field of energy, it relives the event that generated it—to a certain extent. These are the "ghosts" that we chill our spirits with. Through training, or, as in my case, natural ability, some minds are more receptive than others. Lay people call us "mediums". Without vanity, I believe I am among the world's best—but we shall see. I do not expect people to take my word for it; I prefer to demonstrate the truth of that assertion.

'I am now going to remember the event which is plaguing our modern lives and…'

His voice faded into silence.

His pulse slowed.

Before Thomas' concerned eyes he became completely silent and motionless.

Thomas did not dare to approach him but was sure that if

he had, that no sound of breathing would have been detectable.

He sat down and waited.

And waited.

***

'Oh, Marcellus,' the young woman sobbed, resting her head on his burly shoulder, 'It is a cruel world that we have been born into when the gods torment us because we dared to fall in love.'

She was a slight, pale skinned Celt, beautiful as are many of the women of the Britons, especially when they have just blossomed into womanhood. A mass of raven-dark hair cascaded over one bare shoulder, and her dark brown eyes were brimming with tears.

The man was a soldier of Rome, tall, broad and strongly featured. His massive chest was protected by a gleaming bronze breastplate and by his side hung the dread, stabbing short sword known as the gladius; a sword which had sent many a hostile native to the dark halls of the Otherworld. His helmet was lying in the straw, unnoticed as he stroked the woman's tear-stained face.

'We will find a way,' he murmured, 'the gods will relent. Have we not made all the proper observances to them? Did I not offer them the heart of the deer I had slain, the one I had brought down especially for them?'

'But the druid,' she said, looking deep into his eyes, 'he cursed us. He said whatever we did we could not escape the geas he laid upon us; that we would never find peace as long as we were together. All the druids hate you men of Rome, Marcellus, with a hatred that can never be quenched, never die!'

Marcellus smiled grimly. 'Much good their spells and incantations did them when we landed on the Isle of Mona and hunted them down like sheep. We laid them on their own altars and ripped out their guts with our blades. No gods descended to save them then, as I recall. I thought we had rid this earth of their contagion but some of the creatures escaped.'

'Escaped to curse us and me in particular,' she replied. Her Brythonic name was Vindomora but she had accepted the Latin "Alba", as Marcellus had found her native name too barbarous. 'And your father as well…'

'My father?' Marcellus looked dispirited, 'I told him that our peoples are now reconciled together and desire only peace, but..'

'But,' she completed for him, 'You are High Born and I—what am I?' Her breasts heaved under the thin shift with the intensity of her emotion, 'I am just a low born Briton, an uncultured savage, a barbarian. I cannot quote Virgil or Horace, and that damns me in his eyes.' She stood in an angry burst of energy and looked down on him as he lay there on the straw. 'High Born, Low Born—what does it matter to those who love each other! The same colour blood flows in our veins; we feel the same pains. We are still man and woman! Why should anyone enjoy happiness if it is denied to us? I hate the gods!'

Marcellus stood and made as if to push her away but instead brought her closer. In his arms she felt light and fragile, almost insubstantial, a faery woman, woven from mist.

'What do I care for nobility or the ravings of deluded priests! I care only for you, Alba!'

At that moment the door of the barn crashed open and three Roman soldiers burst in.

'Marcellus Magnus!' one yelled, 'Your father desires your attendance. But first he commands you to put this sow of a Briton to death with your gladius—immediately!'

Marcellus retrieved his plumed helmet from the straw and thrust it onto his head.

'That I will not do. Perhaps you'd like to take her from me, Aurelius?'

He reached for his sword and brought the weapon out from its scabbard in a blur of fierce steel. Aurelius laughed and, lifting his own sword above his head, leapt forward, bringing the death-dealing blade down at his opponent's throat.

There was the ring of clashing metal as Marcellus interrupted Aurelius' swing with his own blade and in the next instant it bit into Aurelius' neck, sending him crashing into the reddening straw.

'You killed him!' one of the others gasped, 'A Roman like yourself—for a barbarian!'

For answer, Marcellus leapt towards them, gladius stabbing out like the tongue of a deadly snake.

They turned and ran.

'Come Alba,' he called, pulling her towards him, 'We must go now! My father will kill me for this!'

They ran out into the courtyard. The sun was rising like a bloodied eye behind grey banks of cloud, and in the trees beyond the villa birds were greeting the dawn with entrancing melodies.

But only anger, fear and apprehension were in the minds of the lovers as they raced towards the waiting chariot. Two horses stood in their harnesses, snorting and pawing the ground in their eagerness to be on their way.

Then a crowd of soldiers, led by a bald noble in a white, red-fringed toga, poured out of the villa as the couple climbed into the chariot. With a flick of the reins it shot away from them.

'Murderer!' the noble roared behind them, 'you are no longer my son! I call the furies down upon you and the creature beside you!'

Marcellus and Alba did not look behind them as the chariot swept on down the wide Roman road and as the villa disappeared into the green folds of the southern British landscape Marcellus placed his lips on the trembling ones of his companion.

'For you I would fight all of Rome,' he whispered, 'let my father and the whole miserable tribe of druids do their worst!'

'But where now, Marcellus?' Alba panted as she cast a first, fearful glance behind her.

'Londinium!' he replied, 'and a ship to Gaul where I have friends who will gladly take us in! Then we will be free—free to laugh and love!'

The chariot seemed to leap forward, faster and faster at those words.

***

The walls of Londinium, with a mass of white buildings behind them, came into view beyond a slight hill.

'Not far now, my love,' Marcellus said, allowing the horses to slacken their headlong flight slightly.

She looked up into his face with the adoration she had only felt before when bowing before the idols of her tribe among the harsh hills of the Brigantes. He was so strong, so magnificent— almost like a god himself!

The horses had dropped to a quiet trot as they reached the crest of the hill and suddenly before them lay Londinium in all its majesty!

Alba drew in her breath in a short gasp.

Londinium was vast! —Surely it could not be the work of mere men!

The chariot began its descent of the low hill.

The horses suddenly seemed to leap forward as if being pursued by wolves. Marcellus frowned and tried to reign them in but still they plunged onwards, snorting and turning foam-flecked muzzles back and forth.

Then they were at the foot of the hill and he turned to speak to his lover.

Suddenly a great cart heavily laden with amphorae appeared from a cloud of dust, bearing down upon them.

Marcellus turned the chariot to pass on its flank but it was too late. It was struck a heavy blow and keeled over. Roman and Briton were tossed out like dolls and the next instant the cart toppled onto them.

When the baying of the horses and the screech of the wheels had both died away Marcellus managed to turn his face toward Alba.

'We will meet again in your Isles of the Blest,' he managed to say, before blood filled his lungs.

And then they died.

***

The Mind once named as Cross stirred in the darkness.

So that's what happened, it thought, this was the outcome of the geas of the druid and the curse of the father.

And thus the tormented souls were seeking a retribution for being robbed of the happiness they had been expecting; the bliss that had been snatched away at the last moment. In their bitterness and despair they were forcing their fate onto others.

Well, there was only one thing to do.

The Mind gathered all its strength and power, reaching down into depths of being; into dark strata of existence normally forbidden to mere mortals.

There was a flash of spilt fire, flames that blazed without heat or sound.

And before Thomas' astounded eyes, Cross vanished from the armchair in modern day London.

***

Cross lifted his head. There had been soft grass tickling his face. He moved into a crouching position and saw before him a soft, green landscape framed in a blue sky in which only a few, soft-contoured clouds were drifting. A dusty road was just a short distance away and at the nearby foot of the hill was the crossroads he seemed to know well.

I still have the abilities, he thought with self-satisfaction, *I wonder what Thomas thinks has happened!*

Suddenly there was no more time for thought. He heard the chariot behind him and spun around to see it hurtling towards him. Automatically he raised a hand to indicate that they should stop, and then realised the meaninglessness of that action.

Instead, he brought the power of his mind to bear upon the horses.

He dipped into their brains and there he saw only terror and gibbering horror.

No wonder they would not stop in their headlong flight.

He sent his power into their turmoil, and in a blaze of light that only he and they could see, he drove those phantoms of fear from their minds.

Then he sent an imperious command into the churning equine minds: STOP!

As swiftly as they could, the horses obeyed and the swaying chariot came to a halt.

Marcellus drew his gladius and made to jump from the chariot onto Cross but even as the deadly blade slid out he and Alba looked away, drawn by the sight and sound of the heavy cart thundering past just below them.

All three watched the cart as it rumbled on towards Londinium.

Marcellus stepped down from the chariot and bowed towards Cross.

'I thank you stranger,' he said, 'we are in your debt. If you had not stopped us…'

Cross looked inwardly for a moment, seeking guidance. His time here as a physical entity was limited: soon he would be pulled back to the twenty-first century. As he had expected, there were other Minds nearby, watching him; some benevolently, others less so. He quickly borrowed the knowledge of demotic Latin from one of the favourable Minds and looking back to Marcellus said, 'You must hurry from here, Marcellus. Your father is close behind and his plans for you are not pleasant.'

'How do you know my name?' Marcellus asked, his eyes narrowing, 'your manner of speech is strange. Your clothing…'

Alba had joined them and she looked up at Cross with doubt clouding her features; doubt tinged with another emotion—fear, perhaps.

'Are you a god?' she said in little more than a whisper, 'the way you stopped the horses. And your attire is so strange.'

'No,' Cross said. (*They have to get moving!*) 'I am just a friend. Please hurry.'

'At least, tell us your name!'

'Cross.'

'Cross? What strange names you Britons have.'

35

'He is not a Briton,' Cross heard Alba whisper to Marcellus, 'we do not speak like that. And we certainly do not dress like that!'

'Your friendship is welcome, stranger, whatever distant land you may come from,' Marcellus said, offering a huge hand. Cross ignored it; physical contact with people had to be avoided or he risked being marooned in Roman Britain.

'You really should go,' he said and to emphasise his point he gestured in the direction of the white sprawl of Londinium.

Marcellus nodded and he and Alba climbed back into the chariot. They gave him one last wondering look and then the whip cracked and the chariot resumed its flight to the capital of Britain.

Cross knew that their departure had been just in time. He returned the borrowed knowledge to the watching Mind just as he felt invisible tendrils of temporal force begin to tug at him. Had there been onlookers, they would have seen a sudden, mysterious flash of spilt silent flame and then emptiness instead of a human figure.

Some minutes later another chariot rushed past where he had stood, hurtling on in a vain effort to catch the chariot that bore Marcellus and Alba before it could reach the great city.

***

The ships were tied up against the wharf, rocking gently on their chains on the muddy brown water of the Tamesis. The merchant was protesting loudly that he carried no passengers.

'I will offer you ten denarii,' Marcellus said, meeting the merchant's gaze with a steely stare.

'No!'

'Fifteen.'

'No.'

'Twenty.'

'Very well,' growled the merchant, secretly overjoyed by the bargain he had just struck. 'But I am sailing almost immediately—you'd better get on board.'

'Thank you, kind sir,' Alba said, relief washing over her.

The merchant watched them head out into the bright sunshine and ran a calloused hand over the wiry stubble on his chin.

Those two were obviously in a hurry to quit Britain which meant that they were running away from something. The woman was very good-looking for a Briton and he wondered briefly whether he could have asked for her instead of the money, but the soldier seemed too attracted to her to have risked it. He shook his head wonderingly as he spat on the floor.

What was the world coming to when Roman nobles were reduced to nosing around after native women!

Marcellus and Alba walked briskly along the crowded quayside, heading for the merchant's ship, threading their way through the crowds of sailors.

She found the noise and smells of the bustling port overwhelming; completely unlike her quiet northern hillsides. There were busy people everywhere, lifting bales or guiding livestock onto the boats, and she was amazed to see that some of them had skins as black as jet! She had heard tales of such people but had always believed they were just fables.

But then Marcellus felt her fingers stiffen and dig into his shoulder.

'What is it?' he said, looking down in shock at a face blanched with fear.

'Your—your father,' she said, wide-eyed, 'I thought I saw your father on the ship next to ours!'

Marcellus followed her trembling finger, narrowing his eyes against the sun's glare.

He saw a small ship whose deck was covered with bales of wool. There were men carrying more bales up a gangplank which was bowing under their weight.

But there was no Roman noble.

'You are being haunted by shadows,' he said, smiling, 'my father couldn't be here. How would he know from where we were embarking?'

He held her shoulders and turned her to face him.

'We are safe now, and nothing but happiness lies ahead of us. Safe, do you hear me? Safe.'

He kissed her and they joined the sailors on the ship that would take them to safety, not knowing that the merchant was at that very moment gazing at the money Marcellus' father had earlier given him to keep watch and grinning as he added it to the money that the son had just delivered.

Soon the ship was on its way down the turbulent Tamesis, out into the open Channel.

Alba noticed that there was a fog bank directly ahead of them and shivered slightly.

***

Cross leaned back into the plush fabric of his favourite armchair and gently sniffed the aroma of his wine.

He had earned this rare vintage, he thought to himself. He took a contented sip, careful to savour the richness of the wine and not rush the pleasure.

Thomas was back in the kitchen, and in gratitude for the service that Cross had given had ensured that Cross was to be served only the best cuts of meat from now on, smothered in the most sumptuous sauces.

The shadow of the past had been lifted.

Once again, Cross ran the triumph of his endeavours through his mind and shook his head at the thought that no-one would ever know what he had done—with the solitary exception of Thomas.

But even he had not witnessed anything other than a mysterious disappearance.

He had not seen the glories of Roman Britain or breathed in air that carried none of the pollutants of modern life.

Cross closed his eyes to relive his endeavours, but as he did so a strange doubt began to surface from the recesses of his mind.

Never before had he attempted utterly to change the sweep of history; never before had he dared to interfere in the course of the great river of Time.

Had he overreached himself?

He tried to push the thought away, but it kept floating back to the surface.

He opened his eyes and looked around.

Nothing had changed; his Club was still full of the Rich and Famous who, like him, were enjoying the best that money could buy.

And then, for reasons he could never explain, he put his glass on the nearby table and reached for his computer pad.

His fingers seemed possessed of their own will as he selected the news page.

He stared at the headline for a few moments, and then the pad slipped from his fingers and bounced on the floor at his feet.

The wheel had completed its revolution, for the headline had read:

NEW FATALITIES AT SEA: THIRD COLLISION IN
CHANNEL IN THREE MONTHS!

THE UNSPEAKABLE ONES

Darkness.

Hot darkness.

Rough straw-like material under her back.

Irina Miller slowly opened her eyes, not entirely sure she wanted to know where she was.

For a moment she saw nothing, nothing but grey obscurity before she realised she was seeing the underside of a great dome. Slowly, as her eyes adjusted, she could see massive metal struts crisscrossing the concave surface, looking like the tremendous ribs of some impossibly enormous creature.

She heard noises around her and forced herself up into a sitting position.

She was not alone; there were thirty or forty other people with her in the dome.

There was a man near her; like her, he was dressed in a functional, grey outfit comprising a featureless upper garment and ill-fitting trousers.

His face was grey and sad, seeming to blend into the monochrome gloom around him. He might have been in late middle age, or maybe that was just his demeanour. Miller did not care either way.

'Where am I?' she said.

Her throat was dry.

He looked at her coldly, seeing a tall, strongly built woman; one who was not young but assuredly not old.

'Where do you think you are?'

She forced herself to stand, towering over him as he lay on the floor. It was covered in something resembling grey straw.

'I don't like people who answer questions with questions. I repeat; where are we?'

He tried to smile, but it was as if he had forgotten how to do it properly. There was no life in his eyes.

'You're in a holding pen, of course. A holding pen of the

40

Gorathnar.'

Miller groaned.

She had feared that this would be the outcome when the Collaborators had come for her that night.

She'd fought them, of course; she was reasonably sure she had blinded one, but it had been to no avail.

The fates of most of the conquered had been simple to understand. After the Gorathnar had arrived and defeated the whole of humanity in two days, there had only been a few options given to the survivors: They could work for their new rulers in the perilous bases on the oceanic ridges or the polar regions; they could join the hundreds of thousands who were relocated from the more populated areas to work in the steppes and the deserts, toiling in mines, extracting rare metals to help build the mysterious machines that their masters were constructing: machines carrying enormous cylinders, pointing skyward as if they were the barrels of terrible cannons.

But there were other, more mysterious, possibilities.

For instance, thousands of people, always adults, were regularly shipped off-world to unknown destinations.

This, apparently, had been her fate.

'Who are you?' the man asked, seemingly lacking the strength to raise himself from the floor, 'what's your name?'

'What does it matter,' she said, taking her gaze from him to look around the dim enclosure, 'we're all going to die, aren't we? It's best we don't become too friendly.'

Everywhere she looked, she saw the same thing: men and women in identical clothing, sitting, standing, or lying on the featureless grey floor. All of them showing the same emotions.

Defeat.

Despair.

The exact centre of the enormous room was a circular structure that had channels on its surface, radiating outwards to troughs that fringed the circumference. There were more people around it than elsewhere and they were all standing, looking inwards, apparently expecting something to happen.

41

Miller pointed. 'What are they waiting for?'

He followed her finger. 'You are a newbie, aren't you? That's where we eat.'

'It's almost dinnertime, I take it,' Miller said, 'they're showing more life than the rest of you.'

The man did finally succeed in forming a kind of smile, but it was one Miller would have preferred he had not made. 'It's rather plain fare. Nothing to get too excited about.'

'I'll be the judge of that.' She glanced down at the man, almost with pity. 'You seem to have been here longer than me. You've told me where I am, but I want to know why I am here.' She looked around. 'It's obvious this accommodation is distinctly on the basic side. I guess we won't be here long.' She fixed him with a cold stare. 'Do you have any idea why we're here?'

But before he could answer, she suddenly stiffened and felt her heart race.

'Wait a minute: A holding pen. Are we farm animals? Do they eat us?'

The man finally found the strength to get to his feet.

'No, I don't think so. I used to be a scientist, and I've been observing them since the murderous day they arrived. If they found us tasty, they wouldn't wait to take us off Earth to do it. There'd be abattoirs all over the world. I suspect they're half cybernetic in any case, so meat is almost certainly off their menu. No, they don't eat us—why come all this way just for a meal? And I don't think they experiment on us either, so I'm not worried about vivisection. Their science is so advanced they have no interest in studying our biochemistry or physiology.'

'Then if they're so advanced, why bother with us at all. Why conquer us?'

The man shook his head slowly and lowered his head, looking at nothing but the grey straw.

'I don't know. It's clear they want the planet Earth itself; maybe it has a strategic location in some interstellar war they're fighting and we just happened to be on it when they arrived; like a colony of seabirds on an island that human powers might have wanted, centuries ago.'

Miller in turn, shook her head, but more vigorously.

'No, there's more. I can understand putting us to work, but that doesn't explain taking thousands of people off the planet. There's something else.'

The man was about to reply, but some motion caught his eye and he pointed to the central device.

'I do enjoy a stimulating conversation, but it's time for you to eat.'

Miller turned. 'Fine by me.'

Ignoring her companion, she strode to the central machine, elbowing her way through the throng, and also ignoring their complaints.

She stood looking down at the trough which formed the end of the nearest radial channel to her. There was a cup on a hook just below the lip of the trough. As she took it off the hook there was a gurgling sound and a stream of a viscous green-yellow liquid slowly flowed down the channel into the trough.

She stared at it. 'Is this it? It looks like snot!'

'What were you expecting?' the man next to her said, 'a juicy steak with peppercorn sauce?'

Miller dipped her cup into the glutinous mess and slowly brought it to her lips. She hesitated for a moment and then tipped it into her mouth.

It was warm and slightly salty, but beyond that, little could be said about it: it was basically tasteless. Thank God for that! she thought to herself, although its slimy texture was unpleasant as she swallowed.

There was a tap on her shoulder; turning she found a small woman glaring at her.

'Have you finished?' the other hissed, 'we haven't had ours yet!'

For a moment, Miller considered knocking her senseless, but decided she had better wait to see who was in charge first before taking direct action.

'Here you are, bitch,' was all she said, ramming the mug into the small woman's hands.

She walked back to the grey man she had first seen on waking. Apart from sitting again, he hadn't moved.

'Not hungry?' she inquired casually. She wasn't really interested in his answer.

'I ate some hours ago,' he said, 'we don't move around much here, so my needs are meagre.'

'Just as well,' she replied, 'I'm sure the stuff that comes out of my ass would be better. More vitamins and minerals.'

He looked at her quizzically. 'You clearly think you're something special. Some kind of warrior woman.'

'Compared to you—yes.' She joined him in sitting. 'I'm a bit bored, so tell me—how did you get here?'

For the first time, a ghost of animation crossed his features.

'I was a scientist, specifically an astrophysicist. I'd been trying to prove a theorem on the nature of vacuum energy in relation to the cosmological constant. My second wife and I had developed a new mathematical approach. We hadn't been married long. In 3 BC.'

'BC?'

'"Before Conquest".'

'Oh.' She sat down, stretching her long legs out, pushing the grey straw aside. 'I once heard some religious nut job using those letters for a different meaning. What happened to your wife—she here?'

He hesitated and looked away for a moment. 'No. No, they took her for one of their undersea camps near the Cape Verde islands. I've heard nothing from her. That was in 1 AC. That's…'

She raised a hand. 'I'm not an astrophysicist, but I can work that one out. So the Collaborators got you?'

'Yes. They came around 4 AM. Knocked the door in. Stuck something in my arm. And here I am.'

She yawned. 'My, that was exciting. So what do you think our chances are?'

'What—you and me?'

'No. I know we're fucked; I mean the human race.'

44

He rubbed his chin. 'Look—call me Otto. We've got to try and keep our way of life going, our humanity.'

'OK Otto. I'm Irina. I'm sure we'll be great friends.'

His eyes seemed to light up for a moment. 'We will?'

'No. I was just kidding. We might meet up again as the filling in a Gorathnar burger, but that's probably it. Do you really think we can ever get our planet back?'

His hands made vague movements in the grey straw. 'Perhaps. They're obviously a very intelligent species. There's no reason why we shouldn't share the Earth. We tried communicating with them when they first appeared…'

'What—just before they blasted Washington into red-hot dust, you mean?'

'Yes, just before, during and after!' he snapped, 'We had to try, we have to try! Two species, each possessing high intelligence—it must be possible to find some commonality; to pool our resources to understand this wonderful universe we both inhabit!'

She looked at him coldly, unemotionally. 'You just don't get it, do you? You don't understand the world you're now living in—you believed in all that disinterested science, all that gathering knowledge, all that hope for a future with nice, kindly human beings living in some kind of Kiddies' Playtime Utopia where everybody loved one another. It's all gone, dead as all those losers in D.C. who now make up little bits of the dust that's all that's left of their city. It's over!' Her voice rose to a shout; some people near them looked at her. 'Over! It was all a kindergarten dream. As long as we sat all alone on our little ball of shit, we thought we were something wonderful, something special. We didn't realise that we were just a load of helpless dodos watching a pirate ship show up on the horizon!'

'That's horrible,' Otto said quietly, sadly, 'how can you live believing that?'

She leaned forward, and he recoiled slightly from the intensity of her gaze, 'Because there's one thing that I do care about and that's extending my life as long as fucking possible!

Because that's all there is, all there's ever been! I'd be just the same if the Gorathnar had never come and beat the crap out of us!'

'So that's all you want: living in an alien dome, eating this slop. No joy, no laughter, no human company, no friends, no lovers. Nothing else.'

'Yes. And I can tell you why I'd like that.'

'Please do.'

'Because this stay in the dome is only temporary. The Gorathnar have other plans for us—that's obvious. And it won't be an all-expenses-paid Grand Tour of this Wonderful Universe, and whatever plans they really have for us—they'll be worse than what we have here.'

Otto said nothing, but Miller knew that he'd had these thoughts himself but not had the courage to voice them.

He spoke slowly. 'So what kind of world are we now living in? And what kind of relationship could there be between you and me?'

She stood. 'I'll tell you what it is. It's a rat-eat-rat world. That's our status now—*Rattus so-called-sapiens*. And it's best that we go our own ways—I might have to kill you at some time in the future and right now I feel sorry for you.'

Some hours later the Collaborators came for them all.

***

The planet hung in space fifty astronomical units from a terrible, unendurable blue-white Wolf-Rayet star.

Around a gentler, milder, more forgiving star, the alien world would have become a Jupiter-like planet, but the insane ferocity of the primary's hard radiation, coupled with the endless furnace blast of its stellar wind, had stripped the lighter elements away into the interstellar depths, leaving only the rock and metal core. But that core was still a mighty planet, with a gravitational pull over two and a half times that of Earth.

None of that was occupying the mind of Irina Miller as she

stood on the surface of the hell-planet.

She was well aware that its terrible sun could not be looked at with the human eye, not even a shielded one like hers. No eye could look at that sun and see another object—ever again. The sky itself, in which sat that portal into Hell, was brighter than a direct view of the timid sun of Earth. Standing there was like being under a dome of liquid steel. Had she been in normal clothing, she would have been burnt into a smoking black mass of amorphous carbon by the heat; radiation-scarred by the feral blast of ultraviolet and X-Rays; shredded by the merciless torrent of bone-piercing charged particles; smashed to her knees by the terrific pull of the massive world on which she stood. But the suit that she had woken up wearing was protecting her—she knew not how, but also did not care.

The fact that it was protecting her was enough to know.

And for just a few moments, she had ignored the presence of her dreadful companion.

She had looked around at the bare, repellent brown-saffron plain which stretched from the base of the low hill on which she stood, away to the impossibly distant horizon of this Brobdingnagian planet. It was implacably hostile to any creature as fragile as she, contemptuous of anything built from watery organic matter; it was a landscape both dead and deadly, dead as a fossilised skull, deadly as the interior of a blast furnace.

She had seen enough, and so she turned to face her horrific captor.

It was bigger than a bull, with a shining black carapace blazing with blinding highlights from the ferocious sun. It stood on four pillar-like legs, and from its blunt front end, two powerful arms protruded, terminating in long nail-less fingers. The very end of the body, which Miller assumed corresponded with a human face, was a cluster of waving tendrils, like a transplanted sea anemone. And below that writhing mass was a single, circular protrusion, glowing ruby-red, like a fiery coal: perhaps an eye, perhaps not. Whatever this creature was, it needed no protection from the planet's deadly embrace.

47

It was a gorath; an individual of the mighty race which had smashed humanity into subjection and servitude in forty-eight hours; although, in truth, it had been obvious early in the struggle that they were insuperable.

Miller stared at it for a second or two and then said, 'Is it always so hot here?'

The gorath did not move its body, but a tendril extended from the anemone-cluster, becoming a thin filament whose tip split into a spray of even thinner tendrils. The tendrils reached a metal box-like object that lay on the ground before it and danced over the box's surface.

To her somewhat horrified surprise, a warm contralto voice issued from the box.

'It is still winter here and will be for the next fifteen years. A little bonus for you.'

'You're too kind,' Miller snapped, briefly wondering if the Gorathnar understood sarcasm, 'But perhaps you could explain where I am and why I'm here.'

The creature made no movement; it could have been a statue carved by a madman. But the box spoke again.

'Surely you must have reached the obvious conclusion: you are here to die.'

Miller had suspected as much, but the confirmation sent a sharp pulse of ice through her nerves. She stared at the creature, not knowing if it was seeing her with that red disc.

Her mouth was dry, but she managed to say, 'It seems a long way to take someone for a simple execution.'

'That's because it will not be a simple execution,' the pleasant feminine tones from the communication device continued, 'you are here to be hunted.'

Miller stared in disbelief. Eventually she managed to say, in a voice which was almost a croak, 'Hunted? Are you mad?'

'An accusation which is not made very often against the Gorathnar. I speak literally: you will be hunted.'

'You mean: I run off, you follow me and kill me.' She felt anger begin to replace her fear. 'That's not much of a hunt.'

48

'Indeed, it would not be. That's why you will be equipped with devices which will attempt to keep you alive. Your suit, for instance, will repair most of the wounds which you will suffer when attempting to escape from us. We would not wish you to die an accidental death. Your suit has an outer layer of neon atoms, held in a' <Unknown Word> 'field, which will also protect you from the high radiation level of this world and its corrosive atmosphere; an atmosphere which we will change from time to time, by the way. The pack on your back holds an invertograv unit which locally reduces the pull of the planet on your body. It may or may not be defective; I don't know which. You also have a pack of assorted survival devices, which were chosen by a third, entirely neutral, party.'

'I've only got your word for that,' Miller said, interrupting the obscene parody of a talkative woman.

'Obviously. To continue: There are also small survival domes scattered over the landscape which are keyed to your retinal patterns. They have internal invertograv fields so you can remove the suit for such purposes as defecation. The suit recycles the urine and could handle faeces, but you may wish to dispose of solid wastes completely.'

'You really are too kind, like lovely, cuddly teddy-bears. You've actually given me permission to take a dump. Wow!' Miller said, in what was almost a snarl of hydrofluoric bitterness, 'But what's in this hunting crapola for me?'

'Well, I didn't mention that, as it is an unlikely possibility, but should you survive for at least four of this planet's days then we will release you back into human society and you will not be hunted again.'

Now Miller did snarl. 'Human society! The ass-end of everything we ever had, which you destroyed! Tell me something, you ugly monstrosity, why are you doing this to us? Why this hunting shit? What are you: some kind of fucked-up Big Game Hunters, sticking human heads on your walls? Why!'

The communicator was silent for perhaps a minute.

'That is an excellent question. We have purposes and drives

49

which we cannot explain to creatures with nervous systems as simple as yours but let me make the attempt to explain this one, extremely small part of our nature.

'We are no longer what you would term fully biological. I cannot explain to you what exactly we are; it is unlikely that you would have developed the concepts even if we had not enslaved you. Hundreds of thousands of years ago we were biochemical creatures which struggled to survive in an environment of savage predators. Eventually, we overcame them and rapidly made ourselves into what we are. But even though our brains are vastly different from those of our progenitors, we have a mental substratum that calls us to pit ourselves against other creatures; other creatures that want to fight us, to conquer us, to destroy us. And we have the need to periodically reawaken those fierce desires that we still have within us. We want the joy of conflict. We want to deal out death. We want blood.'

Another silence fell.

Then Miller said, 'And simple animals would not be enough. You want thinking adversaries; things that can plot against you; devise traps, fight back. And yet,' she stepped back and, turning, indicated the barren killing ground which lay below them, 'you bring them here, out of their natural environment so that the odds are stacked against them. You're not supermen, you bastards, you're cowards. Just fucking cowards!'

Another silence ensued; this time longer than the first two.

Then the communicator spoke again.

'I have not told you the name of this planet: Welcome to Hunterland.'

***

Miller watched the gorath depart in the flying machine that had brought them both from the Transfer Station.

It had told her many more things before it had left; mainly about the wonders of her suit, which would protect her from the corrosive atmosphere and the crushing gravitation; how it could heal wounds and even regenerate tissue, as long as the flesh had not been carbonised.

The gorath had taught her other things as well, perhaps unknowingly.

For during the journey from the Transfer Station, Miller carefully had watched how it manipulated the controls on its flying machine; storing the knowledge safely away in a vigilant brain that was on high-alert.

What was the likelihood such knowledge could ever be useful?

The likelihood was not zero and that was enough for her.

Before leaving, the gorath had indicated a cone-shaped mountain, some unknown distance away on the ochre plain. Miller had no idea of the distance to the peak, as the planet's horizon was so much more remote than Earth's, but she had been told she needed to be standing on that mountain, alive and well, after four Hunterland days to win the prize of freedom—if that concept had any meaning now in a world where humans had been reduced to the level of beasts of the field.

She had not watched the creature's flight for long, as the sky was far too bright to stare at for more than a few seconds. She shouldered the blast-rifle she had been given and began the arduous descent to the lifeless plain. Hunterland was sterile, she had been assured, the only things that would try to kill her were her inhuman predators.

And the near certainty was that they would kill her.

But that probability was not unity, and so she began the long march to the cone mountain.

She looked around once she was on the death-trap plain. The air was very clear, and it seemed almost that she could reach out to the mountain and crumble it to dust in her glove. There was a device like a wristwatch on her left wrist and on its display, she could read in human symbols the nature of the atmosphere. It was mostly noble gases but contained trace amounts of things called chloryl fluoride, chlorine pentafluoride and dichlorine heptoxide. She did not know what those things were but assumed they were deadly, part of the sadistic game in which she was an unwilling participant. As such, she did not bother to look at the display again as she began to trudge toward the mountain, the carnivorous sun casting an impossibly black shadow before her.

She leapt over gullies, ravines; ran down gulches and staggered through canyon and arroyo; avoided rifts which dribbled green-yellow gas; carefully avoided mud springs and quicksand. There was no sign of her hunters.

The foreign sun, brighter than blazing magnesium, sank rapidly towards a flanking mountain range, dimming as it sank into the encircling mists until it could be briefly glanced at without pain. The coruscant sky segued into a blue-violet canopy.

Would they attack if she slept?

Suddenly the question became academic: she could not stay awake anymore. Hunterland had a rotation period of fourteen hours, but Miller was not enough of a mathematician to convert local days into Terrestrial ones. But it was irrelevant: four Hunterland days would be an eternity of pain.

To hell with it! She thought and sank onto the sand.

Before her eyes closed, she stared up into the deep indigo bowl of the evening sky of Hunterland and looked upon alien constellations which shone in unrecognisable patterns.

Was the sun of martyred Earth hidden in one of those strange patterns?

She slept fitfully, waking from dreams which promised that the Gorathnar and their overthrow of humanity were simply nightmares, and finding in bitter wakefulness that both were real.

Once she wept.

Then abruptly, the eastern sky glared the colour of lightning and for an instant, before the blaze became too fierce, she glimpsed a small, very brilliant orb rising from the faraway horizon. Then she turned away to prevent blindness from being added to her troubles.

She crossed a desert of white powder which the wind suddenly disturbed into whirling dust devils and towering djinns of caustic dust. For a few seconds she was lost but staggered slowly in the direction she had been heading before the wind had struck.

The dust cleared, and she came to a flat area of bare rock, but rock pocked with short spout-like protrusions, looking disturbingly like puckered mouths. It stretched away in all directions across her path, meaning that she had no choice but to cross it.

She was halfway across the great slab when there was a terrible whistling sound, clearly audible through her suit, and from an orifice directly behind her a solid pillar of roaring yellow-white flame erupted. The air became thick with drifting white clouds of ash. A wall of heat crashed into her and her knees buckled with the shock, but she did not fall. Her narrowed eyes rapidly scanned the ground in front of her: if one orifice could spit fire, so could they all. The towering column of flame behind flickered once, twice, and died.

In her mind she saw a path off the rock, a path that passed the smallest number of orifices, and started running. A spout beside her spat flame, another behind her erupted skywards causing her to stagger off her course. As she fought to stay upright, she glimpsed a bare sandy area which formed a bay in the surface of the rock. She readjusted her plan and leapt towards it. She was nearly there. Then another mouth in the slab blew out a long, feathery lance of flame that caught her side and lovingly wrapped itself around her, sinking fangs of agony into her flesh beneath the suit, before tossing her into the powdery dust.

She screamed and screamed again as the pain sunk deeper into her, seemingly ripping her innards into bloody ribbons of agony. Her mind was lost, lost in a red pit of pain beyond all description. Unconsciousness took her.

But the suit had not been holed or burnt. Its outer layer was made from neon atoms held fast in a flexible network by the incomprehensible science of the Gorathnar; a totally inert surface no flame or acid could penetrate. The heat that had taken Miller into near madness was only a fraction of the feral energies that had seized her. She would live.

Even as she had hit the ground, the suit's automatic devices had spun into action. Anaesthetics were driven into her arteries, dulling the agony into mere pain; regrowth enzymes swept into the burnt areas, preventing tissues from scarring and enabling the rebuilding of firm flesh.

An hour later, Miller stirred, groaned and awoke—a remade woman.

The lustful Gorathnar observers were determined this was not how she would die.

But as Miller staggered upright, she did not display any gratitude. She looked back over the mass of rock that she had traversed. Many of the spouts were showing wisps of black smoke, spiralling into the caustic air.

She looked around, left and right, north and south, knowing that in one of those directions her captors and tormentors must be waiting, watching, gloating.

'I may not be able to kill you,' she hissed, 'but by fucking God you won't kill me!'

A fierce madness came into her eyes and her voice rose to a snarling roar.

'You won't kill me, you bastards! You will never kill me!'

***

Miller did not know how long she had been staggering through the barren landscape. The cone-shaped mountain didn't appear to be a centimetre closer. Obviously, its nearness had been an artefact of the clarity of the intervening air and the unearthly distance of the horizon.

The suit had provided water which held proteins, fats and vitamins but that had no effect upon her feelings of hunger. She knew that soon the water would be her own recycled urine but did not concern her. It was a minor issue. She lisped hackneyed obscenities into the warm confines of her helmet as she walked on. Sometimes she was so weary she forgot to look left and right for approaching death—but not often.

Another night of shallow sleep came and was shattered when the sun came up like a scream.

Sweet Jesus, every day was hotter than the one before!

Then there was no more time to think.

At the extreme edge of her vision she saw a movement where there should be no movement, a blur of motion where there should be no motion.

Instantly she threw herself to the ground, rolling over and over while reaching for the blast-rifle.

Something huge and black hit the ground exactly where she had been standing and then reared up on its hind pair of legs so it stood metres taller than she.

Miller saw that this creature's arm-like protuberances had somehow morphed into appendages which now ended in massive claws; pincers that snapped and tore at the empty volume of air she had just quitted.

She swung the blast-rifle into position and pressed the control.

Nothing.

With sickening horror, she realised she had forgotten the exact procedure to arm the weapon: it had been deactivated to avoid accidental death. And it was still switched off.

She ran, feeling the ground shake as the murderous thing lumbered in pursuit.

The land rose in front of her, terminating in a flat area which was covered in boulders of all shapes and sizes. Hearing great claws snapping behind her, she leapt up the slope, nearly tripping in the sliding scree, and ducked behind one boulder which was perched precariously on the edge.

In this gravity it would become a terrible missile if she could get it moving! Miller pulled the invertograv unit from her back so she could manipulate its controls. She boosted the field so it encompassed the boulder, temporarily reducing its inertial mass. The unit screamed and gave off a blue radiance as it strove to meet the vastly increased demand upon its power. The gorath began to ascend the slope. She must hurry or the boulder would not pick up enough speed! Resting on her back she put both feet against the stone and pushed. The rock shuddered and then broke free in a shower of gravel. Exiting the local invertograv field, it immediately felt the pull of the heavy planet and thundered down the slope onto the ascending gorath. The rock crashed into the thing, flinging it into the air in momentary flight, and as the gorath came down in front of it, it rolled over her pursuer.

Gorath and boulder came to a halt, with the rock half covering the silent enemy.

She breathed a great sigh of relief and rose, shakily, to her feet. Quickly she returned the invertograv unit to its normal level before it failed—or exploded. She was about to descend to examine her slain foe when something made her freeze into terrified immobility.

The gorath moved.

With unbelieving eyes she saw a rolling shudder pass through the exposed part and then the thing heaved itself upright, sending the boulder rolling away as if it were a theatrical prop constructed of papier maché. It resumed its ascent.

A strange calm came over Miller. It seemed as if her hellish environment became cool and soothing. She took her gaze from the ascending horror and looked down at her weapon.

She had been told how to arm it. She knew that. The necessary actions were in her brain, if only she could remember...

She remembered.

The blast-rifle became live. She lined it up on the centre of the blunt anterior end, establishing a trajectory which terminated in the centre of the writhing anemone-thing. She fired.

Instantly the rifle and the gorath became connected by a blazing violet line of fervent extinction.

The gorath did not writhe or shudder or clutch at itself or give out a wail of pain or despair.

It exploded—instantly.

Miller was so astounded she fell backwards, even though the blast-rifle had not given any noticeable recoil. She had never seen a weapon like this before!

She stood and gazed at where the gorath had been. There were a few scraps of tattered black material, turning and tumbling in the furnace-winds. That was all.

Finally she spoke: 'Good fucking God.'

And then she resumed her bitter trek to the cone-mountain.

The meaningless, monotonous hours passed. By the shadows, she could see that the short day was closing. Mostly she looked from side to side, on hairspring alert for any movement which would indicate an approaching danger.

But the mountain was closer now, Miller was sure of that now. She could see deep fissures scarring its sides, see tumbled, broken stone at its foot. She was going to make it. She would stand unbroken, undefeated on its austere surface and claim her freedom.

New energy swept into her arteries, and she began to sprint across a flat white plain, not noticing the ominous little spurts of vapour curling from the footprints she left in its soft surface. She was halfway across when the entire plain erupted skywards in vast gouts of tumbling cloud. The fragile ground was sublimating in one tremendous surge of vapour.

She was tossed around like a cork in a maelstrom, rolling over and over, utterly helpless. Desperately she hung on to the blast-rifle, knowing that if she lost it she would never find it again.

And then it was over.

Miller staggered to her feet, brushing white dust from her suit, dust that vanished into the atmosphere as it sublimated away into apparent nothingness. Then she stood very still; her screwed-up eyes saw something not too far away, something standing upright against the grim vista of the mountain.

A gorath? No, it was too small, too upright.

Then it hit her: it was another human—an ally!

Invigorated by sudden hope, she ran towards the figure,

waving madly as she neared it. The other had seen her because it too began to run.

They met, embracing, pounding each other's back in their joy.

And then Miller got a clear view of her new companion's face through the dark visor of its helmet and was hit by a wave of disappointment.

The newcomer was a woman.

A small, slight woman.

***

The suits allowed clear communication between the two women, and Miller gradually learned much about the stranger.

She was Maria Commatteo and like Miller she had had an interview with a gorath which had instructed her to go to the cone mountain if she wanted to live.

They attempted to have a conversation as they walked slowly over the pitted, arid ground, but the exertion required made speech difficult. Still, Miller made the effort.

'What about your family?' she asked, between gasps, 'do you have one?'

'My mother was killed in the Conquest,' Commatteo replied, 'my brother and I were captured by the Collaborators on the same night.'

'And?'

'I came here; I don't know what happened to Angelo. I never saw him again.'

Miller fell silent; there didn't seem much more to ask on that topic, and she was not given to vacuous expressions of sympathy.

But Commatteo seemed to want to continue the conversation.

'I had a happy life before the Gorathnar came.'

'Didn't we all.'

'Yes, of course, but I loved my job, absolutely loved it.'

Miller concluded she was supposed to show interest and

said: 'And that was?'

'I was a lecturer; in English Literature.'

'English literature?' Miller seemed somewhat surprised. 'What—reading books? That seems more like a hobby than a job for a grown woman.'

Commatteo stopped and looked at the other.

'That's a horrible thing to say! There's a great deal of scholarship involved in really understanding English Lit.'

Miller was bored and was rapidly coming to the conclusion that she had little in common with her new companion.

'Yeah; I daresay you were a big help in fighting off the Gorathnar with the complete works of Shakespeare. By the time they'd finished reading it they just wanted to top themselves.'

Miller could not discern the details of Commatteo's expression behind her tinted visor but it sounded like she'd pissed the other off.

'That's unfair. I suppose you've never read a book in your life!'

'I've read various manuals on stripping and reassembling automatic weapons—so let's just leave it at that, shall we?'

There was silence between them then, broken only by the sounds of their ragged breathing. The land was beginning to slope upwards.

Suddenly Commatteo stopped her laborious ascent and pointed ahead.

'Look—is that a building?'

Miller looked ahead and could make out a white rectangular structure a few hundred metres above them.

'Yes,' she said, feeling excitement rise, 'it's one of those rest stations that fucker told me about.'

'Please,' Commatteo said, in a tone which strongly suggested she was wrinkling her nose, 'there's no need to use that sort of language. It shows you have a limited vocabulary.'

Miller wondered briefly if she should just kill Commatteo there and then and carry on by herself but decided the other woman might just possibly be useful in the next trial of strength with the Gorathnar. Even though, oddly enough, she did not have a weapon.

'Forgive me, Maria; I've had a difficult upbringing. My parents abandoned me when I was five.'

'How awful!' Commatteo said, 'no wonder you're like you are!'

Miller grinned to herself in the hot confines of her helmet. That was a complete lie of course. She'd abandoned her mealy-mouthed parents as soon as she had been able. They'd tearfully begged her to stay.

They finally arrived at the building which was set on a level shelf of rock on the gradually steepening flank of the mountain.

'How do we get in?' Commatteo wondered, looking around in all directions.

'Trying the door might be a good start,' Miller observed dryly and walked up to the faint outline of a door. As she did so, a red beam of light hit her visor and a second later the door opened.

'Retinal recognition,' Miller grunted, 'that's what the mother—the creature—said.'

The door was the outer part of an airlock, a necessary structure given the toxic and corrosive atmosphere of Hunterland. Finally, they were inside and found themselves looking at a table and chairs and a low bed, just big enough for two.

'I'm getting this bloody suit off,' Miller said, 'I need a shit right now.'

Commatteo sighed. 'There you go again.'

Miller continued removing her protective suit, without bothering to reply to the other's comment. Another door led to the lavatory, and after ten minutes she finally emerged from that facility.

'That's better!' she said, and then stopped, looking up and down her similarly disrobed companion; seeing blue eyes, blonde tresses and pert bosom.

'Why are you staring?' Commatteo said, slightly nervously.

60

'Look, sister,' Miller said in a weary voice, 'I've only seen those bloody monstrosities recently. It's good to see a human being again.'

Commatteo relaxed. 'That's all right then.'

There was a cupboard containing water and protein bars and over their makeshift meal the two women looked at each other.

'When do you think this will end?' Commatteo asked.

'End? What's ending?' Miller said, between hearty bites at her food.

'This awful war with—with them.'

Miller stopped raising the protein bar to her mouth and let the latter hang open for a moment.

'End? It ended a long time ago. We're beaten. Knocked flatter than a pensioner's tits. Licked good and proper.'

Commatteo shook her head. 'That can't be right. We must win in the end. They're horrible things. They can't be allowed to win.'

'And how are we going to win? What will come to our rescue?'

Commatteo waved her hand in a vague manner. 'Oh, I don't know. The spirit of humanity or something like that. Our cleverness, our resourcefulness.'

Miller was so startled she put the half-eaten bar back on its plate. She stared in puzzled amazement at her companion.

'Look, if we were going to win, we'd have done it when they first arrived; when we had the resources of an entire planet behind us. Not when we're slaving in the mines or under the sea or scattered God-knows-where throughout the galaxy!'

Commatteo did not meet her gaze but shook her head.

'We'll find a way. We always have.'

Miller scowled. She'd met this attitude before and it annoyed her.

'Maria, we've had it easy up until now. When we fought our way out of the caves, what were we up against? The occasional cave-bear? A wolf pack or two? We've never had to fight something which met us on our own terms, using science,

61

technology, intelligence. When we finally did meet that something, we just caved in. Gave up. We lasted as long as a snowflake in an electric-arc furnace. A few smashed cities convinced us we couldn't succeed. The survivors rose up and demanded that we give in, for God's sake!'

'So what's your answer?' Commatteo snapped, showing her first strong emotion in their time together, 'we just become sheep?'

Miller controlled her own anger and forced herself to speak slowly, quietly.

'No, not sheep. Rats.'

Commatteo looked both startled and, somehow, frightened.

'What! Rats? Are you mad?' For the first time in the argument, she looked Miller full in the face.

'No, I'm serious. Deadly serious. Listen to me—don't turn away, you little fool! Think about it. For thousands of years, rats have lived alongside humans; skulking in the shadows, knowing that every hand is against them, knowing they can't fight us, face to face. And yet they thrive. Rats are everywhere. Even when we can't see them and think we're alone they're there, watching us. That's what we must become if we're going to carry on living. A new type of rat; never directly challenging the Gorathnar; retreating, hiding when they see us but when they are gone we come out and feast on what they throw away. That way we live.'

Commatteo leapt to her feet.

'You're mad! Worse than mad—you're wicked, evil! What kind of life would that be? Better to die!'

Miller looked up at her, stolidly, calmly, perhaps even with a little tinge of pity.

'You say that now when you're alive with your belly enjoying this food. But when it comes to the choice between living as a rat or obliteration—I wonder what you will choose then.'

The discussion ended, and no more was said for quite some time.

They sat on the chairs, studiously avoiding each other's gaze. Eventually, Commatteo went to the bed and lay down.

Then after she had been lying there for about ten minutes, she suddenly said, 'Irina, I feel all alone. Could you hold me for a while, please?'

Miller stared at the prone figure for a while and then joined her on the bed, lying behind her in spoon fashion.

Commatteo said, 'I like that, but please hold me, Irina. I want to know you're there, caring about me.'

Miller placed her hands on the other's shoulders and they rested there for a while.

Then an idea occurred to Miller and, slipping one arm under the smaller woman and the other over her, she began to fondle Commatteo's breasts.

Commatteo stiffened. 'Please don't do that, Irina. I don't want it.'

In that instant Miller reached a conclusion. In a voice that was suddenly gruff and throaty she said 'But I do. Roll over.'

The other obeyed, looking nervously at Miller.

'Take your clothes off,' Miller said, 'Now!'

Commatteo stared back, uncomprehending, hesitant, until Miller repeated, 'Now!'

Hurriedly she obeyed while Miller did the same and then like a predator pouncing, Miller straddled her, forcing her legs apart.

Selfishly, unmercifully, shaking with erotic rage, Miller took her pleasure from the squirming woman beneath her, flinging her head back and shouting as the blissful release claimed her. Then she collapsed upon Commatteo and both lay there, panting.

After some minutes, Commatteo said in a quiet voice, 'Why did you do that?'

Miller grinned as she climbed off the bed, reaching for her clothes. 'Maybe because I wanted to?'

'I didn't ask for it. I've never been with a woman before.'

Miller struggled into her trousers and then went back to the bed to look down on Commatteo's naked form and gave a grunt of amusement at the sight of the small woman's hands firmly pressed over her vulva, shielding it from view.

'Don't knock it, sister. I've told you—this is a different

world. Everything's changed. There's nothing left of the old ways; nothing left of your Shelley and your—I don't know—of your James Joyce, whatever their fucking names are. From now on we take our pleasure where and when we can, with whoever's around, because I'm pretty damn sure there's not much pleasure in store for us in this new life of ours.'

She walked away.

As Commatteo put on her clothes she stared bitterly at Miller.

'You deserve to be hunted,' she said, 'you're nothing but a wild beast yourself.'

Miller shrugged but did not reply.

'"The unspeakable in pursuit of the uneatable,"' Commatteo hissed as she pulled the blouse over her head.

Miller glanced at her. 'That's got a nice ring to it. I suppose it's a quote from your vast store of literary knowledge?'

'Oscar Wilde on the English aristocracy hunting foxes. A cruel bloodsport.'

'Never heard of the bastard. I take it he didn't approve of hunting?'

'You take correctly. And I don't approve of hunting. Nothing civilised could approve.'

Miller sat down and looked at Commatteo with narrowed eyes.

'I've just realised—you haven't had a hunting encounter yet, have you?'

'No. How did you know?'

Miller gave a mirthless laugh.

'Because if you had you wouldn't be standing there, all het up with your prissy little nose stuck up in the air. You'd be a pile of steaming guts and bone. They obviously decided you weren't worth hunting. Maybe that's why they didn't give you a gun. But you could try slapping them with a copy of the "Treasury of English Verse", or some such trash."

'A charming image. Typical of you.'

Miller crossed to the smaller woman.

64

'Come on, it was just a simple fuck. You must have gotten something out of it.'

'Nothing. You raped me.'

'Have it your own way.' Miller pointed to the suits. 'Get yours on. We've got to move out. I intend being on that mountain with all my womanly charms in perfect working order. If you want to live, you'll stick by me.'

'I'll stick by you. I want to beat those Unspeakable Ones, too. For my mother and Angelo.'

'And I want to beat them. For me.'

The brief night arrived and departed.

They left and began the ascent.

***

The going got tougher once they had left the refuge. The slope became greater; the land more rugged with huge boulders perched precariously above them. Each time they successfully navigated a boulder field, there was another.

Commatteo begged Miller to slow down; perhaps rest for a while.

Miller did stop, but only to stare down at the trailing blonde woman.

'Don't you want to get off this fucking planet?' she snapped, 'if you want to rest your bones you might remember that you could be resting your bones here for all eternity!'

Commatteo had long since given up trying to moderate Miller's language. She gazed up wearily at her.

'A rest now and then will help us get to the top,' she said, 'we're not all superwomen like you!'

'You're not wrong there.'

But she did stop. She looked beyond the small woman struggling to catch up.

She saw a vast plain below them; austere, harsh, unforgiving, deadly, feral, fatal.

Yellow, brown, grey; torn, tormented; blasted by the

corrosive world-encompassing hard radiation that passed for sunshine on this killer world.

'I hate this bloody planet,' she hissed. She turned to look up-slope to where the crumpled horn of the mountain peak stood out in grey silhouette against a sky the colour of an electrical discharge. 'And I hate you motherfuckers who put me here! If I can kill you before you kill me I will die happy, delirious!'

Commatteo had caught up. 'What were you saying?' she enquired between pants.

'It doesn't matter. I doubt you could find my words in one of your stupid poetry books.' Miller raised a finger. 'Don't argue with me, don't question me. Let's get on with it.'

They continued upwards, sweat trickling down inside their suits, moisture which the suits would capture and return as drinking water.

They came to a reasonably level area, covered as usual with jagged boulders seemingly carved from obsidian by a sadist. In one promontory of fissured rock, there was a cave entrance.

'We could rest in that cave,' Commatteo said. Miller could hear the hope dripping from her words like glucose syrup.

'No,' she said, 'we go...'

She did not finish the sentence.

Without warning a great twisting, blue-white bolt of lightning flashed down into the ground mere metres from where the pair stood, sending shattered rock fragments spinning through the air like volcanic bombs. Some smashed into Miller's suit but rebounded, frustrated, defeated.

But a direct hit by a bolt—the suit might not withstand that.

'The cave!' she shouted, 'Move!'

More bolts struck as they ran for the cave; terrible, eye-wrenching serpents of actinic flame. It was as if the terrible sun was flinging spears of its own incandescent flesh at them.

The brightness was so great that their vision almost failed to resolve any details in their surroundings, but Miller knew in which direction the cave had lain and she ran for it. Some momentary weakness in her made her pull Commatteo behind her. A great bolt hit just behind them as they rushed into the cave, sending its interior into an overexposed black and white vision of Hell.

They carried on running until the cave came to an end. There was a shaft of bluish light coming down from a natural chimney in the roof. Miller realised Commatteo was crying. She grasped her shoulders and shook her.

'Stop that! It won't help. Don't you understand no-one's coming to help us. This planet is made to terrify us, to soften us up, to make us surrender, beg for death!' She shook her again, more violently. 'We're on our own! No sweet Jesus is going to rescue us!'

Commatteo's tortured features were dimly visible through the visor. 'I...'

The world fell in around them, huge chunks of stone crashing down next to them while the ground cracked into a spider's web. Miller spun around, her features contorted into a snarl.

A gorath was standing in the cave entrance, its bulk reaching from floor to ceiling. Commatteo was between her and the monster.

'Get out of the way!' Miller roared, but Commatteo stood motionless, unable to believe that this was reality. Miller knocked her aside and brought her blast-rifle into position.

And fired.

And nothing happened.

She fired again.

Nothing happened. The gorath lumbered on, its snapping pincers now resembling those of a titanic scorpion.

Miller desperately examined her rifle. Was it jammed in safety mode?

No. But she saw a message on her wrist monitor.

SUPPRESSOR FIELD DETECTED.

The gorath was using a local energy field to prevent the rifle from firing.

Miller knew what to do.

'Up the chimney!' she yelled and, without seeing if Commatteo had broken out of her trance, pulled herself up into the natural orifice. Gasping, grunting, snarling, blaspheming, she pulled herself higher. It narrowed, and it began to look as if she would be stuck in its stone throat. The protrusions she was using to pull herself up rapidly became smaller, and she had to turn and jam her back against the rock in order to jerk her body upwards.

Then she was out.

She rolled herself over until she was looking down on the cave entrance.

Half of the gorath's body was still outside.

She looked at her wrist monitor. The message was gone. She was outside the suppressor field's range.

Her rifle was alive again.

For reasons she could not explain, she yelled: 'Hey fucker! I'm up here!'

The monstrosity stopped its inward movement and pulled its massive body out of the entrance. It looked up at her, glinting in squat power in the blaze from the sky.

Sweating and panting with the lust to kill, Miller rammed the blast-rifle to her shoulder and took aim. She saw the writhing anemone organ above that disc which shone like a red-hot coal.

She fired.

A leaping pencil of irresistible obliteration tore into the gorath's body. An undetectable instant later its entire body thundered into raging combustion. The beam carried on through the empty space which had held the hunter's body and by the time Miller released the pressure on the trigger it had volatilised the rock on which the creature had been standing into a shallow crater.

Miller collapsed onto her back and lay still for some time.

When she finally forced herself upright, she saw Commatteo standing not far from the crater which marked the gorath's annihilation. She had not followed Miller up the chimney.

Miller said nothing when she rejoined her companion.

There was nothing she wanted to say, and she waved the other into silence as she started to express her gratitude.

The peak and freedom was not far now.

They staggered on, spent, exhausted. Miller was sure her adrenal glands had been squeezed dry. She could, she thought, feel no more, emote no more.

And then the land flattened out and they found themselves standing on a flat area from one side of which the final, sharp tip of the mountain rose up, ten, perhaps twelve metres higher. The region was featureless except there was an overhanging shelf of rock from which granite stalactites hung, looking unnervingly like the fangs of a ferocious beast.

'What now?' Commatteo said.

Miller was scanning the refulgent sky. 'We see if the Gorathnar keep their word.'

And then she saw it—a black dot against a background of incandescent fury.

It grew rapidly until Miller could see it was a Gorathnar flyer, like the one that had brought her from the Transfer Station to this desolate killing-ground.

A flyer with enough room for its pilot and one human.

It landed a few metres from them and its horrific pilot dismounted.

It came towards them and Miller felt Commatteo shrink behind her. She threw her companion one glance, in time to see her backing away until she was under the stone overhang.

Miller held her ground, blast-rifle armed and ready.

The gorath stopped a few metres away. Miller looked for a few moments at the writhing anemone tentacles and then at the powerful arms. She was relieved to see they terminated in hand-like structures, not deadly pincers. Relieved that is, until she saw one of the hands was holding a compact blast-rifle. It also bore a communication device, positioned between the anemone and the red disc.

It spoke.

But this time not in a pleasant contralto. It spoke in a voice so deep and resonant it was as if the rocks themselves were speaking. Miller could feel infrasonics shaking her innards.

'You have done well, Irina Miller. Better than I expected.'

'And now?' Miller demanded. 'Do I get to leave?'

'No. I am going to kill you.'

'What! You promised!'

'Some did promise that. Most of my companions agreed to spare you; even to take you off Hunterland. But I, being the strongest, overruled them. And hence I am here.'

'But why do you want to kill me?'

'Because I can. Perhaps you don't realise one simple fact: You are ours, ours to do with as we please. Do you think that this ridiculous hunting is the only plan we have for your species? Or even the main one? We have many more subtle designs for *Homo sapiens* once we have fully domesticated you.'

Miller raised her blast-rifle, aiming squarely at the red disc that might, or might not, be an eye. She fired.

Nothing.

'I have of course deactivated it. There was a little more power in its pack, enough to have killed me but I have deactivated it remotely. And that is not all I can deactivate in response to you and your companion's continued existence.'

Instantly Miller's invertograv field failed and for the first time she felt the full strength of Hunterland's gravitational pull. Her legs buckled beneath her and she found herself on her knees with the foul creature looking down on her. Behind her, unseen, unregarded, Commatteo collapsed like a tower of playing cards.

'Why don't you just kill me with that weapon of yours?' Miller panted. It felt like her head was being pulled through her shoulders into her chest. Her heart seemed to thunder under its increased burden. Her vision blurred into a red background covered in dancing white sparks.

'This thing? Oh no, we Gorathnar prefer to kill with our bodies, not like a coward at a safe distance with a mechanical contrivance. But I could have killed you with it.'

It lifted the arm that held the gun and fired at the overhang sheltering Commatteo. An invisible beam of energy instantly shattered it, sending spears of stalactites rolling over the ground in all directions. But a large slab fell onto Commatteo and even through her suit, Miller heard the cracking noise as Commatteo's femur disintegrated.

The gorath moved closer.

'You are ours. We are the masters of this arm of the galaxy. You will never escape us. Never. You are ours.'

Miller felt something bump into her thigh. She glanced down.

One of the stalactite fragments had rolled onto her leg.

And under Hunterland's 2.6 g she rose with that stone spear in her grasp and with the last of her strength rammed it into the centre of the red disc. She did not care if she lived or died.

The gorath shuddered and then went rigid.

Miller screamed her hate and with redoubled strength she thrust the stone deeper through that disc, gouging further and further into the creature's interior. Colourless ichor began to spurt around the penetrant spear. And still she thrust, grinning with each additional centimetre of insertion.

And then the gorath gave one last convulsive shudder and its legs gave way, and like a repulsive, lifeless gargoyle carved from ebony in a drug-crazed delirium, it fell.

And was still and silent.

Miller collapsed on top of it.

'Never corner a rat,' she whispered to herself, as she hovered on the brink of madness.

Then she heard a little weak voice calling to her. Begging for help.

She turned and saw Commatteo lying with the stone on her leg; a leg which was bent into a truly impossible angle.

'Help me, please Irina! Help me!'

Miller looked at the flyer. It was similar enough to the first one that she was sure she could fly it. And now the original pilot was dead, there was enough room for two.

She looked down at Commatteo.

'You know Maria, I've wondered about you from the first moment we met; how a snowflake like you could survive for more than a few minutes on Hunterland without a weapon. Then it hit me: you're part of the test; you've been put here to see whether pity for you would weaken me, make me vulnerable. It was only ever me they were interested in. But I pass the test: I won't take you, Maria. I can't let you slow me down, you'd be just a dead weight. I can't afford that.'

'What! What do you mean? Help me!'

Miller smiled a slightly sad smile. 'I can help you, Maria. You see no-one's coming for you, to save you; but starvation is a very bad way to die. Just take your helmet off. This planet's air will kill you in an instant. It'll be a good, kind way to go.'

Miller could dimly make out Commatteo's expression through the visor. Her eyes were wide and staring.

'You can't mean it! Not after what we did together!'

Miller turned and began to walk to the flyer.

'Maria, you gave me a slightly better cum than I could have gotten from my hand, and I thank you for that. But that's my help. Take it or leave it.'

She heard Commatteo's last, despairing wail. And she heard her yell: 'You're the Unspeakable One! You!'

Miller flew off through the savage sky, heading for the distant Transfer Station through which she had passed an eternity ago, knowing she must now search in whatever passed for sewers in the world of the Gorathnar, looking, searching for the free humans, the human rats that must be living there; rats living in the dread shadow of the masters they would have now and forever; rats hiding from the guns, the blades, the traps, the poison.

But she knew she would eventually find a nest and that its members would rapidly learn to love their new Queen.

CYCLE OF THANATOS

Being a psychologist, Sally Richardson had no difficulty identifying the nature of her feelings: it was a gnawing anxiety, not quite fear yet but not too far from sliding into that disturbing emotion.

It was not difficult either to identify the cause of that anxiety. It was the fact that she was at the bottom of a column of six hundred metres of black, icy water in a small—in fact, a four-person—scout submarine.

Ahead shone two converging beams from the powerful searchlights that the vessel possessed, which were revealing the jumbled rocks of the fissured seabed. Boulder after boulder came into view, each one retreating into the darkness as the motion of the scout carried it past. Everywhere there were ooze-covered slabs of basalt, which had been thrust up into shapes not unlike gigantic tombstone teeth.

They were not far from the furrowed slopes that led up to the summits of the Mid-Atlantic Ridge as they traversed a depression that lay between Jan Mayen Island and Iceland. They were on the last part of the curved track which had taken them out into deeper waters but was now (hopefully!) taking them back to the base.

She glanced at her new husband, relaxing as she saw how in charge he appeared, his large, strong hands resting in apparent unconcern upon the controls. He was in full profile; his face lit into a patchwork of light and shadow by the craft's internal illumination. And he was looking straight ahead, but with the occasional glance left or right (or should that be port or starboard—she was never sure if naval terminology applied down here).

'No sign of any upthrusts,' he said, apparently to himself.

'Couldn't have been a big quake, then Greg,' she said, adding for her own benefit, 'we don't need to hang around, do we?'

He glanced at her, a broad smile illuminating his face like an internal power source.

She loved that smile and felt her nervousness melt away.

'Don't tell me you've had enough of the North Atlantic seabed? I could stay out here all day—as long as I was with you.' He reached over and gave her hand a quick squeeze.

She smiled back. God, she loved this man!

'Spoken like a true geologist,' she said, her eyes sparkling in the shifting patterns of light, 'sometimes I think you're more interested in these stones than you are in me.'

'If I ever see a stone I'd like to take to bed, then I might agree.' He returned to the controls, grinning, sending the craft up; upwards towards the hidden sun.

Content, reassured, she settled back into her chair and looked into the oceanic darkness, seeing nothing but the endless, tortured, broken submarine seascape, but also occasional swirling flecks of descending organic matter, looking like snowflakes as they entered the beams.

Greg caught her thoughts and said, 'It's called marine snow, I believe.'

'I think I prefer the real thing,' she said in a dull monotone.

He gave a slight shrug and returned to guiding the sub.

Once she saw a fish. It flashed silver in the searchlights and then was gone.

Involuntarily, she shivered slightly.

Greg saw it. 'We'll be back soon. I didn't know you were so claustrophobic.'

She gave an unconvincing smile. 'I'm not really. I mean, in normal circumstances. I mean, I'm not nervous in the base, and that's cramped enough.'

He laughed. 'The base! I'd hardly call that normal. It's like being a sardine getting smothered in tomato sauce and squeezed into a can.'

She laughed at the image and then felt a wave of relaxation wash over her. She pointed into the dark gloom.

'Thar she blows!'

Ahead, a structure gradually revealed itself from black

obscurity—The International Research Base.

It comprised four domes connected to each other by circumferential tubes and by similarly sized spokes to a central, much larger globe.

The scale could not be determined at this distance, but she knew the base stretched over four kilometres. In the gloom beyond, she knew, but could not see, were the great enclosures that held the mutant fish.

'Home, sweet home,' she breathed.

As they approached the nearest dome, she noted the globular escape pod perched on its upper surface.

Hope to God I never have to use one of them! She thought to herself, and then wondered why these thoughts kept recurring.

There was a bump and then a slight shudder as the sub docked, and soon they were standing in the corridor of the Geological Dome.

Greg looked down at her. 'You OK?' he asked, 'you seemed unusually uptight out there today.'

She frowned. 'I was. And I don't know why.'

'You don't? I thought you were the psychologist around here.'

'I am; that's what's annoying me. Maybe it was the quake. I know it hardly registered, but it seems to have shaken me up. It reminded me we're near the bottom of the Atlantic Ocean and not too far from the pole.'

Greg pursed his lips. 'Well, Sal, you're the one who's supposed to be monitoring the mental state of the rest of us. Do you want to go Topside?'

She shook her head. 'Of course not! It's just when I'm out there. I'm fine when I'm back here with the gang.'

'OK. Let's meet the rest of the Happy Throng.'

She touched his arm. 'I'm OK, Greg. I really am.'

He nodded, and they headed down the corridor to the Meeting Room which resided at the centre of the Geological Dome.

The others looked up as they entered. Sally looked them

over automatically, searching for any signs of stress or depression. It was her job.

She ticked them off as she regarded them.

Igor Kurchatov: Nuclear Technician—looking miserable and somewhat lonely. But no more than usual.

Tick.

Marie Beauvoir: Ichthyologist—looking bored. Studying her nails. No change there.

Tick.

Harald Sigurdsson: Oceanographer—reading a technical manual. As he always was.

Tick.

Ricardo Alvarez: Geneticist—giving Greg and Sally a big Hollywood smile, although it was directed more at her than Greg. Same old Ricardo, leaning nonchalantly against one of the cabinets holding the pressure suit equipment. Everybody else was seated, of course.

Tick.

Joan Hicks: Medic—staring admiringly at Alvarez. As usual.

Tick.

'Did you see any damage out there?' Alvarez said, apparently to Greg, although his eyes remained on Sally.

'No, nothing at all. No landslides or new fissures,' Greg said, taking a seat and stretching out his long legs.

'I meant the fish pens. We don't want mutant tuna getting loose. I can see the headlines now: Frankenstein Fish Run Rampant, Eating Old Ladies.'

'If there had been, it would have been the first thing I'd mentioned,' Greg said, with just a tinge of irritation in his voice.

'Of course,' Alvarez said, finally switching his gaze to Greg. 'I just want to be sure. They're my life's work, after all.'

'Give it a rest, Ricardo,' Beauvoir said wearily, 'we all know you're the most important person down here.'

Sally looked sharply at her. Was she showing the signs of hypoglycaemia? Probably not, Sally concluded, like all people who had been Type 1 since childhood, Beauvoir wouldn't make

76

that kind of mistake. But there was definitely tension in the room, and it was her job to defuse any situation before it developed. When tightly confined in an unnatural environment, the smallest of grievances could build up and fester.

'Ricardo,' she said, coupling her sweetest voice with her sweetest smile, 'I've never quite understood what you're doing here. Perhaps you could go over it again for me.'

Out of the corner of her eye, Sally saw Greg look at her sharply. Of course, she knew what Alvarez's work was, and Greg knew that. Obviously, he was taking her literally, not realising she was at work. She tapped his thigh gently to warn him not to say anything. She continued to smile at Alvarez.

She was gratified to see his face relax. He had fallen for it.

'Well,' he began, 'you know that the bluefin and yellowfin tuna are major sources for protein in the modern world.'

'I suppose I do, Ricardo.'

In order to deliver his lecture, Ricardo had decided it was best to be sitting down and was now leaning back in his chair, the perfect image of relaxed authority; the others had all found something else to do. Kurchatov had left the room.

'Tuna are remarkable animals,' Alvarez continued, 'unlike most fish, they have a degree of homeothermism. They…'

'Sorry, Ricardo. Could you put that in terms that a country girl like me can understand?'

Alvarez's smile became so broad that Sally became worried that the bottom part of his face might detach.

'Sorry, Sal. It means that they are warm-blooded. Like you. But not quite as warm-blooded as a beautiful woman like you.'

Sally felt Greg stiffen slightly, but she carried on smiling.

'In what way?'

'They use a countercurrent exchange system in which heat from the venous system is transferred to the arterial system. The bluefin tuna does it better than the yellowfin, but neither is up to your mammalian standard.'

'And that's what your genetic engineering has given them.'

'Exactly! Bright girl! The world is suffering from a protein shortage as the population continues to increase. But overfishing had almost exterminated the great food fish like the tunas and the salmon. By altering their genetic code, I can make them more like mammals. I can make them more resistant to deep-sea pressures. And that means we can farm them in huge pens right up here in the Arctic; out of the way of the industrialisation of the oceans. So you could say, I'm the saviour of humanity.'

'I was going to say exactly that, Ricardo.'

He laughed, and Sally relaxed. The mood had lightened.

Greg stood up. 'Well, now we know what you do for a living, Ricardo; I think it's time to eat.'

They chatted over the meal, which, as usual, was heavily fish-based, along with various preparations of seaweed. Sally noticed Kurchatov mournfully pushing his portions around the plate.

'Not liking the meal, Igor?' she enquired.

He looked up from the plate, his face seemingly devoid of any emotion, his eyes dull and lifeless.

'Tuna. I'm sick of tuna. If it's not tuna, it's salmon. I'd like a lovely steak every now and again, with lots of English mustard, soft brown onions, asparagus tips in melted butter. I dream about it sometimes.'

Beauvoir tittered. 'What! You dream you're going to be a billionaire! Nobody eats like that these days!'

He ignored her and returned to his plate, studying it with such intensity that it looked like he was trying to magic a juicy steak into existence.

'If it's not fish, it's TVP or some other monstrosity. God, I hate mycelial protein!'

'There are lots of people who don't even get that, Igor,' Sally reminded him, 'that's why we're here so we can give people a better life.'

He nodded slowly. 'You're right. I'm just being selfish. I'm sorry.'

He returned to pushing the fish pieces around his plate, but occasionally he would raise one to his lips and chew morosely, staring into the distance. The others soon learned to ignore him and carried on with their conversations.

Sally looked at him with pity in her eyes.

Poor Igor! He was the kind of guy who was always in the kitchen at parties.

She had tried to bring him out of himself, to reassure him, to get him more animated; he had much to offer. All of her techniques had failed. But she would not give up. It was her job.

She took her gaze from Kurchatov and ran it over the others. Alvarez was sitting next to Joan Hicks and telling her a very convoluted story about how his genius had been recognised at an incredibly early age, to which Hicks was nodding in a regular fashion, all the while lifting strips of glutinous seaweed to her mouth.

But apparently Hicks' admiration for Alvarez had its limits, as the glazed quality of her expression was visible to Sally even at her distance from the pair.

Greg was nominally in charge of the station, due almost entirely to his longstanding undersea experience. Occasionally he would attempt to bring the group together to discuss progress. Despite Sally's advice, he had a habit of trying to do that at mealtimes. Now was one of those unfortunate times.

'So Ricardo,' he essayed, 'any developments with the—ah—crop?'

Alvarez turned from Hicks and was about to speak when Beauvoir leaned towards Greg and said, 'Excuse me, Greg, but Ricardo's involvement is rather in the past. As the ichthyologist in this team, I think you should address that question to me.'

Sally groaned inwardly.

He'd done it again! Didn't he realise how important status was to these people; how fiercely they defended their positions?

'Ah, yes, I'm sorry about that,' Greg said, looking between the two experts, 'I thought we weren't entirely sure how the new genes were being expressed.'

'That is true, Greg,' Beauvoir continued smoothly, 'but I am of course, more than adequately educated to be able to report on any developments.'

'Well, no one here is doubting your academic achievements, Marie,' Alvarez interrupted, 'but we're talking about more than spawning behaviour here. I'm sure Greg realises...'

'I beg your pardon, Ricardo, but that is a very simplistic interpretation of my field of study.'

Sally realised that, thanks to Greg's ill-advised question, the mealtime was spiralling into a full-blown altercation. Throwing an exasperated glance at her husband, she said, 'Did anybody else feel that quake earlier? It scared the bejesus out of me!'

Alvarez laughed. 'I can tell you're not a San Franciscan like me. I've been through ones so strong that they brought down buildings. Why, I lost my car into the mother of all big cracks that opened up...'

Sally let her interest fade. Soon the diners were swapping earthquake stories, each trying to outdo the other in the horrors they had lived through. She let them get on with it. It was not a competition she wanted to enter.

Later in bed, after another fruitless battle with the malfunctioning air conditioning, she turned to Greg and said, softly, 'You've got to be more careful with those people, darling.'

He grunted. 'Huh. They're just a crowd of overgrown teenagers, always trying to get one over on the other.'

'No, that's not good enough. You have to soothe them, stroke their egos. This place is a tinderbox. You've got to understand that. The unnatural environment. The feeling of enclosure. We're all subject to those pressures, even if we don't admit it.'

'It doesn't worry me.'

She sat up, the blanket falling from her small, firm breasts.

'That's just it! For God's sake, I can see why this place needs a psychologist! It's not about you—it's getting the team to perform at their best. You should have married a rock, not me. You wouldn't have to worry about those messy emotions then.'

He sat up as well and looked at her in the dimness.

'OK. I'm a man. I don't do emotions. Except with you.'

She smiled. 'Yes, I know. But that's another thing. Has it occurred to the slab of basalt between your ears that they might be jealous of us?'

'Jealous? How? What are you talking about?'

'Greg, we're the only couple down here under kilometres of black water. They have their flirtations, I've seen them, but no-one's teamed up. They're alone with just their work.'

Her fingers made a brief, butterfly-kiss on his penis. 'They can't do things like that. You have to be careful, think beyond just the work, collecting the data, filing the reports. They're people—and not particularly happy people.'

'Helping millions avoid starvation isn't enough for them, then?'

She frowned, but in the dimness he did not see it.

'That's an abstraction. They don't see millions of people. They just see each other. And us.'

Greg had thought about making love that evening, but they did not.

And soon they were asleep.

**

Sally dreamt she was in the grip of an angry giant.

She was held fast in his mighty grasp, and he was shaking her back and forth, laughing in a voice like thunder.

She woke up.

She was shaking. The entire room was shaking.

Greg was already out of bed, looking at the monitor on the other side of the room. The glow from the screen made a green nimbus around him.

'Greg!' she yelled, 'what's happening?'

He did not turn.

'Another quake. A big one, this time.'

She was out of bed and beside him in an instant.

'Are we in danger? Is the base safe!'

He turned and gave a little smile.

81

'Yes, we're safe; The Ridge is having a minor hiccup, that's all. There'll be a few landslides on the slopes, but this base was designed to move with the flexing and bending of a moderate quake.'

'But the reactor? If that should be damaged…'

He turned fully, so he was facing her.

'Look, darling, I wouldn't lie to you. Everything's been thought of. It would take a quake a thousand times bigger than what's happened to put us in danger. And we have the escape craft in any case. So don't worry. Go back to bed.'

She thought about it. The shaking had stopped. Then she shook her head.

'No. I'm wide awake now. I'll make some coffee.'

Of course, the quake was the only topic of conversation later that morning over breakfast, except from Kurchatov, who was as silent as a stone.

'The Ridge isn't particularly volcanic these days,' Sigurdsson was saying as the Richardsons came in.

'What about Iceland?' Beauvoir said, 'that's part of the ridge.'

Sigurdsson nodded. 'Yes, but as it's my homeland, I think I am more than qualified to talk about it. There are still eruptions, but they are few and far between. There are places on Earth far more active. And more dangerous. If the Yellowstone Supervolcano ever goes off…'

Sally walked past them.

'Can we change the subject, please?' she said, as she collected her plate from the dispenser, 'I'm just glad it's over.'

Beauvoir raised an eyebrow as she looked at her.

'You're a bit nervous, aren't you? Haven't you got any psychological tricks to calm us all down?'

'I'm an academic psychologist, not an Agony Aunt,' was Sally's scathing reply as she sat down; a reply she regretted instantly.

After all I said to Greg—now I'm upsetting them!

She summoned up a smile to deliver to Beauvoir.

'Sorry, Marie, I didn't sleep very well.'

Beauvoir shrugged, and turning, began to talk to Alvarez, who, to Sally's immense annoyance, resumed his stories of San Franciscan seismic horrors.

Greg caught Sally's mood.

'We'll go out in the sub later and take a look around.'

She glared at him.

'That's just what I need—looking at earthquake damage. We're rather monopolising the sub, aren't we?' She looked around at her bored companions. 'I'm sure somebody else would like to go out.'

No answer.

He lowered his voice and in exasperated tones, said, 'Sal, you'll see that very little happened. There're always little tremors near the Ridge—it's perfectly normal. It's just another day at the office.'

Sally felt that the attention of the crew was being directed at her.

She must affirm her authority as the centre of mental calm.

'Yes, that'd be wonderful,' she said, feeling like an actor just about to fail an audition, 'absolutely wonderful.'

***

The quake had kicked up a quantity of terrigenous ooze, which was only then beginning to return to the ocean floor. As a result, the water ahead of the sub had an opalescent quality into which the headlights carved two columns of misty light.

'Apart from the disturbance to the ooze, there doesn't seem to be too much going on,' Greg said, giving his tensely rigid wife a quick, reassuring glance. 'I told you it wasn't a big one. Now that the stress has been released, things should quieten down again.'

'Let's hope so,' Sally said, hoping her voice didn't sound too strangulated.

Greg nodded automatically; he wasn't really listening.

'We'll go out a few more hundred metres, then start to curve back.'

'That would be nice,' Sally said, realising that her voice did indeed sound strangulated.

Just then, the massive grey flank of the Mid-Atlantic Ridge hove into view behind the curtains of slowly descending particles.

'Everything where it should be,' Greg commented, apparently to himself, 'Just a little—hey!'

'What? What!' Sally said, abruptly straightening herself in her bucket chair, 'What's wrong?'

'Nothing's wrong, Sal,' he said, in a slightly schoolmasterish tone, 'look up ahead, where the beams meet.'

She looked. Against the drab grey rock was a black patch. A deep black patch.

She informed Greg it was only that which she was seeing.

'It's a cave, dear,' he said, with a vague air of disappointed expectation, 'a very big cave to be visible this far away. And more than that, it's a new cave.'

'That's nice,' Sally replied, 'well, I guess it's time to be heading back.'

'Not till I've had a good look,' was the reply.

Sally's heart sank, but it was the reply she'd been expecting.

The black patch soon resolved itself into a huge gash in the furrowed rock. Above the entrance, a mighty slab hung precariously.

'It's a new gash,' Greg muttered, 'but there looks to be a pre-existing void beyond. I think I'll go in.'

Suddenly alarmed, Sally reached for his arm. 'Don't be silly, Greg. If it's just opened, it could collapse at any moment with us inside. And I don't like the look of that big overhanging rock.'

He turned slightly and gave her the kind of smile a parent would give to a nervous child. 'It'll be fine. As far as I can see, the hole is new, but there's a cavern beyond. The quake wouldn't have torn a rent of that shape and depth. It has to be an old cavern; probably a very old one.'

His hands gripped the controls tightly. Sally slumped in the chair, knowing it was now useless to argue.

The sub nosed slowly past the jagged teeth of the entrance, passing directly under the massive overhang.

Greg let out a low whistle. 'It's gigantic, absolutely gigantic.'

Sally agreed; the void was so deep that the headlight beams almost met before giving up their unequal fight with the darkness and without revealing the opposite wall of the cave.

'I think I can see movements,' Greg said, 'I'll set her down and switch off the headlights.'

The sub slowly settled onto the cavern floor, and with the headlights extinguished darkness swept over them like a tossed cloak.

The only light was the slightly green glow of the cabin illumination.

We'll be on our way soon, Sally told her herself, it won't be long.

But then she saw something flash past in the gloom, something that had a row of blue lights along its side.

'There's life in here,' breathed Greg, 'bioluminescent life! What a pity Marie isn't here!'

Yes, instead of me! What a pity!

As their eyes became adjusted to the low levels of light, it gradually became apparent that the cavern was thronging with abundant lifeforms. The darkness was transformed into a tapestry of shifting constellations of bluish stars; some moving slowly, others fast; some belonging to creatures the size of shrimps, others to creatures the size of sharks.

'It must be an ecosystem that's been isolated from the outside world for thousands, maybe millions of years,' Greg said in awed wonder. 'What a find for science!' He turned to Sally. 'And there's you worrying about little quakes! This is wonderful! And I discovered it!'

He turned back to the controls. 'I'll turn the cameras on, they may pick up details our eyes can't register.'

But Sally must have had vision superior to Greg's because

she said, 'I can see lots of fish. Shoals of very tiny ones, then much fewer medium-sized ones, and every now and again, a really big one. Too big for my liking. Let's get out of here.'

Ignoring her request, Greg said, 'You can see all that? I can see your medium-sized ones, which I thought were the smallest ones, and I can see the big ones. This is wonderful—look at all those lights dancing and flashing around!'

They sat there for some time, and Sally gradually became resigned to the situation and looked more intently into the star-shot dimness. Slowly she became aware of behaviour patterns within the churning groups of fish.

'That's odd,' she finally said, 'I've seen it happen three times now.'

'Eh—what?' Greg muttered, looking up from a display she hadn't seen active before, 'What are you seeing?'

'I've seen groups of two or three of the tiny fish going right up to the open mouths of the middle-sized fish.'

'Cleaner fish?'

'No. They dart in and the big fish closes its mouth and starts chewing. They deliberately chose to get eaten.'

'That would be odd if it was true.'

Sally frowned. 'Thanks. And what is that display panel you've been messing around with for the last ten minutes?'

'It's the control for the asset retrieval facility—a.k.a. the Grabber.'

'What? You're going to try to catch one of the fish?'

'Not try, dear. Marie will be so glad I've brought her back a specimen, she'll be all over me.'

'Keep your mind on your job, I...'

They both became motionless.

A large black fish had just swum up to the sub's canopy and was now hanging there, kept in position by flickering movements of its fins. It had bulbous eyes, standing out some distance from its head, even though they appeared to be shut. Lights flashed along its flanks from its massive head to its tail, disappeared, and then began the journey again.

But what was really holding Sally's attention was its mouth. It opened periodically in a regular rhythm, and each time it did, she was rewarded with the sight of a seemingly endless display of ultra-sharp teeth shaped like miniature steak knives.

'Greg,' she said slowly, unaware she was trying to push herself through the back of the chair, 'let's go. Now!'

Abruptly, the great fish rotated ninety degrees, giving them a splendid view of the convoys of light along its sides.

It opened its mouth wider than Sally had thought possible.

And another, much smaller, fish swam directly into that horrific gape.

The mouth closed.

And chewing motions began.

Sally put her hands over her eyes and said, very quietly and earnestly, 'Greg…'

Suddenly she heard an odd noise, and looking up she saw a mechanical arm dart outwards; an arm that terminated in a net. The net enveloped the large fish and it disappeared from view as the arm retracted, storing the creature in a tank below their feet.

Sally could feel the vibrations from its thrashing making the floor shake under her feet.

'Great,' she croaked, 'Now I'm sharing this tiny sub with a Devil Fish.'

Greg was grinning again. 'Don't worry. I've done enough. Back we go!'

The journey back seemed much longer than the outward journey, and all the time Sally could feel the fish thrashing madly a few centimetres below her feet.

***

Sally had never been gladder to be back inside the base. The weird fish had been rapidly transferred to a glass-sided tank in the main BioLab, pressurised to the outside level, and most of the crew were now staring at it as it swam around in a restless, agitated fashion. Occasionally it would rest its snout upon the glass and hang there motionless, apparently staring at the humans, even though it was now obvious it was blind.

When Sigurdsson commented 'What an ugly bastard,' he was speaking for most of them, but not Beauvoir, who was so fascinated that when the creature rested its head upon the glass, she pressed her nose on the other side in fascinated wonder so both heads were separated only by the transparent casing.

'That is a very uneducated comment, Harald,' she said, without moving her head, 'I expected better from you.' Forgetting about Sigurdsson, she stared at the fish for some minutes. Then, seemingly discussing the issue with herself, she said, 'In appearance, it resembles Chauliodus sloani, but is much bigger and appears to be totally blind. I can only conclude that it is a species new to science.'

'Wonderful,' muttered Sigurdsson, 'you can name it uglymotherfuckeris beauvorii, or some such moniker. I've had enough of it. The best thing you can do with it is to serve it up with some French fries—but take that head off first.'

Just then the light gave a flicker, dulled to yellow, and then snapped back to full illumination.

Greg looked around. 'Where's Kurchatov? He said the reactor was back to full function.'

No one knew. Alvarez made a tasteless comment about Kurchatov performing unlikely sexual acts with the control rods, but no-one laughed.

They went back to studying the tank.

But in the few seconds that the light had malfunctioned, the fish had gone wild. Its thrashing was now frenzied, and with increasing frequency it flung itself against the side of the tank, causing the whole structure to shudder. Automatically they backed away, even though they knew the tank's tensile strength was far greater than any fish of the creature's size could deliver. But as it hit the side, its mouth gaped wide, displaying serried ranks of razor-sharp teeth.

'It's trying to get you, Harald,' Alvarez chuckled, 'it maybe can't see, but its hearing seems fine.'

Sigurdsson tried to grin but did not quite succeed. Sally, however, did achieve a quick grin as she observed him surreptitiously work his way to the back of the group. Just then Beauvoir said, 'Oh no!' and Sally whirled around to see the animal slowly sinking to the bottom of the tank, its mouth agape but not moving.

Beauvoir pressed her hands against the tank as she stared at the fish as it slowly drifted down, finally resting on the floor of the tank, with its open mouth turned in their direction.

'If fish could be said to hate,' Sally said quietly, 'I'd say that fish hated us.'

'I'll have to do a dissection,' Beauvoir said, 'I thought we had the pressure just right, but maybe I overlooked something in its environment. Perhaps the salinity, damn it!'

Sally shrugged. 'I guess it didn't like being held captive by people.'

'No anthropomorphism, please Sally,' Beauvoir said. 'We've lost the chance to study its behaviour, and that's a blow to science.'

Sally's response was never to be heard as at that moment Kurchatov appeared, walking down the corridor from the central nuclear furnace.

'What's going on, Igor?' Greg demanded, 'I thought you said that damn reactor was working fine!'

Kurchatov did not meet his stare.

'It's just a little blip,' he said, examining his shoes as if he had just seen something unpleasant attached to them.

'We don't want "little blips" with a fission reactor, Igor,' Greg said.

Kurchatov looked up, and it surprised Sally to see that his eyes appeared to be moist. 'Leave me alone! I know what I'm doing! There's no danger—why don't you believe me? Do you think I'm not a professional like the rest of you here?'

'Of course, we don't doubt your professionalism, Igor.'

'Then leave me alone.' His voice had become a whine. 'Don't you know who I'm named after?—THE Igor

Kurchatov—the one who designed the Obninsk nuclear power plant; the first of its kind in the world! The father of the Soviet atomic bomb!'

'OK, OK, Igor. Can you confirm the reactor is working completely safely now?'

'Yes, of course. It always was. I know what I'm doing!'

The others had drifted away, back to their studies or the coffee machines. Only Sally and Greg were left with Kurchatov. Greg threw Sally an exasperated glance and walked away.

Sally crossed to Kurchatov, who seemed to shrink away.

'It's alright, Igor. No-one's getting at you, we all trust you.'

'Yes, but you don't like me, do you?'

'Why do you say that?'

'I've seen you looking away when I come in; I've heard you talking about me. Just because I can't talk about football with Sigurdsson or women with Alvarez. I wish I hadn't agreed to come down here to this horrible place, Mrs Richardson.'

Sally dared to place a hand on his shoulder; he flinched slightly but did not move away.

'Relax Igor, just take it easy. You're probably the most important person in this base. Relax. Just enjoy the company, find something in common with the rest of us. It's not that difficult.'

Kurchatov nodded. Sally saw that his eyes were indeed moist.

'And two small things, Igor.'

'Yes?'

'Call me Sally.'

'OK—Sally. What's the other thing?'

She smiled tenderly. 'It's probably best if you don't have as a hero the man who invented the Soviet atomic bomb.'

***

There was no-one in the BioScience Dome other than Marie Beauvoir, and at that exact moment she was staring down at the corpse of the weird fish from the cavern.

One eye was below her scalpel and would have been returning her gaze had it not been sightless.

Expertly, she removed the organ and placed it under the magnifier.

It clearly had evolved from the standard vertebrate eye but had atrophied in the darkness of its subterranean environment.

So far, so normal. Most cave fish were sightless. The combination of oceanic depth and a subterranean lifestyle was unusual, but there were other examples.

She opened the skull and spent some time looking at the brain. She rubbed a sore patch on her chin under her surgical mask. Something a bit different here. The brain was distinctly larger than she would have expected. Intriguing.

The scalpel sliced into the tissue, her expert movements peeling away the outer layers to reveal the glistening interior.

The minute movements of the blade stopped.

There was a black mass there.

And it was moving, quivering, pulsating. Rippling shivers swept over its surface.

Only the region of her eyes was visible above the mask and her eyebrows moved downwards as she frowned.

This was unusual; very unusual.

Her heart rate quickened. This was a genuine discovery; something to get her noticed; get her higher in the echelons of biological science so she'd never have to do this kind of skivvying again!

That annoying itch under her mask had worsened. She pulled the mask up and rubbed the irritated flesh.

Just then, the lights in the lab flickered once and then went out.

She stood transfixed, looking down at the dissected fish. Its sides were still bioluminescent with a lambent blue glow.

It was beautiful.

She leaned in closer to get a better view of the lateral organs from which the soft radiance was emanating.

As she did the black mass in the brain rose slightly; so very slightly only an observer closely studying it at that precise moment could have noticed.

Perhaps even such an observer would not have noticed a small puff of black particles that shot up from the mass; in the semi-darkness and with her attention focused on the bioluminescence Beauvoir did not. So small were the particles that she did not register that a few of them had attached themselves to her nasal membranes.

The light came on again.

Beauvoir straightened up as the creature's soft glow was no longer visible.

She felt suddenly exhausted; she would continue her studies tomorrow.

Yes, tomorrow.

***

Kurchatov sat looking up at Greg. He was visibly wilting under the latter's wrath.

'One more foul-up, and you're out,' Greg was saying, his voice brittle with anger. 'The safety of this entire base is at risk from your ineptitude.'

'I'm not inept, Mr Richardson,' Kurchatov finally said, in a voice hardly above a whisper, 'The reactor has been running fine for days now. I was experimenting with the control rods when it happened and I reduced the power too much. The base was never in any danger.'

'So you keep saying. No doubt you'll still be saying that when tonnes of arctic water are pouring into the corridors. Alright, get out of my sight, Igor.'

The small man rose unsteadily and started to walk out of the Meeting Room.

'Don't forget—one more foul-up!' Greg yelled after him, leaving the threat hanging.

When Kurchatov had disappeared, Sally tapped Greg's arm.

'Aren't you being a little hard on the poor man?' she said softly. 'He's got very good recommendations.'

Greg turned to her. 'Sally, darling, you're too soft-hearted for your own good. I know you like him and feel sorry for him. I guess it's not his fault he's such an introverted little weed.'

'Greg!'

He grimaced. 'Sorry, that was a bit strong. But look, all our lives depend on that bloody reactor working perfectly. I can't pretend it's not important. We should have had a back-up for Kurchatov, but no, those bean counters Topside claim the budget wouldn't run to it, so we're all dependent on one man.'

'Try encouraging him a bit more,' Sally suggested, 'instead of brow-beating him. He's very unsure of himself.' She raised a finger to forestall his next irritated comment. 'And don't forget you're talking to a psychologist. We're all professionals here!'

He shrugged and looked around the room, his gaze resting on a coffee machine.

'God, I wish they'd allowed alcohol down here. I could do with a real drink instead of this bloody dishwater they call coffee!'

'Yes, drink-driving under nearly a kilometre of ocean. That's a really good idea.'

He grinned. 'Now, you said you'd never mention my little peccadillo ever again.'

"And you said you'd listen to me in future!'

They both smiled, kissed, and were about to leave the room when Beauvoir walked in.

Sally immediately noticed something different about her; something about the hair…

'Are you OK, Marie?' she said as the other woman passed on the way to the coffee machine.

'Yes, why shouldn't I be?'

'You look a little…tired.'

'Hah!' Beauvoir sat down with her cardboard coffee mug, turning her back on them, 'Why shouldn't I be—I do all the work around here.'

Sally was concerned. Beauvoir was not the easiest woman to

get along with, not the kind Sally would choose to accompany her on a Girls' Night Out, but she seemed a little more brittle than usual. And the hair. What was it...?

'Sorry to annoy you, Marie,' she started to say and then she realised what had caught her attention earlier.

'Marie, your hair, it looks like you've been pulling lumps out.'

Marie turned to face her. 'Don't be ridiculous. My hair gets a bit thin sometimes. If you suffered from diabetes like me, you would have known not to ask.'

Sally knew better than to push the issue. But she also knew that Marie's hair had not suffered from a consequence of diabetes: it was obviously thinner in well-defined patches.

The woman had quite definitely been pulling clumps out.

So what could the reason be? Why was she denying it?

Sally knew that such behaviour was usually the sign of some mental distress. Her professional duties kicked in. She would have to get Marie involved in a one-to-one, to find out what was upsetting her.

And yet she had seemed so excited to be dealing with that bloody fish; so convinced she had made a scientific discovery.

'Marie, you do seem a little down, dear. Is it something to do with the fish? Is it a well-known species after all, is that it?'

To Sally's amazement, Beauvoir flung the half-full cup across the room, narrowly missing an astounded Greg. She stood in front of them; her face contorted with fury.

'Shut up, you stupid woman! You don't know a whale shark from a goldfish! Just keep your nose out of my affairs! Call yourself a psychologist!'

And with that, she was heading for the open door only to recoil slightly as Kurchatov came through it.

'You!' Beauvoir exclaimed, 'I've been looking for you! There's something wrong with the AC in this hellhole.'

Kurchatov took two steps backwards.

'Well, I know Mr and Mrs Richardson have...'

'No, not them! Me! There's a terrible stink in my lab, and I want it seen to.'

'Is it the fish?' he enquired, innocently.

'Of course not, you fool. Look, are there service areas in the ducts near my lab?'

'Why yes, I think so, but...'

'Then I want to look inside, and you'll show me. Now!'

Kurchatov gave Greg an apologetic look and departed, with Beauvoir extremely close behind him.

The Richardsons waited for a few moments to be certain the other two were sufficiently distant, and then Greg turned to Sally and in a hollow voice said, 'What in the name of all that's holy was that all about?'

Sally shook her head. 'Something's gone wrong with her studies of that goddamn fish, I think. She was like a schoolgirl at her birthday party a few days ago, but now... I'll have to have a word with her, but it looks like I'll have to pick my moment very carefully.'

'Well, I hope you can sort her out. I can't have hysterical women running around the place.'

She glared at him. 'Did you actually say what I thought you said? Marie is a first-class scientist. If she's upset, then there'll be a reason and I'll find out what it is and help her get over it. Got that, Mr Neanderthal?'

He grinned, slightly sheepishly, and held out his hand.

'Spank me, Miss. I've been a very bad boy. Please.'

She stared at him for a few moments and then burst out laughing. She slapped his hand playfully.

'Oh, you!'

But after she had finished laughing, her gaze returned to the doorway.

'But something is wrong.'

***

The next morning was "lifeboat" drill—as everyone called it. Although they were sufficiently far into the mesopelagic zone

95

to be unaware of the diurnal cycle, the base adhered rigorously to a 24-hour cycle, although one set to the equatorial rhythm rather than to their actual latitude.

Sally's voice came over the intercom, distinctly muffled and with a tinge of nervousness.

'I can hardly move in this damn thing. And I don't like looking like the Michelin Man.'

Greg had to agree there was a resemblance. The pressure suit was very bulky, and its joints were extraordinarily rigid, requiring no small effort to flex the limbs. And Sally had already complained about the weight of the oxygen-helium tanks more than anybody else.

Sally's face was dimly visible through the faceplate, but not so dimly that he could not see the desire on her face to be released from the heavy protective suit.

'OK,' he said, 'you've proved you can get into the suit. Now prove you can get out. It's not going to be very sweet smelling in there if you can't. Not to mention us having to feed you through a tube!'

Sally could get out of the suit—although once again, there was no danger of her losing the record of being both the slowest person to get into a suit, and also the person slowest to get out of one.

When she was finally out she was confronted by several people looking at their watches in mock anger—at least she assumed it was not genuine.

'I don't ever want to get into one of those fu—those damn things again as long as I live!'

'Well, I can't promise that,' Greg said, with a wicked smile playing on his lips, 'but I won't ask you to do it again. For a while.'

'Could you remind me of the pressure tolerance of these suits?' Alvarez asked, his eyes not straying from Sally, as she stood there panting with the effort of escaping from the suit.

'Up to forty bar.'

'Now, that's very interesting. As we're at six hundred

metres, I believe that means the pressure outside is about sixty bar. Any particular reason for the slightly alarming gap between the suit's strength and the pressure of the water, water which is only separated from us by a thin steel shell?'

Greg looked at him with annoyance written plainly on his face.

'I believe you've asked that question before, Ricardo. My answer is the same as last time: The Powers-That-Be decided that the extra cost would be too much of a strain on the budget. Plus the fact that to strengthen the suit up to sixty bar would make it almost possible to move in it. These suits will be OK for short excursions.'

'And I believe I pointed out that the phrase "up to" is meaningless. It simply specifies a range from zero to forty—and zero is not excluded.'

A tense silence fell.

The other people in the room looked either bored or embarrassed.

Eventually, Sigurdsson broke the silence.

'Look, as long as we play by the rules we'll never need to get into one of those things. So can we move on, please.'

Greg nodded, showing his relief to be rescued from the situation.

But Alvarez was not so easily silenced.

'If the four survivors' (Greg frowned at that word) 'wanted to escape in the sub, but the power was out, how would they get to the sub?'

Greg looked briefly up at the ceiling, in a theatrical "Give Me Strength" gesture.

'As I said last week, Ricardo, the sub's airlock can be entered mechanically, as can the outer door, for that matter. Would it help if I wrote all this down on your hand?'

'Time for your lecture on the escape pods, please,' Sigurdsson said, with the air of the man who has suffered enough of a very tedious lecture.

'OK, on to the escape pods,' Greg said, wishing he could

97

escape from Alvarez.

Each escape pod held two people, which, as Alvarez never tired of pointing out, was a little inconvenient as the base personnel amounted to seven individuals.

'Each dome has an escape capsule; you do all remember I took you to the Escape Room, next door?' Greg pointed out yet again, 'and as there are four domes that means—if my arithmetic is correct—that we have the capacity for eight individuals.'

'If we have access to all the domes,' Alvarez returned, 'doesn't it all depend on what kind of disaster we'd be facing?'

'Two people is the recommended number, but at a squeeze they could take three,' Greg said, 'I can't imagine what kind of crisis would knock out two domes.'

'The Mid-Atlantic Ridge blowing its top?'

'Now you're just being provocative for the sake of it,' Greg snapped, 'we've had two minor tremors we'd not even have noticed if we'd been Topside. All indications are that the stresses have been released and things have settled down.'

Alvarez smiled. 'I guess you're right. My Ma back in Frisco would have carried on serving up the enfrijoladas without a second's thought. And perhaps Joan might like to sit on my lap—that would make four people in a pod.'

Sally was amused to see a faint blush colour Hicks' cheeks at that comment.

Greg returned Alvarez's smile, glad that the latter's needling had finally ended. 'OK. That's that. Let's get on with the drill.'

Beauvoir looked completely uninterested, Sally thought, and she had still not managed to get the woman on her own, but she didn't want to make a formal request for a discussion—as yet.

Strangely, Sigurdsson also looked completely uninterested; not simply bored with a routine he had done many times, but— what was the right word—disdainful.

But as she had expected, Greg had not noticed the unusual attitudes of those two and was demonstrating to the others, who at least were trying to feign interest, how to pull down the access ladder and open the entrance hatch to the escape pod.

Then Hicks asked a question that nobody had ever asked before.

'What if we were trapped outside and the base was uninhabitable? Could we get into the escape pod then?'

Greg's brow furrowed, and he went quiet. Sally could tell he was running the manual past a mental eye; not wanting to admit to his crew that he—heaven forfend—didn't know!

Then he smiled.

'There's a mechanical control panel on the outside that can eject the pod from the dome. You'd be able to get in when it had separated.'

Alvarez put up a hand.

'Great, Teach. But the pod doesn't have an airlock. It's only meant to be accessed from inside this complex.'

Greg looked annoyed. 'Please, Ricardo, you're clearly enjoying being difficult. If you were outside, you'd obviously be in the pressure gear. You remember—the one Sally has just demonstrated? The electrics inside the pod are completely sealed. And once you're inside, the systems kick in to pump all the water out.'

Sally thought it was time to ask an intelligent question.

'What if you didn't have a pressure suit? Say I was wearing scuba gear?'

Greg slapped his forehead theatrically. 'Sal, Sal. Without a suit, you'd be squashed flat and in hypothermic shock simultaneously! It's sixty bar out there, for God's sake.'

Sally winced. 'Sorry. Please carry on Greg.'

Greg did carry on and eventually everyone agreed that they knew how to get into the escape pod.

That is, the ones who were still talking. Greg had to ask Beauvoir and Sigurdsson to confirm they understood the procedure and, eventually, they both nodded their assent.

Later, Sally confided in Hicks that she was concerned about Beauvoir.

Hicks pursued her lips and then said, 'Yes. I thought it was me, imagining things. But if you've seen it too…'

'Could it be her diabetes going haywire?'

'Could well be. I'll ask her to provide a blood sample. It's the only way to be sure. We certainly don't want any emergency cases down here.'

Reassured, Sally left Hicks to do the arranging, pleased she had done her duty and Beauvoir would soon be getting the care she needed.

Returning to their room, she found Greg getting ready to go out in the sub.

'Fancy a spin?' he said, smiling lopsidedly.

She threw a cushion at him.

'Get lost! I don't want to be out in the water ever again! Take Alvarez with you. It'll stop him leering at me!'

He gave a normal smile. 'OK. You can have a lie-down and rest.'

'What in this stuffy steam-room? Why don't you get Kurchatov to do something useful about the AC, instead of switching the lights off and on, like a kid playing with the remote control?'

'You told me to go easy with him.'

'Oh, you're impossible,' she said, but only half-angry, 'you remember everything I say except the things I want you to remember!'

He kissed her on the cheek as he left.

'Welcome to married life.'

***

The sub hung in the cold darkness with its motor idling, as Greg and Alvarez stared at the great net fence a few metres in front of them. They had checked the enclosures which held the salmon and the yellowfin and now was the time to meet the stars of the show—the splendid bluefin.

Bluefin which now were even more splendid since Alvarez's alterations to their DNA.

Alvarez was in conversational mode.

100

'You know, I suppose, what we're doing here has been foreseen for a long time.'

'What—what, pisciculture? I didn't know that; I thought we were the first.'

'Well, on this scale we are. And with genetically modified fish. But fish farming had a long history. I think salmon farms in the Norwegian fjords were the first real attempt.'

'Yes. I've heard of them. But it was all very small beer.'

Alvarez nodded. 'I read a book once about this kind of thing. The Deep Range, I believe it was called. The writer got a lot of things right but one very big thing wrong.'

'Oh?' Greg wasn't really interested, but he knew that taking an interest in his people was crucial in keeping them motivated.

'Yes, he had the farmers rearing and slaughtering whales. Although to be fair, by the end of the book they are considering stopping the slaughter.'

Greg slapped his thigh. 'God! And now we're trying to talk to them! Times have certainly changed!' He looked ahead at the swirling motion behind the net. 'I hope things don't get so bad Topside that we ever go back to that sort of thing, I really do.'

'That's why we're here, Greg,' Alvarez said soberly, 'to make sure that never happens. The human race can't seem to stop having babies, so we're here to make sure they don't starve.'

Greg nodded as he thought Alvarez's words over. 'You've got hidden depths, Ricardo. And there's me thinking you were only interested in making babies.'

The other grinned, the soft interior lights casting his face into a relief map of light and shadow, but said no more.

'Well, I guess it's feeding time,' Greg said and sent the sub nosing towards the great gate in the fence. Its components slid apart, sending out an ultrasonic pulse as they separated, deterring any fish from seizing the opportunity to escape. Immediately they were surrounded by silvery, streamlined living torpedoes as mighty bluefin tuna swept around them. Great eyes examined the men as the superb fish hurtled around the submarine in dizzying helices, occasionally passing so close to the canopy that the sub's occupants could see themselves reflected in a staring eye.

'How big do these bloody things grow?' Greg said, his knuckles white as he grasped the controls, 'Are you sure you didn't incorporate orca genes into them, you mad scientist?'

'The median length is now around four metres, but even before I started monkeying around with their DNA they occasionally made three metres.'

'Occasionally! Anything that small would be gobbled up in an instant. Please, Ricardo, don't make them any bigger!'

'I'm glad you approve,' Alvarez said, his justly-famous smile once again endangering the lower part of his face.

The sub hummed contentedly further into the pen, while around it the silver kaleidoscope of its powerful denizens continued to whirl and circle. Slowly a great pillar came into view in the headlights' misty radiance.

'It's malfunctioned once before,' Greg murmured, 'It's almost time now. Let's see what happens.'

The sub hung in the darkness, its motor ticking gently, and with its gyroscope ensuring it was stationary in all three dimensions.

Then all over the surface of the pillar, holes appeared, for a moment looking disconcertingly like hungry mouths. And then the mouths began to eject a steady stream of small, brownish blocks.

Those blocks had no time to descend to the ocean floor because the pillar immediately disappeared behind a roiling mass of silver frenzy as the tuna went wild for the food.

'Protein, fats, vitamins. They love it,' Alvarez grunted in self-satisfaction, 'all my own recipe. Scientifically proven to add on kilos of hard, red muscle.' He gave Greg a sly poke with his elbow. 'Perhaps you should try it, Greg.'

'Very funny. Any time, Ricardo.' Greg stared at the tumultuous mass of hard-muscled eating-machines. 'I wonder what would happen if these mothers got out into the open.'

'God help anything smaller than a humpback,' Ricardo said, 'they'd be the kings of the sea in nothing flat.'

'Hmmm. Well, it'd better not happen on my watch.' Greg straightened himself in the chair and, looking away from the feeding-frenzy, said, 'well, everything's working fine here. No signs of parasitic load. Back to the Hotel Paradiso, I think.'

The sub made a slow turn, Greg being careful not to bump into the writhing mass of piscine power, and they began the return to the gate.

It had just come into view when Alvarez made a strange, gurgling noise. Greg turned to check on him when the other suddenly grabbed the controls.

The sub rolled badly as it tried to obey Alvarez's demands and Greg was thrown to one side, with Alvarez slamming into him an instant later. Righting himself, he tore the other's hands off the controls, sending the craft pitching straight down into impenetrable darkness.

Then just as suddenly as he had snatched the controls from Greg, Alvarez made the same liquid, bubbling sounds and slumped in the chair.

Greg got the sub horizontal again just as the grey ooze of the sea bottom came into view.

Keeping one hand firmly on the controls he shook Alvarez with the other.

'What the fuck was that about, you idiot! If that was some kind of joke, I'm sending you Topside as soon as we get back. Answer me, you bastard!'

Alvarez's eyelids, hitherto clamped firmly shut, flickered open and he looked around, a haunted expression contorting his face.

'Greg, I don't know! Something inside seemed to reach up and take over my hands! I knew I was doing it but I couldn't stop myself! You've got to believe me, Greg! I didn't want to do that! It wasn't me!'

Greg stared at his companion and for some time the only noise was the reassuring purr of the engine. Then he spoke.

'Maybe it's some kind of rapture of the deep. It shouldn't be, but maybe you're susceptible, more than the rest of us. I know one thing, Hicks is giving you a thorough medical as soon as we get back. You do nothing until she's examined you, inside out. You hear me?'

Alvarez nodded dumbly.

Greg flicked the telecommunicator into life, going straight to the medical lab.

Hicks appeared on the screen. Looking strangely tired.

Greg barked instructions on what he wanted her to do as soon as they arrived.

She nodded, without making any comment, and the screen went dark.

The rest of the return journey was made in utter silence as the fish pen slowly receded into dark invisibility behind them.

***

Kurchatov knocked on the door of the central laboratory in the BioScience Dome.

'Ah, Ms Beauvoir? You wanted to see me?'

Beauvoir looked up from the tray on the desk before her. It contained various animal organs sitting in a fluid that was tinged a murky shade of red.

'Igor—please come in.'

He obeyed but stopped a few metres from Beauvoir; his gaze focused on an indeterminate patch of the floor.

She made a tutting noise.

'Now, don't be silly. I don't bite, you sweet little boy. Come closer.'

Once again, he obeyed.

'Is it the air conditioning, Ms Beauvoir? I've already shown you how to look into the conduits. I do agree the smell seems to be getting worse, but…'

She put down the scalpel and turned so she was fully facing him. Then she indicated the tray with the unidentifiable lumps of flesh sitting in the reddish liquid.

'Do you know much about biology, Igor?'

He shook his head. 'No, Ms Beauvoir. It has never interested me. I much prefer things that can be properly controlled, things with electric currents, conductivity, resistance, machines that do what they're told to do.'

She gave a big smile. Kurchatov realised he had never seen her smile before this moment. He liked it.

'Igor, that's almost poetic. You must have hidden depths.' She giggled. 'I suppose that's a silly thing to say, considering where we are!'

Then she laughed; an unusual throaty laugh.

He looked on, unsure of what reaction was required.

She motioned him to come nearer, and when he was standing next to her, she turned and prodded the lumps of tissue with the scalpel.

'I've dissected that fish, Igor. I know a great deal about it. It's a remarkable creature, Igor, very remarkable. Take a look at this.' She prodded a small sac of stringy black tissue. A stinging stench of formaldehyde rose from it, making him gasp and pull away.

She caught his arm, holding him in place.

'We animals have things that your machines, your circuits, don't have, Igor. For instance, this little black pouch of flesh. Do you know what it is?'

'Ms Beauvoir, I think I…'

'Igor, I asked you a question. Do you know what this is?'

'No, Ms Beauvoir.'

'It's a sac which contained the animal's testes. They make the spermatozoa. For fertilisation of the female. Men have testes as well, Igor, although we usually call them "testicles." But they also produce spermatozoa. Lots and lots of the little devils.'

Suddenly she placed her hands on his shoulders. They were about the same height.

'Would you like to use your testes on me, Igor? Would you like to fertilise me, Igor?'

He pulled away, forcing her arms down to her hips.

'Stop this! We are professionals; this is not appropriate!'

With surprising strength for one so slight, she easily broke his grip and pushed against him. She held his head and forced their faces together. To his horror, he felt a tongue thrust its way between his lips, carrying a load of salty saliva with it. The tongue danced in his mouth, and he felt her strangely cold breath flood his features.

Frantically, he pushed her away, so she crashed back against the workbench, sending some of the liquids from the organ tanks splashing to the floor.

She stood looking at him and then began to laugh.

Louder and louder, she laughed, holding her hips as she was seized by a paroxysm of hilarity.

'It's OK, Igor, I've done what I wanted. I won't trouble you again. You can go now.'

Needing no further encouragement, he turned to the door.

As he rushed out, he heard her mocking voice echoing down the corridor.

'I think you can call me "Marie" now, Igor!'

***

'That's done now, Ricardo.'

Hicks held up the syringe to the light. It contained a dark red liquid.

'Is there any blood in that alcohol, do you think, Joan?'

She looked blankly at him for a few seconds and then smiled.

'Sorry, Ricardo. I don't have much of a sense of humour, I'm afraid. That was very funny.'

'You think I'm joking?' he said, rolling the sleeve of his sweatshirt down a hairy arm, 'you don't know me very well.'

She smiled again. 'I've got the measure of you now, Ricardo. I'll let you know what proof your blood is later. Off you go.'

With a grin, Alvarez rose from the chair and headed out of the Medical Dome. For a few seconds, Hicks looked in the direction he had gone, unaware that she was stroking the fabric over her left breast.

Ricardo arrived in the Meeting Room just as Greg had begun his daily report to the authorities on the surface—known to everyone in the base simply as "Topside".

Greg was typing at the console as Ricardo moved just behind him, making as little noise as possible.

He saw the words appear on the screen as Greg typed.

"As reported yesterday, there was a minor tremor near the base of the Ridge. I confirm the epicentre was at the coordinates I supplied earlier. Alvarez and I checked the three pens in the order of distance from the epicentre, namely Salmon, Yellowfin Tuna, Bluefin Tuna. There was some sign that a slight displacement had occurred to the western side of the salmon pen but it was less than a metre and no tear was discovered so I decided that no action was necessary. The other pens were untouched, and Alvarez and I checked that the feeding problem in the Bluefin pen has been resolved. The situation is nominal, and no further action is required on the tremor issue. Richardson out."

He pushed his chair backwards, colliding with Alvarez, who had not moved quickly enough.

'Ricardo! What are you doing there! Oh, don't tell me—you were checking to see if I'd mention your little brainstorm to Topside, weren't you?'

Ricardo spread his arms and assumed his best penitential expression.

'Sorry, Greg. I couldn't help it. This job means a lot to me. If we succeed here, they'll roll out facilities like this over all the world's seas and oceans, And I want to be there. Leading, directing. This is just another diving job for you, but I've staked my reputation on getting this right.' His voice dipped. 'Any whiff of a problem—that I might be unreliable, well, you know…'

Greg looked at him and folded his arms.

'If I think that I need to tell Topside about any "whiffs", I will tell them. But I'll tell you first. Got it?'

Ricardo now felt genuinely penitential.

'Yes, Greg. Sorry.'

Greg placed a large hand on Alvarez's shoulder. 'Forget it. Did Hicks say anything about…' He looked around briefly 'it?'

'No. It'll take a while to run the tests. She'll let me know.'

'OK. I understand your concerns. Let's hope everything's clear, and it was just a one-off.'

Alvarez's smile was slightly lop-sided. 'Yes. Let's hope that. You know us volatile Latin types.'

Later that night, Greg and Sally lay on the bed in their room. Both were naked.

'I thought Kurchatov was supposed to have fixed the bloody AC,' Sally muttered, 'this room is making me feel like an oven-ready chicken that the cook's forgotten about.'

'I'll have a word with the little twerp tomorrow,' growled Greg, 'I agree this is ridiculous. How can we be expected to sleep! And just think there's a gazillion tonnes of ice-cold water just a short distance away!'

Sally turned her head. 'I wish you'd stop saying things like that. You know it upsets me!'

'Look darling, do you think I'd be down here if it wasn't perfectly safe? You fly in planes, don't you? You don't mind being in a metal tube hurtling along with nothing but the stratosphere to support it. It's just the same.'

'No, it's not. You're a diver; this is your job. When you say things like that it reminds me of all those tonnes of cold, black water pressing against the walls of this place. We're like an empty eggshell held in a vice; just turn the screw a little and—pop!'

Greg rolled, so he was looking down at her dimly lit face.

'You know I'd protect you.'

She shook her head. 'No, there are some things no one can protect against. The ocean is one of them.'

Greg had intended to make love with his wife that night. But they did not.

**

Kurchatov felt a rising excitement as he entered the central structure of the base, the massive sphere which held the small modular reactor which gave the researchers all their power. Half of the reactor was below the catwalk in the lower half of the sphere, leaving the bank of controls easily accessible in the upper half.

Kurchatov walked up to the controls and checked the readings. Everything was on the button. There was no problem with the coolant, which was simply seawater. Once in the heat exchanger the boiling water, which had been heated by the fissioning uranium, readily gave up its borrowed energy to the icy exterior. No problems at all.

He moved a little to the left to where the outer casing of the containment structure was exposed. He ran his hand over the smooth metal. It was slightly warm.

He knew that inside the structure, neutrons were bombarding rods of U^{235}, splitting them into lighter elements and in the process giving off torrents of energy, more than enough to run the base.

But for the first time, a new concept came to the surface of his mind; something that had not occurred to him before. There was something else inside the containment structure, and that something had a very old name.

And that name was DEATH.

There was death not far from his fingertips, blazing, incandescent death. Death from metal-softening heat; death from hard radiation—high-energy photons which would blister the skin and, like invisible needles, burrow deep into the marrow.

Why had that not occurred to him before?

Why—he was the Master of Death! He held in his powerful grasp the lives of all these poor little creatures which infested the base.

How could they be so stupid as to sneer at him and think him inconsequential—when he was the Master of Death!

The idea fascinated him, and for several minutes he stood

motionless as idea after delicious idea swept through his brain.

Then, with a jerk, he broke the spell and returned his attention to the controls.

But there was much to consider after this new epiphany. Very much indeed.

***

'Have you managed to map the new stress patterns, Harald?'

Sigurdsson did not reply and, motionless in the chair, continued to stare into infinity.

'Harald?' Greg said again.

Sigurdsson moved his hand to his chin and began to rub it slowly. He let out a long sigh.

Greg planted himself directly in front of the other man and said in a low, authoritative voice, 'I'm talking to you, Sigurdsson. I'd like an answer.'

Sigurdsson seemed to be looking at a point some metres behind Greg as if his interlocutor was invisible. He let out another sigh.

Greg was not famous for the length of his temper, and leaning down, he shook the other man quite strongly.

Suddenly Sigurdsson looked up, fixing him in an eye to eye gaze.

'I wouldn't do that if I were you, Richardson.'

'I beg your pardon?'

Sigurdsson stood. He was only slightly shorter than Greg, though not so heavily built.

'I think it's best you leave me alone.'

'Leave you alone?' Greg was astounded. Everyone—except perhaps Greg—knew Sigurdsson to be direct in speech and somewhat brusque, but point-blank insubordination was a new one. 'You're here to do a job: map the seabed, calculate the fault stresses. I didn't realise you'd become a tourist.'

Sigurdsson smiled, but here was something wrong with the expression. Greg found himself staring into the face of a not

110

particularly friendly head-teacher, who had grown tired of a particular student's continual solecisms. But Sigurdsson's voice became mild and no longer confrontational.

'Look, Greg, what does it all matter? What's the point? We're just wasting our time down here.'

'We are?' Greg found himself unable to do anything other than utter his question in a kind of squeak.

'Yes, old friend.' And to Greg's horror, Sigurdsson gently patted the side of his face as if he was dealing with a naughty pet, 'It doesn't really matter, does it, my little friend? Nothing's important anymore, is it? None of us are getting any younger, if you know what I mean.'

Greg was used to subordinates trying him out, checking to see if he was all talk, but this behaviour was outside his experience. He remained trapped in stunned silence, and then Sigurdsson yawned and said, 'It's been lovely talking to you, but I think I'll go to my room now. I need a bit of a rest.'

Greg watched him go and then turned away, uncertain of what he should be doing. Alvarez had been watching in silent amazement but then said, 'What the hell's got into him?'

Greg sat down and resumed staring at the corridor into which Sigurdsson had disappeared. 'Damned if I know.' Turning, he looked sharply at Alvarez. 'Another rapture of the deep? Looks like people are starting to copy you, Ricardo. How are you feeling now? Have you got your results back?'

'I have. All my blood readings are within normal limits.'

As Greg looked into the San Franciscan's smiling face, an unusual thought occurred to him.

Within normal limits? But within normal limits of what?

But he said nothing. It was not his field.

Instead, he looked up at one of the air vents high in the wall and snapped, 'I thought Kurchatov was supposed to be doing something about that smell!'

Alvarez's smile stretched to Cheshire Cat proportions.

'Looks like you might have a mutiny on your hands, Captain Bligh.'

Sally and Greg lay on their bed in the hot, damp darkness. The room was so oppressive that they had left the door open. She was listening to his report of the recent events, particularly with Alvarez and Sigurdsson.

'Well, you're the psychologist, people aren't as easy to understand as tectonic plates,' he was saying, somewhat peevishly, 'so you tell me what's going on?'

In the darkness, her sweat-streaked brow furrowed.

'It's unusual behaviour. I don't like it.'

'What do you mean? I asked your opinion, expecting to be told there's nothing to worry about. What do you mean?'

'I don't know these men as well as you, but for them both to present atypical behaviour at approximately the same time— that seems significant to me.'

He stirred uncomfortably. 'I was hoping you wouldn't say that. It's disturbing, and I don't like things that disturb me. What could be causing it?'

She looked in the direction of the ceiling, not seeing it in the darkness.

'There can be a number of causes. Some anomalous behaviour can be caused by infrasound, below twenty hertz. It's difficult to shield against it as it can get around obstacles without much dissipation. It can cause mental disturbances; feelings of being watched; an increase in aggression or fear. It's been shown to be behind some reports of hauntings.'

'And where would this infrasound be coming from?'

'Perhaps from machinery running out of alignment. You'll have to ask Kurchatov.'

'OK. Anything else?'

'Changes in air pressure. Some taint in the food. Or…'

'Or?'

'Perhaps people are reacting against this unnatural environment. Look, I know it doesn't worry you, but not everyone's as unimaginative as you.'

'Thanks.'

'Sorry, Greg, but this is unnatural. We're under nearly a kilometre of arctic water, confined in a restricted environment, unable to go outside for a walk, see a sunset, hear a bird. We see nothing but grey steel walls, except when we go out in the sub. And then we just see darkness, penetrated slightly by the sub's searchlights. For God's sake, that is unnatural!'

'So what can be done?'

'Get out of this hell hole, ASAP!'

In the humid darkness, he shook his head.

'That's just selfish. This experiment is vital for mankind. A new source of protein for the starving billions. They need us— we can't just give up because we're afraid of the dark!'

Silence fell.

Then she felt his hand explore a breast.

'Sal, we mustn't argue. I can't deal with these men if we two aren't right. Instead of just giving in, we've got to work out what's happening and deal with it.'

She said nothing for some time while his hand toyed with a nipple.

Then she made up her mind, and she turned so that they were facing each other.

'You're right. If we're OK, then everything is OK.'

Then they made love.

She awoke in the darkness. Greg was asleep beside her and was covered by a thin sheet with only his shoulders and head protruding.

There was a hand in the sweaty cleft between her breasts, and it was not Greg's.

Looking up, she saw a male silhouette against the dim light in the corridor.

They had forgotten to close the door.

A hand covered her mouth while the other hand began to fondle a breast.

Twisting her head, she bit down on the hand on her face; hard. She was vaguely aware that the skin felt odd, as if it were covered by something.

But everything was happening so fast!

There was a high-pitched yell, and both hands were rapidly removed. As Greg began to stir, the unknown assailant disappeared into the corridor.

Greg sat up, looking around blearily.

'What—what's the matter?'

'Greg, there was someone in the room. A man!'

'A man?' Greg seemed to be having difficulty with the idea. 'A man? What did he want?'

'He wanted me! Me! Greg, I'm frightened!'

He leapt out of bed and switched the light on. The sudden brightness hurt her eyes. He went to the door and looked up and down the corridor.

There was no-one there. He came back.

'Did you see who it was?'

'No. It was all over in a second. But I could tell it wasn't a very big man.'

He sat on the edge of the bed. 'Anything else?'

'Yes. I bit his hand. There might be marks.'

'A mark, you say. Then I'll check in the morning.'

He closed the door and held Sally until they were both asleep.

**

Beauvoir stood in the dissection room in the BioScience dome.

In her slim hand, she held a medical scalpel.

She raised it to the light, rejoicing in the way that the burnished steel reflected the light in brilliant rays of glory. If she held it in precisely this orientation, she could see a lovely azure colour, just like the warm Mediterranean of her childhood, far, far away from the cold darkness that lurked hungrily, not very far from where she stood.

And if she held it this way, she could see a rich ruby glint, like the sun when it seemed to sink into the water, beyond the

Pillars of Hercules.

She placed a finger on her neck, and there, just below the soft skin, she could feel the familiar pulse as the rich blood ascended from her heart to her brain.

How strange to think that shortly that pulse would be no more.

She placed the very tip of the scalpel against that regular beat.

So cold the steel.

And so hot was the blood as she severed the artery.

She thrust deeper, slashing in a mad frenzy in the last seconds of her life.

Then her body crashed into the steadily widening pool of her blood.

***

'I want everyone in the Meeting Room!' Greg thundered into the intercom. He looked at Sally. 'Don't worry, darling; I'll sort this out. Whoever the bastard was, I'll get him.'

She nodded, dumbly looking at her interlinked hands.

Hicks appeared first, looking enervated and withdrawn. Greg ignored her.

Then Sigurdsson arrived and sat down, becoming as motionless as a mannikin and looking blankly into infinity. Greg crossed to him and pulled a hand up from Sigurdsson's lap.

There was a red mark on it. Greg pulled him to his feet.

'So, it was you, you bastard!' He drew back a mighty fist.

Sigurdsson looked at him blankly, unmoved, dispassionate.

'What are you talking about?' he said in a flat, unemotional voice.

'The mark on your hand—it's where Sally bit you last night!'

'Oh, is it? Take a closer look—does it look like a bite?'

With an expression of deep suspicion, Greg brought the hand closer.

After a few seconds, he said, 'It looks like a cut.'

115

'Perhaps because it is. Now take a look at this.'

Sigurdsson rolled up a sleeve, and on his left arm were three long red lines, fresh and weeping in the pasty flesh.

'You've been cutting yourself?' Greg whispered, 'self-harming? Why, for God's sake?'

Sigurdsson was back in his chair. 'Why not? What else is there to do? I've got to pass the time until it's time to go.'

'Go? Go where, you madman?'

The other did not look at him and stroked his wounds.

'Look at yourself, Richardson. What do you think you are? A living, breathing man, a man's man, a leader of men? I'll tell you what you are: you're a skeleton, a skeleton wearing a temporary coat of meat, a skeleton that thinks it's a man.'

Greg stood over him. 'How dare you speak to me like that! What's got into you, you fool! Pull yourself together!'

Sigurdsson did not look up. Neither did he speak again, but resumed his contemplation of infinity. Greg drew his fist, but Hicks crossed to him and restrained the arm before it straightened into Sigurdsson's face.

'Stop it, Greg! Can't you see he's not well!'

Greg went back to Sally, but casting backward glances at the seated man as he did so.

Sally held his hands as he sat beside her.

'Greg, there's something wrong!'

'I can see that,' Greg growled, again looking back at Sigurdsson.

'No, no, not just him. With everybody! With this base—something's wrong with this base!' She looked at Hicks. 'Tell him, Joan, tell him there's something wrong!'

Hicks gave a start, as if she had been locked in her thoughts before Sally's plea had drawn her back.

'Yes, yes, there seems to be a spreading dysphoria.'

'Dysphoria?' Greg snapped, 'what the hell is that?'

'A kind of infectious depression, lassitude, despair—oh, I'm running out of words! You know what I mean!'

Greg said no more but stood motionless, looking around

angrily.

'Where're Kurchatov and Alvarez?'

As if on cue, Alvarez appeared from one of the corridors but seemingly having left his smile behind.

'Where have you been?'

'That's for me to know and you to find out,' was the laconic reply as he sat.

Sally could see a vein throbbing in Greg's temple and knew her man was not far from exploding into violence. She crossed to him and said, 'Hi, Ricardo. Have you seen Kurchatov?'

'Nope. He's probably playing with himself on top of the reactor.'

'Watch your mouth, Alvarez,' Greg roared, 'or I'll be feeding you to the bluefins!'

Alvarez did not respond.

Greg crossed back to the intercom console.

'Kurchatov!' he roared, 'get to the Meeting Room! Now!'

After a few more minutes, Kurchatov appeared from the opposite corridor to Alvarez.

There's something different about him! was the thought that flashed through Sally's mind.

Indeed, Kurchatov did not appear to be suffering from dysphoria. Instead, he looked somewhat pleased with himself, and his face was wreathed in a big grin. Suddenly, Sally realised that she had never seen him smiling before.

He sat in the nearest chair, his right leg hanging over an arm, and looked up at Greg.

'You called?' he said sweetly.

'Show me your hands.'

Kurchatov obeyed. He was wearing gloves.

'Take them off.'

He took them off. Sally inspected them. There were no marks.

'Why are you suddenly wearing gloves?'

'I've developed a bit of a rash; contact dermatitis, I believe.'

'I don't see a rash.'

117

'That's because I've been wearing the gloves for protection. I was wearing them all evening. And at night. They've worked wonders.'

Greg moved away, looking apologetically at Sally. Then he spun back to the others.

'I don't know what you wise guys think you're playing at, but it stops now! Now, do you hear! By God, if you ever want to work again, you'll start behaving like adult men instead of giggling behind these stupid games. You seem to think you can play me for a mug, but you won't. I'll take you all on, one at a time or all together, it doesn't matter a fuck to me! Do you hear!'

Sally was only slightly surprised when the other men showed no reaction at all; no admission of guilt, no apologetic expressions, no anger at an unjust accusation—nothing.

Then Hicks said, 'Has anybody seen Beauvoir?'

Ten minutes later, Hicks and the Richardsons were staring at Beauvoir's body as it lay there in the centre of a great scarlet patch. A scalpel lay a short way from an outstretched hand.

'What happened?' Greg muttered, looking from one woman to the other, 'why did she do it?'

Hicks shook her head slowly. 'I don't know; I just don't know.'

Sally looked wild-eyed at her husband. 'Greg! This is it! We've all got to get out of here! Can't you see that something very bad is happening? You and I are still alright, but how long before we go under! There's been a death on the base; you can't just say "business as usual!"'

Hicks glanced at Sally. 'Yes, you two do appear seemingly as you've always been—unlike everybody else, including me. Why would that be?'

Greg shrugged. 'Maybe I'm not a hysterical woman, like everybody else.' He stopped and looked at his companions. 'Sorry. No offence.'

'None taken,' Hicks said with the faintest of smiles, 'but you've got to report this, of course. Immediately. I imagine they'll agree with Sally, that we have to evacuate.'

Greg's mighty shoulders drooped. 'I guess that's what has to happen. What a terrible pity, just when we were getting somewhere. Now we'll have to start again. Probably with an entirely new crew.'

Sally ignored Greg's musings and looked at Hicks. 'Do you have the facilities for an autopsy here?'

Hicks looked startled. 'No, my lab is just for dealing with injuries or decompression problems.'

'Could you do an autopsy?'

'I'd rather not. I'm not exactly qualified.'

Silence fell, eventually broken by Hicks.

'What are you getting at, Sally?'

Sally took a few steps away so she could see the other two without turning.

'Are you both blind? Something is wrong, terribly, terribly wrong. Everyone is acting out of character, massively out of character! There's something here in the base that wasn't here before, and it's affecting us!'

Hicks pursed her lips. 'And what exactly would that be?'

Sally turned her head from side to side, thinking, thinking desperately.

'What has happened recently? Let's work it out. What has happened in the last few days that hadn't happened before?'

Greg was silent, looking down at two clenched fists, seeming to want no part of the discussion. Then Hicks said, 'The quakes.'

'Yes, the quakes. What could they have done to cause these peculiar behaviours? A release of volcanic gases?'

Greg remained silent. Hicks continued, 'No, how could any type of gas get into the base? We're completely, hermetically sealed. We have to be under this pressure.'

Sally held her head in her hands, her mouth working silently as her mind raced, proposing, and then almost immediately rejecting, possibilities. Then she looked up.

'The fish! That fucking monstrosity of a fish!'

Now Greg spoke. 'Sal, that's ridiculous! It was only here for a few hours before it died! Do you think a zombie fish got out of the pressure tank and roamed around, biting people in their sleep!'

'No, no, of course not.' Sally looked around desperately. 'We're missing something, something vital. But it's to do with the quakes—it just has to be!'

Hicks interrupted. 'In the meantime, I've got to clean this place up and get Marie stored away so an autopsy can be performed when we get back to Topside. And you, Greg—you've got to tell them that entire base needs to be evacuated! '

He nodded, with obvious reluctance. 'Yes, I suppose so.'

Sally stared at Hicks. 'It's not as simple as that, Joan. Whatever it is, it's spreading, which must mean it's infectious. I think it's best to assume it's airborne.'

Hicks looked slightly surprised. 'You're right—I should have thought of that.' She looked around as if trying to find something. 'Why didn't I think of that?'

'Well, let's stick to the point—have we got any masks?'

'Yes, there're surgical masks in the lab; I'll dish them out when I get back.'

'We'll get them now. Just tell me where they are.'

Hicks complied and after the Richardsons had helped her put Beauvoir into cold storage, they left her cleaning the BioLab and returned to the Meeting Room. It took Sally some minutes to collect the masks, but when she returned she found Greg sitting still, his chin resting on a fist.

'Have you told Topside yet?' she asked, feeling a cold chill on seeing his immobility.

Had Greg suddenly become one of the anomalous cases?

To her relief, he acknowledged her, but then shook his head. 'No, not yet.'

'Why not?'

He looked at her with staring, slightly bloodshot eyes. 'Sal, Sal, you don't understand what this project means to me. It was my chance to get really noticed; to carve my name into the history books. So much is riding on this; it's no exaggeration to say the future of the world depends upon it.'

She rushed to him and, to his amazement, beat her small fists on his chest.

'Listen to yourself! A man whose lifework is studying stones—you're like a bloody stone yourself! This isn't a vanity project, you fool! Our lives are in danger! And think about me for once—I've got to get out of this place, it's destroying me! I feel like I'm trapped in a small steel box with thin walls that are bending in. And out there, it's the sea, all that horrific black water, thousands of tonnes of it, trying to get in, to crush me, to crush us all! I've got to get out! Got to get back to the sunlight!'

He stared up at her. 'That's just silly emotionalism. This base is impenetrable. I expected better of you.'

'Impenetrable!' She turned away, pulling at her hair in her frenzy, 'Impenetrable! Something has penetrated it, you fucking idiot, and it's driving all of us mad! Call Topside—now!'

Suddenly Greg was standing next to her, standing over her.

'That's enough! I'm in charge here! I think you'd better take a lie-down for a while!'

Sally stared up at him for a few seconds in utter disbelief.

Was this the man she had joyfully married not so long ago?

Reluctantly, she realised that he was serious and, choking back a sob, she swept out of the Meeting Room, back to their living quarters. She flung herself face down on the bed, and then the tears did finally burst out. The sobs wracked her body for some time until, unwillingly, she fell into a nightmare-haunted sleep.

An unknown time later, she felt hands on her shoulders. She must make it up to Greg, try to explain why he had to call for help.

She rolled over and froze, staring wildly up at the face that hung over her.

It was Kurchatov. And he was wearing gloves.

For a few fleeting moments, neither moved nor spoke, giving Sally time to study the man's face. It was Kurchatov but at the same time the face of another. No longer was the face that of a hesitant, diffident individual. The expression was one of strength, of confidence, of determination. And a hungry desire.

'Get out,' she said quietly, and then in a shout, 'Get out!'

For answer, a gloved hand was clasped over her mouth, and her assailant said in a strangely thick, throaty voice, 'Now, now, Mrs Richardson, we'll have none of that shouting. I've come here to help; to give you what you really want. You've been stuck with that eunuch for long enough. Now he's going to be a cuckold as well as a eunuch.'

Horror burst into her eyes as the import of his words struck home.

'No, no,' she said, 'No!'

Kurchatov laughed and, straightening, peeled the gloves off his small hands.

'Enough of those, I think. No need for subterfuge now. It's time for flesh on flesh.'

He bent over her again, tearing her mask off, and clawed hands reached for her breasts.

She rolled under his hands, tumbling off the bed in her haste. As she crashed onto her back on the floor, he reached for her again. Sally's mind whirled: there was no more time for civilised niceties, no time to weigh up consequences, to consider options. As he came nearer, she drove her knee into his crotch with as much energy as her small frame could muster. He doubled up with a deep grunt of pain, bringing his chin involuntarily nearer to her. Her fist drove onto the point of that chin, and he fell backwards, trying to hold onto the bed to steady himself, but the sheet came with him and after hitting the doorframe, he slid down it into a heap.

Get out now! her mind screamed but he was blocking the doorway, still conscious and now very angry. She looked around for a weapon, anything! But there was none.

He was slowly getting to his feet, one hand clutching his crotch and the lust in his eyes was now accompanied by murder.

'That wasn't at all nice, Mrs Richardson,' he said, apparently speaking with some difficulty, 'No wonder your husband doesn't want you; you're a very nasty, spiteful little bitch, aren't you?'

Sally backed away, but soon there was no space left to back into.

'Greg will kill you for this; you know that, don't you, Igor? So stop now while you still can.'

He shook his head. 'No, that's not the way it will be. There will be killing, Mrs Richardson, but I shall be doing the killing. And after I have done what I want with you, I shall kill you. And then I shall kill Mr Richardson. In fact, I don't think once I've started killing that I shall want to stop. The thought of it is wonderful because I now realise that the killing is necessary. There has to be killing: it is the way.'

'You're mad,' she whispered, 'something has driven you mad.'

'No, Mrs Richardson, not mad—awakened.'

She made one last desperate look around the small room for something to fight off this maniac, but there was nothing. And then he was on her.

His face came horribly close and a grey, slime-streaked tongue protruded from his lips, trying to force its way between hers. She tossed her head from side to side, stifling a desire to scream, which would have proved easy ingress for that probe of almost reptilian flesh.

It was almost touching.

And then two large hands suddenly appeared on Kurchatov's shoulders, and he was plucked away from her and thrown like a rag doll against the wall. He bounced off it and lay seemingly stunned at Greg's feet. Greg looked at her.

'You alright?'

'I am, now. Greg, he's insane! Something's driven him mad!'

'Well, I'm going to drive him all the way to hell.' He pulled Kurchatov to his feet with one hand and, glaring into his eyes, roared, 'You're finished, mister. I don't think I'm going to wait to report you to Topside; I think I'll just beat you into a blood-stained mess right now!'

'Greg, no! We've got to find out what's happened to him!

You know this isn't the real Igor; something terrible has gotten hold of him. The same thing that made Marie kill herself. We need to find out what it is so we can stop it before it kills us all!'

Greg hesitated and took his attention from his captive to Sally. 'I…'

But Kurchatov had recovered somewhat. With astounding agility and speed, he twisted in Greg's grasp and drove an index finger into the other's eye socket. Instinctively Greg pushed him away, and in an instant Kurchatov was out of the door, the sound of his running echoing off the metal walls. Sally leapt towards Greg simultaneously as he moved towards her.

'Are you alright, darling?'

'I'm alright. Are you alright?'

They hugged each other while Sally examined Greg's eye.

'No serious damage, but you must get Joan to take a look at it.'

'After I've taken that little bastard down.'

'No. Leave him for the time being. We've got to work with Joan to work out what this thing is. We don't know how much time we have left.'

He stopped halfway to the door and looked back at her. 'What do you mean?'

'Greg, Greg, why do you think we're immune? Whatever this thing is, how likely is it that it isn't getting to us? It must simply be that—for reasons I don't understand—we're not as far down this horrible one-way road as everybody else is. We can't waste a second!'

He stood motionless for a few moments, then: 'You're right. I'll talk to Joan after I've given that twerp a taste of my fists!'

Sally followed him to the door and watched him run down the corridor, standing motionless except for biting her hand in her agitation. Then she shook her head and went in the opposite direction, back to the Meeting Room.

It did not take Greg long to reach the entrance to the Reactor Sphere, but he did not enter. He did not enter because a great slab of shining steel had replaced the entrance.

He beat his fists against it in impotent rage for some seconds until a voice from a grill above his head caused him to look up.

'Sorry I can't entertain you at the moment, Mr Richardson. I am busy inserting myself into every electrical circuit in the base so I can better control them. And control them, I will. You see, Mr Richardson, it takes more than big biceps to be successful in the modern world. It takes a brain, and I have that particular organ in spades. And when I have taken care of you, I will introduce Mrs Richardson to another organ I am lucky enough to possess. Thank you for your time.'

Greg glowered at the grill, searching for threats which were not empty. And he found one.

'I will kill you, you know.'

There was no reply and eventually he too returned to the Meeting Room.

He found Sally deep in discussion with Hicks.

'Where're those other two bastards?' he snapped, 'Do we have to do everything around here? No—don't bother with my eye, Joan; there's no serious damage.'

'Greg, Joan has had an idea,' Sally said, reaching for him.

He brushed past her. 'Yeah, so have I. Find the other two and knock some sense into them.' He whirled to Sally. 'We have oxy-acetylene on the base, don't we?'

'Yes, but that's not what we need now. What we need is…'

But Sally was abruptly prevented from explaining what it was that they needed. At that moment, a bright red light blazed out on the control panel. Greg muttered, 'What the fuck…' and ran over to it.

'It's the goddamn sub airlock,' he said, 'what's going on now, for Chrissake?'

His strong fingers flashed over the controls, and a monitor flared into full-colour life. And in it Sigurdsson's unsmiling face appeared.

Greg flipped the intercom switch. 'Harald,' he gasped, 'what are you doing in the sub? There're no excursions planned!'

'No, not by you,' Sigurdsson replied in a dull, flat voice, 'I'm

125

taking her out for one last journey.'

'No, you're not! I authorise the excursions. Power down, and get back here—now!'

Sigurdsson's face was replaced by the back of his head and the camera showed him walking to the front of the sub and sitting in the main control seat. He made some movements that were partially hidden by his body, and then through the sub's canopy powerful cascades of dark water could be seen jetting into the airlock.

'He's taking her out, God damn him!'

And the twin doors of the airlock parted; the camera displaying nothing but black emptiness, black nothingness.

Except that nothingness was the dark immensity of ocean water under iron-hard pressure.

There were no points of reference to show that the sub was actually moving, but on the control panel, Greg could see a display which showed an ever-increasing velocity.

'Where does he think he's going?' Greg murmured, 'what's his game?'

He flipped the intercom switch again.

'Harald, explain yourself. Where are you going?' Greg swallowed. 'Please come back.'

Sigurdsson did not turn his head, but his voice was clear and strong.

'I'm leaving behind all this futility, the meaningless of this thing we call life. I realise now that there is no point; there is nothing to strive for. Vanity, vanity, all is vanity sayeth the preacher.'

Greg covered the mike with a hand and glanced at Sally.

'Can you make sense of what he's saying?'

'It's a quote of some kind,' Sally said, 'I'm not sure.'

Greg returned to the mike. 'Harald, come back. Whatever's wrong, we can work it out, man to man. Just come back.'

'No. There is no point, no purpose, no plan, no reward except one, and that reward is oblivion. I go to her gladly now, since the scales have fallen from my eyes.'

126

'He's picking up a hell of a lot of speed,' Hicks said, looking over Greg's shoulder.

Greg frowned. 'Damn right. I've never taken her up to that speed.'

But then Sally seized his arm and yelled, 'Look!'

For the image of a great grey mass had crystallised out of ebon infinity.

The massive flank of part of the Mid-Atlantic Ridge.

'He's going to hit it!' Sally whispered, 'he's going to bloody hit it!'

And so he was.

The flank grew bigger and bigger; more and more detail becoming clear in the centre of the view as objects at the perimeter rushed ever outwards. Mesmerised, they watched faint, thin lines become gaping, jagged fissures, pebbles become boulders.

There was the terrible noise of rending, shattering, tearing, buckling metal, and the display for an instant showed nothing but flashing coloured zig-zags.

Then blackness.

'He killed himself,' Greg said, in a voice which struggled to be more than a whisper.

Sally straightened herself and looked meaningfully at Hicks. 'Another one,' she said.

Hicks showed no emotion. Her gaze seemed to be focused on some point far away. But she replied to Sally. 'Yes. The pattern is simple.'

Greg looked up. 'What bloody pattern? What are you babbling about? A man has just died. A friend.'

Hicks sat down, placed her hands in her lap, and fixed them with a cold stare. 'As I said, the pattern is clear, childishly obvious. A brief period of euphoria in which uninhibited behaviour is displayed. Then dysphoria, accompanied by self-harm or increasingly risky activities. Then finally, suicide and/or murder. A clear pattern.'

Greg glared angrily at her. 'What you—you deduce that

from two cases? Two cases?'

'No. Of the remaining men, both have shown euphoria followed by dysphoria. Alvarez performed a dangerous action in the sub when you last went out. He almost crashed it. And he had no explanation for his action. You told me that. And Kurchatov—is he the milk and water character we've known since we got here?'

'Alvarez hasn't shown any dysphoria.'

'He will.'

Sally gently, carefully, touched Greg's shoulder. 'And there's something else. You realise that now there's no easy way we can get off this base. We're trapped.' Uttering that dread word seemed to unhinge her momentarily, and she began trembling, first in the head, and then all over her body. She turned staring eyes to the ceiling. 'Trapped!'

Greg leapt up and crushed her to him. 'Stop it, Sal, stop it. Nothing's going to happen to you, nothing!'

Hicks watched the couple silently for a minute or two and then said, 'Sorry to interrupt, but we now have very little time to waste. Greg, you really must contact Topside and get them to send down the transfer sub. It can take all of us in one trip.'

'All of us except Kurchatov,' Greg snarled, 'that bastard is staying.'

'Greg, Greg,' Sally said, 'he's ill. It's not him doing all those terrible things. These people are our colleagues, our friends. Everybody's got to get out of this place—everybody! We've all got to get Topside where there are proper medical facilities so that they can find out what's gotten into us and then cure us. Cure us all, including Kurchatov.'

Greg nodded slowly. 'OK. I agree we've all got to get out; sorry I didn't do it earlier. I should have done, but I just don't want to give up on this project. Goddammit, I've never quit on anything before!'

Sally smiled, with relief evident in her relaxing features. 'I knew you'd come through, Greg. Let's do it.'

All three crossed to the comms station, and Greg pressed

the button which caused the monitor to rise from the desk and the keyboard to unlock. He sat, pushed his mask up to take a lungful of air, turned to smile briefly at the watching women, and began to type.

They watched him in growing alarm as consternation began to contort his features.

'Greg, what's wrong?' Sally said; there was a sensation inside her as if her heart had leapt into her throat, 'why aren't you typing?'

Greg looked at them. 'I am. Look.'

His hands flew over the keyboard, but nothing appeared on the screen.

'The keyboard isn't working,' he finally said.

'Not working?' Sally said, feeling her head begin to spin. She clutched his chair to steady herself. 'Is everything connected properly?'

'Yes, of course it is! There's power in it. It just isn't working.'

'Kurchatov. He'll know what to do,' Sally said, before realising the stupidity of what she had said.

'It's OK, it's OK,' Hicks said, in a flat calm voice that contrasted massively with Sally's, 'When we don't contact them at the normal time, they'll send down the transfer sub to see if we're alright.'

Immediately words began to appear on the screen.

"Routine report. No further quakes. All fish pens are intact and all feeding stations working as required. The situation is nominal, and no further action is required on any issues. Sorry to be so boring. Richardson out."

The three stared blankly at the screen as if the monitor had magically acquired a consciousness of its own. Greg was the first to recover, and for some reason started looking around the room. Having apparently seen that for which he had been looking, he crossed to a storage cabinet and took out a harpoon gun.

The two women drew back, fearing that perhaps he had become mentally disturbed under the pressure. But he ignored them and took up position near the corner of the room, put the harpoon gun to his shoulder and fired. Faster than the eye could follow, the harpoon flashed up and into a small box near the corner of the room, and that target disintegrated in a shower of hissing blue-white sparks.

Sally seemed to have lost the power of speech, but Hicks said, 'What was all that about? Are you trying to let the water in?'

Greg turned to her, his expression even grimmer than before; if such a thing were possible.

'Didn't you think it was something of a coincidence that the fake message was sent a few seconds after I tried to send mine? Each one of these rooms is covered by closed-circuit TV for security reasons. Kurchatov has obviously hacked into that system and has been watching and listening to us all this time. We've got to destroy all the cameras and mikes in every room we're in.'

Just as he finished speaking, Kurchatov's gloating voice came over the intercom.

'Well done, Mr Richardson. I wondered if you'd guess I was watching you. Now, of course, you have both blinded and deafened me but it matters not the slightest jot. You can't escape, and no one is coming for you. In the meantime, I will proceed with my plans for bringing this unhappy little melodrama to a satisfactory conclusion. I'm sure you must be tired of these unsatisfying roles that you have been forced to play and are longing for something new. That I can deliver, I assure you. Bye-bye. For now.'

Hicks looked at Greg. 'Do you think he's telling the truth when he says he can't see us anymore?'

'Maybe, maybe not. One thing is certain; we mustn't underestimate him. The one person who can get into the base's systems and I can't get at him.' He brought a great fist down on a nearby table which shuddered visibly under the impact. 'Damn! Damn!'

Just then, he felt a light touch on his shoulder, and turned to see Sally looking plaintively up at him.

'Greg, can we go now? I don't like it here anymore.'

He stared. 'Go?'

She moved closer. 'Yes. I want to go back up to Topside now. I really do, Greg, I really do.' Two small hands reached up and rested on his shoulders. 'I want to go home now, Greg. I want to see the blue sky and the clouds. I want to see the trees swaying in the wind. I don't like this place. I've got to get out!' Her voice rose to a banshee screech. 'I've got to get out! I've got to get out! The water—it's all around me; it's coming in, I can feel it! Greg, take me home!'

Greg felt his eyes moisten as he stared down at his distraught wife. He took her hands from his shoulders and held them, feeling their warmth, their softness. He gently pulled her towards a chair, sat her down and then knelt before her, rubbing her hands.

'Sally, Sally, you've got to come back to me. You've got to remember what's happening. It's our only way of getting out of this. We've got to work as a team, the three of us. Retreating into yourself won't help, darling; we've got to face up to it. I want to get home as well, but there's only one way to do it, and that's to fight!'

Near silence fell, broken only by the gentle soughing of the air-conditioning.

Minutes passed. Then Sally's head gave a sudden jerk, and she looked directly into his eyes; eyes which were now the only visible part of his masked face.

'Yes,' she said very slowly, as if she were communicating in a foreign language, 'yes, I understand now. I'm sorry, Greg, sorry for worrying you. I know where we are and what's happening.'

They lifted their masks, kissed and, somewhat shakily, she stood.

Greg looked at them. 'OK, so Kurchatov can send fake messages that everything's normal but Topside like to have full-scale video conferences from time to time; sooner or later, they'll call for one of them. I can't see how he could have the equipment to fake a full-on video meeting.'

131

'Sooner or later,' Sally murmured, apparently to herself, 'but we don't have later.'

Greg did not reply but picked up the harpoon gun.

'I'm going to the other domes and take out the cameras in them.'

'Be careful, Greg' Hicks said, 'we don't know where Ricardo is.'

He shrugged and disappeared into a corridor. Some minutes later, the women heard the faint sound of the gun firing. He reappeared and, saying nothing, went into the other corridor with the same result.

'Are you feeling better now, Sally?' said Hicks, while they waited for Greg's return.

'Yes, I think so,' she said, and ran a hand over her forehead, 'my head aches terribly.'

'That's understandable.' Hicks paused. 'I wish I could think of something I could do to help but my mind seems to be getting fuzzier and fuzzier. All I want to do is lie down and sleep. Sleep, yes—perhaps forever.'

Sally looked sharply at her. 'Don't you start, Joan. One mad woman is enough. Think, Joan, think! What have we overlooked? There must be something, something so simple and trivial that we've not noticed it.'

Hick's brows knitted under Sally's command. The act of thinking seemed to have become painful. Finally, she said, 'There was something odd about that fish.'

The hairs on the back of Sally's neck lifted themselves from the flesh. She hadn't thought about the fish and didn't want to start again.

'What about it?' she said, eventually.

'Marie had dissected it thoroughly. I found the parts stored away and neatly labelled. But there was one part missing.'

'And?'

'The brain was missing. I couldn't have overlooked it because everything else was there and professionally catalogued. But no brain.'

Sally put her hand under her mask and rubbed her chin. 'I don't want to sound like a parody of Sherlock Holmes, but if it wasn't where it should have been, then it must be somewhere else. There's no way for it to have been taken off this base unless Harald took it with him. Why would the brain have been put somewhere instead of being left in the lab?'

Greg had returned. 'You two seem to be in deep conversation. Care to cut me in?'

'We're trying to think of something that's changed since just before all this kicked off.'

Greg sat and stretched his legs out. 'Perhaps you can think of where we've put the deodorants. The smell in the BioLab area is getting unbearable.'

To the others' amazement, Sally leapt to her feet.

'That's it! That's the thing that changed before all this started!'

Greg stared at her. 'What? A foul smell? We're being stalked by a bad smell?'

Sally did not answer directly. 'Is the camera out in the BioLab? Yes? Then let's take another look.'

They spent some time in the lab, examining drawers, looking in tanks, reading notes, switching computers on, taking the lids off containers and hurriedly putting them back on again.

Nothing.

'I can't do this anymore,' Hicks said quietly, 'I really do need to lie down.'

'Perhaps not in the lab itself,' Sally muttered, ignoring the other woman's plea, 'but maybe near the lab. Let's go back out into the corridor.'

They returned to the corridor and Greg and Sally stared at every available square centimetre. Hicks leaned against one of the walls, and took no part.

Then Greg said, 'That panel up there is out of alignment. Someone's taken it out but not put it back quite right.'

'Take a look at it, Greg!'

Greg went back into the lab and returned with a chair which

he gingerly stood on, lacking any handholds to steady himself. He pulled at the misplaced panel, and it fell instantly into his hands. A wave of nauseating rottenness struck all of them; their masks proving no barrier. It was rank beyond most forms of description, except that the stench carried the promise of death.

'Good God, it's vile in there!' he spat through closed lips.

"What can you see, Greg?'

'A small black mass. It's—it's…'

'What, Greg?'

'This panel is over the air conditioning duct. This thing's been polluting the air in the entire base!'

"Can you get it out?'

'I'm not damn well touching it, but there're specimen bags in one of the drawers. Bring me one and some kind of tongs. Good God, I'm not touching that!'

With as much care as if he were manipulating nitroglycerin, Greg finally got the black mass into a specimen bag, and when he was safely down, they stared at the repulsive black object.

'The missing brain,' Hicks said finally.

'Well, we now know how the infection, whatever it is, has spread.' Greg looked quizzically at Sally. 'But how did we manage to escape?'

'We haven't escaped,' she said, giving a small shiver as she raised her eyes from the decomposed brain, 'we're simply at the start of our journey. But I do know how it is that we'll be the last to go.'

'How?'

'Two things: firstly our room is the furthest from the BioLab and so the spread was weakest when it reached us. But more importantly, our AC has been malfunctioning, don't you remember? So we've had the least contact with whatever it is this thing is giving off. But we've been walking about without masks for some time so we sure as hell have it inside us now.'

Greg grimaced as he turned to Hicks.

'Joan, you've got to find out what's causing all this trouble. What did you check for when you tested Beauvoir's and

Alvarez's blood?'

She did not answer and remained staring unseeingly into infinity.

He shook her and Sally said. 'Joan! We need you! What did you check for?'

She turned her head slowly to face them. Her gaze seemed blank, as if she had been replaced by an automaton that closely resembled a real human being.

Closely, but not exactly.

'For Marie, I checked blood glucose but nothing else. I ran a more detailed analysis on Ricardo: cortisol, adrenalin, major metabolites, but more importantly I checked for bacteria and viruses.'

'And?'

'I didn't find any. No viruses or bacteria. He's a healthy man.'

'Apparently not. We've got to get back to the MediLab, and you've got to re-run those tests and this time look for everything, anything, that's even slightly out of the ordinary. Something is picking us off, one by one, and if we want to live, we've got to find it.'

Sally waited for Hicks to reply but she did not.

'Let's go!' Greg said, pointing the way back to the Meeting Room. From there it would have been a short walk to the MediLab, but Hicks made for the nearest chair and sat down, placing her head in her hands.

'Joan, get up,' Greg demanded, 'we can't waste any more time. Do the tests!'

She looked up. Her face looked as if it had been constructed by a sculptor possessed of only mediocre talents.

'No. I don't want to. I'm tired, so bloody tired. I just want to sit here. Sit and wait for him.'

'Who?'

'Ricardo. I know he loves me. Then we'll go into the world beyond together. Man and woman, together forever.'

Greg stared down at her for a few moments. As she stared

at them, Sally thought they resembled waxwork exhibits in a peculiar tableau, so still were they both.

Then Greg moved. He crossed the room to where he had left the harpoon gun, reloaded it and returned to Hicks. Standing back slightly, he levelled the weapon at her.

'Do the tests or I'll kill you.'

But Hicks simply gave the ghost of a smile. 'Go ahead. I want to leave here in any case. Now or in a few minutes, what does it matter? Ricardo will find me even if we don't go together. Go ahead. Let's end this meaningless farrago.'

Greg lowered the weapon, defeated.

Sally crossed to Hicks and knelt in front of her.

'Joan, we don't want to keep you from Ricardo. You love him, and he loves you. You'll be together soon, forever, just like you said. But before you go, could you do this one little thing for Greg and me? Just do this, and we won't ask you to do anything else. Please, Joan.'

Joan's lack of expression was unchanged. 'I'm not sure I remember what to do.'

Sally smiled. 'We'll do it together. I'll help, come on, just us girls together.'

At last, a small smile altered Hicks' expression. 'Alright, Sally, I'll do this one more thing and then I'll go.'

The two women left for the MediLab, leaving Greg alone, still holding the speargun. After a while, he sat down, the gun across his lap. He looked into the room at nothing in particular, and his head slumped once or twice. And then he slept.

He awoke to face two ashen, stone-faced women staring at him. He was not surprised by Hick's expression, but the one staining Sally's face shocked him and sent a bolt of alarm down his spinal cord.

'What is it?' he finally managed to say, not at all certain that he wanted an answer.

'We know what it is,' Sally said without a hint of human inflections in her voice, 'come with us.'

In the MediLab, the women stood in front of a bank of

136

medical equipment.

'Well?' he said, 'the answer is…?'

'Fungi,' Hicks said, 'parasitic fungi. That's why I couldn't find the infectious agent. It never occurred to me to test for fungi.'

'Fungi? Fungi in the sea? I've never seen any mushrooms down here.'

'A common misconception,' Hicks replied, 'I've done some research while you've been asleep. Fungi are, in fact, extremely common in the world's oceans, indeed cetaceans in particular are prone to a range of fungal diseases. The things are everywhere,' she glanced at a printout on her desk, 'it says here that Ascomycota, Basidiomycota and Chytridiomycota have been found in ocean sediments as much as two kilometres below the surface. It has even been shown that they reproduce faster under high pressure.'

Greg found a chair and seated himself. 'OK, I'm taking this one step at a time. I know that fungi can kill you if you eat them, but—infectious fungi? That's a new one.'

'Not surprising, I doubt if fungi play much of a part in a geology degree. Fungal diseases are incredibly dangerous: in the twentieth century a fungal disease basically exterminated the European elm, a disease with nearly one hundred percent mortality. There are many fungal diseases which affect humans. In fact, it has been suggested that part of the reason why the human body is at the specific temperature that it is, is to help it resist fungal infection. But as the world warms, that will become much more likely.'

Greg looked increasingly concerned, even behind his mask.

'But what's happening to us, the mental disturbances—that doesn't sound like a regular disease.'

Hicks looked at Sally. 'You explain the rest of it, Sally, I've got to sit down.'

Sally looked down at Greg. He returned the gaze and somehow there was pleading in his eyes.

'Greg, we're dealing with a very clever, ruthless opponent.

One that can outsmart many more developed animals. Back in The States, there's a fungus called Massospora that waits seventeen years for cicadas to emerge from the ground. It invades their back ends and injects them with an amphetamine that keeps them active while their bodies dissolve. It also makes the males behave like females so that other males get infected when they attempt to mate.'

'I'm not famous for acting like a female,' Greg said stolidly.

'Take this seriously, Greg! This is the life and death you've been talking about! All I'm telling you is true—I wish to God it wasn't!'

'Sorry.'

She tried to give a smile of forgiveness and failed. She continued: 'But that's not the worst of it. We have interrupted a cycle.'

'Meaning?'

'Greg, your mother was a cat lover. Have you heard of a parasite called Toxoplasma?'

'Yes, but I don't know much about it.'

'It's a protozoan, not a fungus, but don't worry, I'll get back to them. It's a parasite that has two hosts: cats and rodents, let's just say mice. The protozoan reproduces inside the cat but has to transfer to the mouse to complete its life cycle. And here's the thing, Greg: it alters the mouse's mental state, it makes them unafraid of cats. And what do you think happens then?'

'The cat eats the mouse.'

'Exactly. And much more frequently, as the mouse basically walks up to the cat, begging to be eaten. Do you see where this is leading?'

'Yes. And I don't want to.'

'Bear with me, just one more example and one which is even more relevant to where we find ourselves.

'There is a fungus called,' once again a quick look at the printout, 'called Ophiocordyceps which parasitises ants. They pick up spores from the forest floor which multiply to form a fungal mass around the brain, and which secrete various metabolites which take over its nervous system. It then forces the ant to climb the nearest tree and bite into a leaf, a bite of unnatural force, which means they can't be easily dislodged. It's called the death grip.'

'Charming.'

'Wait for it. The death grip prevents the ant from falling after the fungus has killed it. The fungal mass then sends out a fruiting body from the ant's head, which releases more spores into the environment. It has been known to wipe out entire colonies. Need I say more?'

Greg was silent for nearly a minute. Then he said, 'Yes. I understand the examples, but I want you to spell it out in detail. This is all strange to me.'

Sally drew a chair next to him and sat.

'Greg, do you remember in the cavern how I noticed that small fishes were simply offering themselves up to the bigger fish?'

'Yes.'

'They were caught in a parasitic cycle, just like the mice. They wanted to die, to be eaten. The large fish were the top end of the cycle. The fungus would use their bodies to create spores which would be released back into the water, perfect food for the small fish. And so they go, round and round, never ending. Until we got accidentally inserted into the cycle.'

'How did that happen?'

'It must have been Marie when she was dissecting that damned fish. Maybe she cut herself—I don't know. There was virtually nothing left of that brain—it was just a mass of mycelia. We burnt it. But none of that matters now. We know exactly where we are. We've been sucked into the cycle, but we're a dead-end host. The fungus is trying to reach the top of the cycle in order to reproduce sexually, but that top is not there; we're blocking the way. It's using the same mind control tricks as it does in the real cycle, the only tricks it knows, but because we're not the right host, it's misfiring. It causes erratic behaviour, first irritability and thrill-seeking, danger-seeking behaviours—

euphoria. But it gets confused and sometimes goes for murder rather than suicide. But as the fungus becomes dominant in the body, it switches permanently to dysphoria and the desire for death—the host's death. Freud talked about a desire in humans for risk-taking, love of danger and ultimately the desire for death itself. Later writers termed it Thanatos.'

'What—psychoanalysis? I thought we were all scientists here!'

'No, this is not psychoanalysis. This is a real, demonstrable fact. We are trapped in a cycle, a cycle of Thanatos.'

Greg leaned forward and slowly put his head on his hands.

'Is there anything we can do?' He looked up. 'Now that you've found the agent, surely we can attack it with drugs! Joan!'

Hicks had been asleep, but the sound of her name jerked her awake.

'Joan! Antifungal treatments! We can destroy this damn thing!'

Hicks looked around groggily and then as Greg's words finally registered, she said, 'There are no antifungals in the base. Why should there be? We weren't expecting to deal with any.'

'What about the fish? They must be at risk—from being in close confinement.'

'No, the pens are so big that they're basically free-swimmers. And part of Ricardo's genetic engineering was to confer fungal resistance. But we can't alter our genes, I'm afraid.'

'There's one thing we can do,' Sally said, 'one thing we must do. Topside can cure us.' Then once again, her voice rose to a scream. 'We've got to get out of this fucking base!'

'We're no longer people,' Hicks said in an odd, dreamlike voice, 'we're just organic items, drifting near the bottom of the food chain. What an honour! To be subsumed, absorbed, integrated into something greater than ourselves. I am content.'

'Well, I'm not. Come on Sally, let's leave "organic item" to her dreams.'

Greg and Sally emerged into the Meeting Room. To find Alvarez standing there, with his trademark grin nearly splitting

140

his face.

'I see you're still in the euphoric phase, Ricardo. Could you perhaps tell me where you've been hiding?' Greg snapped.

'I told you not to ask that,' was the nonchalant reply, 'I could say I've been taking a walk in the North Atlantic Drift, but you wouldn't believe me.'

'Well, you're back now. I'm sure I can find you something useful to do.'

Alvarez took one step towards them.

'No, you don't tell me to do anything anymore, Richardson. Those days of pushing me around are gone. I'm sure you know by now that we're all going to die, and I mean very soon, not in forty years, drooling in an old folk's home.'

'Rumour has it,' Greg said, watching the other man very warily.

'Well, I have decided to appoint myself as the Agent of Death. Talking to my new friend has made everything very clear that death is the answer to everything. 'Tis a consummation devoutly to be wished.' He stopped and cocked his head, looking at the ceiling. 'Did I think those words up myself or is it a quote?'

'Who's your new friend?' Sally asked, although she was reasonably sure she knew the answer.

'You know who he is. He is the skull held by the Prince of Denmark, he is the invisible worm that flies in the night; he is the ruler of this universe and every other.'

'You're talking nonsense,' Greg said through gritted teeth.

Alvarez switched his gaze to Sally and, with pity in his eyes, said, 'Sally, how did you come to marry this boor? He doesn't understand any of my literary allusions.'

Greg took a step towards him, but Alvarez raised a hand to forestall him.

'Not yet, Greg. I will visit you once again before the end and the next time I will have a gift for you. Until then, adieu, parting is such sweet sorrow. That's a lovely line—I must write it down before I forget it.'

And then he disappeared into a corridor, leaving his

audience standing in wide-eyed bemusement.

'He's gone mad,' Greg said.

'We're all going mad!' Sally snapped, 'that's why we've got to get out! Now, now, now!'

Greg turned to her and, to her horror, shook his head.

'No. I think we should sit this out until they send the transfer sub down. I've got too much riding on this. Sal, you know me—I've never quit in my life, and I'm as sure as hell not going to start now!"

'Greg! You've changed your bloody mind again! Have you forgotten all I've said!'

He held her. 'Sal, do you feel any different? I don't. Maybe we're immune. Not everybody reacts to infection in the same way. A look at the recent pandemics proves that; there are always some people who don't get it, and I'm one —I know it!"

'No! You didn't see that brain! Greg, there was hardly a neuron left in it; it was a just a mass of foul black mycelia. And the same thing's happening to our brains as we stand here.'

'One thing will prove it.'

'And what's that, my newly qualified mycologist?'

'We take the blood test, then you'll see I'm right. I'm not expecting both of us to be clean, but I'm sure the infection will just be starting in you. I mean, do you feel like slashing yourself with a scalpel or running around spouting some weird kind of poetry? We'll wait until Topside realise something's wrong, and come and take us in the nice, comfortable transfer sub. '

'I'm not going to argue with you, Greg. We'll get Joan to do it.'

But Hicks refused.

'No, I'm too tired. I want to be with Ricardo. I thought I heard him outside the lab not long ago, but it couldn't have been him because he must be dead by now.'

'So you won't help us?' Sally said, feeling her eyes sting with sudden salt.

Hicks looked at them and then said, 'I will help you. I'll give you the equipment, and you can do it yourselves.'

'We've never done blood tests!' Sally cried, 'We're not medics!'

'The syringes, needles and everything else is in that drawer. Get two packs and sit in front of me.'

Reluctantly, they agreed.

Hicks began her lesson: 'Take the syringe out of its wrapper, and the same for the needle. Screw the needle on the body of the syringe; make it tight, but not too tight so you break the thread. Choose an upper arm for the insertion. Greg, make a fist and keep opening and closing it. Sally, find the most prominent vein and palpate it. Wipe the skin over the vein with the betadine antibacterial liquid.'

'I can't do this!' Sally wailed.

'If you can't then, that's it. I don't know why I should help you. You're keeping me from Ricardo.'

Sally leaned over Greg who looked up at her, and silently mouthed, 'Come on, Sal.'

Hicks continued. 'Bring the needle up to the vein and go in with a shallow angle. Then slowly draw back the plunger and watch the blood fill the syringe up to the last gradation mark. When you've done that I'll instruct you on the testing equipment.'

Sally gave Greg a quick glance and then, trying to steady her trembling hand, slowly pushed the needle into a now bulging vein. She saw him wince, but he remained silent.

Finally, after much more wincing and "Sorry's" the blood was transferred to the testing machine.

Sally and Greg stood by the printer; Hicks remained in her chair and never spoke again.

The printer made a faint chattering noise and a sheet of paper moved jerkily out of a slot. Sally tore it out and spent some time staring at it. Then her shoulders sagged and, wordlessly, she passed it to Greg.

He stared at the words and numbers and then Sally said, 'Well, satisfied now? Happy? We've got it. It's in our blood in large numbers, which means it's in our brains. Growing, spreading. Sending little tendrils though our tissues.'

'But I feel alright!'

'You do now, you stupid lummox! But it won't last, and when you succumb there'll be no way back! No way! Already I can feel my thoughts getting duller, clumsier, and I'm certain you must be feeling the same thing, if only you'd man-up and damn well admit it! Now, will you listen to me, for Chrissake?'

More minutes passed. Sally could see the muscles of his jaws working under the skin. Then he said, 'We'll ask Hicks. There must be some treatment.'

They crossed the room to the silent doctor.

And the real reason for her silence was instantly obvious. She was surrounded by empty medical vials and between her feet was a large syringe. Showing no emotion, Sally picked up a vial and read the wording.

'Marie's insulin. She's given herself a massive insulin overdose.'

'Is she still alive?'

'I don't know, and I don't care. There's no way we can pull her back, even if she is still alive. Let's go. We've got what we came for.'

Returning to the Meeting Room, they sat facing each other.

Sally looked at her hands and said, 'So this is it. This is what it's like to be in an Agatha Christie murder mystery. One by one, the characters are killed off. The difference is we know the identity of the murderer. There's no need for Hercule Poirot to gather us all together in the withdrawing room for the big reveal.'

'OK,' Greg said, 'so we'll escape.'

'In what?' Sally racked her brains, trying to think of what Greg could be getting at.

She could not.

'The escape pods. The clue's in the name.'

A flicker of animation crossed Sally's face.

'Of course! We haven't been thinking straight—it's that fungus dulling our brains, trying to kill us! Why are we sitting here? What are we waiting for!'

'It would be a bit crowded in there if there were four of us, but two people will have plenty of space. Kurchatov and Alvarez can find their own way out; I don't give a damn about them anymore.' He made an attempt at humour. 'So there'll be no need to get up close and personal. What a pity, eh, Sal?'

She did not react. She simply stood and said, 'Let's go.'

The Escape Room was not far, and they were soon looking up at the pod's rounded base protruding from the ceiling.

Greg said, 'No need to look for airlock controls. The door behind us is a pressure door. As soon as the pod is blasted free, it'll shut. This room will flood, of course, but we can't waste precious seconds on airlock controls.'

'And just how do we get in?' she said.

'Sal, you've forgotten the drill, haven't you?'

She made a face but said nothing.

'We climb the ladder. We press the "E" key. The hatch you can see swings open. We get in. We start the ejection process. This room becomes a flooded airlock. Explosive bolts blast the pod free, and after twenty minutes we'll be on the surface with our emergency beacon blasting away, and rescue craft making a beeline for us.'

'Sounds good. So what are we waiting for?'

'Nothing you want to take?'

'Just my ass. Let's go!'

He managed a smile. 'Ladies first.'

Her heart hammering, she climbed the ladder to the base of the pod.

There was a large red "E" embossed on the shining metal.

Eagerly she pressed it.

Nothing.

She stared at it and pressed harder.

Nothing.

Tears burst from her eyes as she hammered the letter with small fists, swearing, cursing, blaspheming, begging.

Nothing.

Greg watched her as she fought with the recalcitrant letter

and then helped her from the ladder. His face was impassive, seemingly carved from stone.

He also ascended the ladder and also hammered with all his strength on the letter which would save them.

Nothing.

They returned to the Meeting Room in utter, abject silence.

Sally was the first to sit. She bowed her head and wept, seemingly forever. Greg watched her, helpless, hopeless.

Then she raised her head, ran a hand over moist eyes and drew in a great ragged breath.

'That's it, then. This really is it. No more clever plans. Killed by a fish, a bloody, fucking fish. And we'd just started. Everything was in front of us. So much we were going to see. So much we were going to do. The whole world. Everything, we had everything. And now it's all taken away by a fucking, fucking fish!'

He remained silent.

She wiped away more tears. 'There's one consolation in all of this: when the madness comes, we won't fear death—we'll love it, want it, embrace it! Like Marie, Harald, Joan, we'll hold out our hands and kiss the skull.'

Greg said nothing for some time and then he pointed to the corner of the room and said, 'Drag your chair over there.'

She stared at him blankly, but after some seconds joined him in the corner, both facing the wall.

'Why are we doing this?' she said.

'Kurchatov is a very clever little troll. It's possible that he's still watching. Even if he hasn't got audio now, he might be able to lipread.'

'So what! It's finished. We're all out of clever little schemes. All out.'

He touched her arm, but she moved away slightly.

'Sal, I want to apologise for being so pigheaded, so wrong. Everything you've said about me is true. It's just rotten bad luck that you had to find out this way. I want to say I'm sorry.'

'Sorry!' she exploded, 'we are way past sorry! Sorry is what

146

you say to someone when you bump into them in the shops, not when you've got them into a situation which will kill them! Sorry doesn't even begin to cut it.'

He hung his head for a moment then, raising it, he whispered, 'There's still one possible way out.'

'The Easter Bunny's going to whisk us all away in a magic egg basket. Greg, you're a fucking genius.'

'No, listen. It's possible to release the escape pod from outside.'

'What? How?' Her face contorted as she rocked her head from side to side. 'Greg, I can't remember! The fungus doesn't want me to remember!'

'It's the system which allows for people to be rescued if they're unconscious and obviously can't operate the controls.'

'How does it work? Magic? Are we allowed to call King Neptune on his cell?'

'Keep your voice down. No, there's a keypad on the surface of the thing just above the hatch and it will be accessible from outside the dome.'

Memories of the lifeboat drill tried to fight their way to the surface of Sally's mind. She could almost reach out to them, almost remember.

But something was blocking their increasingly desperate attempts to break into her consciousness.

Something hidden, something insidious, something implacably working towards her destruction.

And so in dull monotone, she said: 'And?'

'Press the Star and Hash keys on the pad simultaneously. Twice. Has to be simultaneous to avoid the system being activated accidentally. The bolts will fire and the pod will eject. After a two minute delay, the hatch opens.'

'Won't the pod fill with water?'

'Yes, of course. But the electrics are sealed. After one minute, the hatch closes and the pumps start automatically.'

'One minute doesn't sound like a long time.'

'It isn't, they only expected the procedure to be needed if

the pod was near the surface. That's why you need to press twice to get the bolts to fire.'

She rocked back in the chair, staring at the wall.

'One little problem. We're inside the dome, not outside. We can't teleport ourselves out.'

'The sub airlock. Obviously Kurchatov has switched off the interior controls for the escape pods because he knew we'd go for them. But he might not have overridden the sub airlock because there's no sub anymore. And as the exterior controls on the pods are purely mechanical, he can't disable them. But if he knows of our plan, he'll seal the sub airlock. Hence this secrecy.'

For a second Greg saw hope light up his wife's eyes, but then she continued: 'But we're not near the surface. The pressure suits won't survive the pressure this far down. And how do we get to the pod?'

'We'll emerge not far from it, where the slope is shallow. A service ladder runs from just below the airlock to the top of the dome, and the pressure will work in our favour for a short time.'

'How so?'

'If we press ourselves as flat as possible, there'll be a net force pushing us onto the dome surface.'

'And my point about the suits not being up to the job; you know, the little thing I mentioned in passing? That's one thing I do remember!'

'There's no way around that. They will fail. But they will hold for a while.'

'How long?'

'I don't know. There's only one way to find out.'

Silence.

Then he said, 'We both have to know exactly what the procedures are if this is going to work, in case something happens to one of us. You know how to operate the sub airlock, don't you?'

'Yes.'

'Then let's get our suits on and get the hell out.'

They had both wriggled into the bottom halves of the

148

pressure suits when a great voice boomed through the intercom. It was Kurchatov's voice, but tremendously amplified. And it carried a confident, masculine timbre.

'The time is near! My friends, you have not heard from me for some time as I have been grappling with a major problem that has taxed even my brain. But now you can rejoice!

'For many a time, I have been half in love with easeful Death, but now there is no more doubt. I am fully committed to her, and we will join in blissful union. Now my love for Death is full and complete. From our new vantage point, she and I can see what life really is: an absurd playlet written by an incompetent playwright. Life is a meaningless stain on time and space, an unfortunate side-effect of the ability of certain minor organic chemicals to make copies of themselves.

'It would have been better if life had never arisen in this universe, a self-sufficient continuum which is clearly designed for higher things than this multiplying chemical madness.

'The Greeks were right when they said: Happy the man who is not born! And now I have come to put that mistake right. Mr Richardson, I am no longer your rival. I understand why you are like you are, and I forgive you. Mrs Richardson, our love would have been in vain and I would soon have left you for my beloved bride, Death Herself.

'I am now going to put right that terrible mistake and un-birth you. I have found out how to evade the passive safety features of the reactor. I am about to remove the moderator rods, and very soon the uranium fuel will become an all-devouring ball of liquid metal. At nearly two thousand degrees it will melt this entire complex into impure iron sludge and meet a magnificent end when the deep sea rushes in upon it. Even I am awed by the beauty of that consummation.

'I now bid you adieu. You were foolish infants, trying to cling on to life, but, of course, you knew no better. Once again, adieu.'

Greg and Sally stared at each other in abject horror, shocked into impotent immobility.

Then Greg snapped, 'Come on! We can still make it!'

They resumed their struggles into the pressure suits, but now with fingers that no longer seemed to obey their brains, that seemed not to want to obey their brains. Finally, the helmets snapped into place. The inter-suit comms link booted at once and Greg's voice boomed in her ears.

'To the sub airlock, jump to it!'

Just then, Alvarez burst from the corridor and raised the object he was carrying, so it pointed at Greg. It was a speargun.

Greg dove to one side as Alvarez fired, but not quite fast enough: the spear took him in the right side, bursting two-thirds of its length out of his body in a spray of blood. The force of the impact threw him against a table, and he and it together collided with the wall.

'Greg!' she screamed as she ran over.

But Alvarez barred the way. His voice was very muffled by Sally's helmet, but she half-heard, half-read his words.

'No more taking orders! I'm free. See if you can save your man, Sally, but I fear you will not be able to. Adios amiga!'

And with that, as quickly as he had come, he disappeared into the corridor.

She dropped to her knees beside Greg and screamed, 'What can I do!'

The helmet moved slowly from side to side, and a weak, gasping voice came over the intercom.

'Nothing, Sal, nothing. Even if I could be saved, you don't have the equipment. Even if you had the equipment, you don't have the time. Go, go now. One of us must survive to tell them what happened, to warn them of the danger down here. Go.'

'I can't leave you!' She wailed. 'I can't!'

'You must. If you stay, you die along with me, and I don't want that. Do this one little thing for me, for the sake of our marriage. Please go. Do it for me.'

She moved so she could see into the helmet and said the three words which needed to be said, words which seemed to burn her tongue with their finality. Then she stood and, without looking back, made her way to the sub airlock as fast as the awkward pressure suit would allow.

Ensuring that the correct buttons were activated was not easy with the clumsy gloves but she managed it and vibrations in the floor told her that the heavy pressure door had slid shut behind her and the airlock cycle had begun. She took a quick glance at the small control pad on her left wrist.

Her tanks were full of the helium-oxygen mixture, so there was no danger of her dying from asphyxia.

Not immediately, at least.

There were more vibrations making the floor shudder, and she looked up to see powerful gouts of dark green water crashing into the airlock, water so dark it was almost black. The chamber would not take long to fill.

Nor did it, and soon the outer pressure door slid back revealing an ebony nothingness beyond. As soon as she started to move, she could feel the resistance of the dense liquid, as if a great hand were trying to hold her back. For a moment, she wondered why she was making such a ridiculous effort when failure was virtually guaranteed.

No! Greg told me to do it! I won't let him down!

She reached the lip of the exit and looked out. There was still nothing, no sense of scale, of distance, of movement: she could have been looking at a huge black curtain.

She swung herself out and onto the ladder which ascended from the side of the airlock exit to the top of the dome to where the pod was sitting; inert, immobile. Now that she was fully out of the dome, a terrible vertigo seized her and for a moment, it seemed as if she could feel the crushing weight of nearly a kilometre of water pushing down on her like a tremendous boulder that she would be forced to carry on her shoulders.

But more alarming than that was she could both hear and feel the suit being strained by the great pressure. The entire suit had moved inwards and where there had been a space between the suit's inner lining and her ordinary clothes, in several places she could feel that the two were now in contact, making

151

movement even more difficult. There was also a faint groaning noise as the suit fought to stay rigid in the vice-like grip of the ocean. It was a fight that the suit would eventually lose; she was only too well aware of that.

She began to climb, keeping as little water between her and the rungs as possible. The ocean's great fist was pressing her against those rungs, threatening to push her through them, turning her into slices of human salami.

But as Greg had promised, her emergence point was not far from the top of the dome and the gradient was shallow.

Not far! Every movement up the ladder tore at her muscles as she almost burrowed her way through the viscous black water; the only things she could see through her faceplate were the ladder and her arms. The suit creaked and groaned alarmingly.

Then the gradient flattened, and she realised that she was at the top. And in the murk was the faint curving outline of the escape pod. Her heart, already hammering under the tension and physical strain, beat even stronger. There it was! No Kurchatov! No Alvarez! People who had been friends but who had now become deadly enemies. How was that possible? How was any of this possible! She drove them from her mind and struggled on towards salvation.

Now that she was almost horizontal, she could pull herself along the ladder, and the pod rapidly became more clearly outlined. It was three quarters out of the dome's surface, almost a complete globe. It had four portholes at the cardinal points on its equator, and there were various handholds at regular points on its meridians. The pod was sitting in a collar that went right around its base, a structure that would blast it free and send it up through increasingly bright and transparent water to the real world, the world of uninfected humans, of peace, of calm, of the restitution of normality. Her rescuers would take her and subject those foul mycelia, now worming their way through her brain, to the full force of twenty-first-century medical science. In her mind, she could see those strands of insidious death wilting, shrivelling, perishing.

In the glory of her image, she yelled into her helmet, 'Yes! Let's see how you like it, you bastards!'

It was then she felt a spot of icy water on her calf, and she knew that the suit was giving up its unequal struggle with the crushing pressure.

She must move and move fast!

She was at the pod, searching wildly for the keypad which would free it and send it hurtling up into the blessed sunlight.

Where was the fucking thing? Where?

It must be on the other side.

Keeping herself low, she crawled around the pod, trusting to the pressure to keep her pinned to the surface.

She could see the rectangular outline of the hatch, the hatch that would open, must open, under her probing fingers. And there next to it was the pad, embossed with thick symbols. For a moment of near madness, she couldn't remember what characters she had to press. She howled her grief into the helmet, a dying animal caught in a trap of cold black horror.

She stared at the pad and slowly extended a trembling arm towards it.

The symbols danced in her mind, an insane kaleidoscope of meaningless shapes.

A cold drop of water fell onto her chest.

She tried to remember Greg's voice, tried to remember his instructions.

Suddenly four more jets of liquid ice hit different parts of her body, and she could feel the suit wrinkling like a decaying apple.

Gloved fingers rested on two symbols and pressed them simultaneously, twice.

Immediately there was a brief ring of fire around the pod, which was almost instantly replaced by curtains of bubbles, and then it jerked upwards. For a heart-ripping instant it looked as if it would shoot past and ascend without her, leaving her weeping on the surface of the dome, but instinctively she grabbed one of the handholds as it flashed past and she and the pod began to ascend together.

Even so, the ordeal was not over. She had two minutes to position herself over the hatch and try to get inside when it opened for one, brief minute. Hanging upside down, she pulled herself down the side until she was over the now fully rectangular outline of the hatch. What if it shuts as I'm halfway in? she thought, is there a safety mechanism or will it cut me into halves?

But it must have taken her two minutes to get there, because no sooner had that thought crossed her mind when the hatch opened.

She need not have worried about taking too long to get inside because she found herself at the business end of an irresistible piston of water that rammed her into the interior. In seconds, the pod was full of water and now, with negative buoyancy, fell back onto the dome, sliding down its side towards the abyssal plain. She was tossed back and forth in a seemingly endless whirl of motion, hearing terrible metallic crashing noises through both the pod walls and her suit.

But the pumps cut in, pushing the water back to its allotted place, and as the water jetted back out, the pod began slowly to ascend.

As the last of the icy water disappeared, she removed her helmet, realising that it had saved her from serious head injury during her chaotic fall.

She sat in a bucket seat next to a porthole, waiting for sunlight to make its first feeble appearance in the water.

'Greg,' she whispered, 'Oh Greg.'

At a steadily increasing distance below her, Kurchatov leaned back in his chair, and smiled.

The moment of apotheosis had arrived. Soon he would meet his bride and eternity would be theirs.

There were no more thoughts.

Released from the confinement of the moderator rods, the uranium fuel had been building up greater and greater levels of heat.

Now it had liquified into a great sphere of blazing liquid

154

metal. It burned its way through its concrete shell and expanded through the corridors linking it to the outer domes.

Nothing could stop it; structural steel met it, glowed, sagged, softened and joined its ineluctable onslaught. The hellish sphere devoured the base turning it into a titanic, incandescent amoeba and then began to sink towards the core of the planet. The ooze and rock parted like ice under a blowtorch.

And the sea? It rushed in, confident in the strength of its pressure, the power of its frigidity.

It met the sphere and was instantly transmuted into superheated water vapour.

More poured in to fill the hollow left by that destruction and met the same fate.

A great hemisphere of unbelievably potent, raging gases began to rise to the surface.

For Sally, the first indication of the impending cataclysm was that the water beyond the porthole was suddenly lit from below by a terrible yellow-white glare.

And then the eruption was upon her.

***

Reuters Report 16:09: there are reports of a large explosion near the International Research Base near Jan Mayen island. Reports indicate that great numbers of mutated fish have escaped into the surrounding waters. No reports yet of casualties.

Reuters Report 17:30: Two escape pods have been discovered on the surface. One has been opened and regrettably the occupant has been declared dead. The other pod is being opened now and we will bring you the occupant's condition as soon as we have it.

WE ARE SUCH STUFF

I know I'm dreaming.

I know I'm dreaming because I'm in a world which can't possibly exist. There is nowhere on earth which looks like where I think I am at this moment. These soaring towers, seemingly made of emerald and illuminated by gentle, lambent light from within. The broad thoroughfares in which silent, streamlined vehicles thread themselves through the traffic, coming within millimetres of other hurtling machines, but there is never a collision, never a scrape.

And the sky—jet black and featureless except when a shiver, a shimmer of blinding light flashes across it from horizon to horizon.

I think it is meant to be a city, but—if you pardon the obvious—one that could only be glimpsed in a dream.

And yet there is something odd about this dream, odder than the city I am supposed to be in.

The dream is not like others where events follow no logic, where there is no cause and effect, no discernible rationale.

You know the kind of dream I mean, the kind where you think you're talking to your wife, and then you realise she's turned into a hippopotamus. (Or does that only happen with my wife?)

I've only had this dream for the past few nights, and each time I dream, it feels like it's of greater duration. The first time I just had a brief glimpse of those emerald towers, and then the usual meaningless phantasmagoria took over. I thought at the time that I was just seeing a re-run of The Wizard of Oz. But the second and third time; I was actually interacting with that city, walking along one of the smooth sidewalks, knowing that I was hurrying to meet someone, someone that I really wanted to meet.

And then I woke up. Like I've just done now, just after I started talking to you.

***

Murchison's eyelids fluttered several times, and then the gummed-up flesh finally parted, and he found himself looking at the ceiling. A grey early-morning south London light was attempting to come through a crack in the curtains.

'What time is it?' he said in a thick voice. The voice surprised him until he remembered the somewhat excessive consumption of cheap burgundy the previous night.

His wife was already up and was sitting in front of the mirror, trying to straighten her frizzy, greying hair with a brush that, like the two occupants of that bedroom, had seen better days.

'Time you were up, Mr Sleepy-Head,' she said, not taking her eyes off her duplicate behind the glass.

'It's Saturday, isn't it?' he replied, with a mixture of irritability and hope. He didn't feel like going into his workplace at the moment.

'All day,' she announced. She turned to face him. 'You were really knocking it back last night. Why can't you just have a glass or two like everybody else?'

He swung his legs out of bed and sat on the edge. 'It's about the only excitement I get around here,' he muttered.

She shrugged. 'And why's that, I wonder? You're not exactly Love's Young Dream yourself anymore, Brian. What do you expect out of life?'

He shook his head as if trying to clear it. 'I don't know, I just don't know. I feel something is missing, something I'm supposed to be doing, something important.'

'Well, there's the lawn you've been promising to mow for weeks,' she replied, referring to the nondescript green rectangle behind their house, 'if the grass gets any longer, people will start looking for a lost city in all that vegetation.'

Ignoring the criticism, he half-stumbled into the en-suite and spent some seconds staring at his stubble-patterned face.

Not too bad for my age, he thought, patting his jowls. His reflection stared back at him wordlessly, his green eyes subdued from their usual brilliance by the room's half-light.

After running an electric razor over the stubble and applying an electric toothbrush to his dentition, he called to her from the en-suite; unfortunately while very noisily attempting to use the plumbing facilities—much to his wife's annoyance.

'I had that dream again, Joan.'

'What—the one where you're young and handsome with a harem of blonde cuties?'

'No. I only had that dream once, and I wish I'd never told you! No, the one of the city. The city with the tall green towers.'

She shrugged. 'It didn't sound very exciting. Just looking at a city. You really are losing it, my love. You'll be dreaming about playing dominoes and fancying pigeons next.'

He had emerged from the en-suite by then, looking slightly enervated by his struggles on the WC, and was reaching for his underpants.

'Well, I agree it wasn't exciting, but I had a feeling that it meant something, that it was important. And why do I have it every night?'

'Well, I know why you had it last night. It was the wine talking. Ask it for a better dream next time.'

He shook his head and dropped the topic.

However, over scrambled eggs and bacon, he found his thoughts returning to the images he had seen. The dream hadn't felt like the usual meaningless farrago that he was familiar with.

It was as if he had been standing there in that exotic place in another reality, and there had been a thought running through the disturbed mind of his dreaming alter-ego.

And that thought was about bad news.

Somehow he had failed.

***

As Murchison got off the commuter train in Uckfield on a damp Monday morning, the magnificent radio telescope was already starkly visible, dominating the small East Sussex town with its massive bulk. Its tremendous dish was angled completely horizontally, so he knew it was scanning the zenith of the radio sky. Nothing was visible to the human eye at that zenith, of course; as usual, the vista over southern England was overcast, as if a giant had flung a grey greatcoat over the dome of the sky. But that was no concern to the men and women who cared for the Hawking Telescope; its eye was unaffected by most atmospheric disturbances. Very little could interfere with its examination of the momentous events in the far reaches of the cosmos: the merging of black holes, the fierce energy outbursts from quasars, the hiss of electrons trapped in the spiralling magnetic fields of supernova remnants. It captured them all within its vast, calm gaze.

Murchison was not thinking of any of these distant phenomena as he got off the shuttle bus. He was wondering if he had remembered to pick up his security pass before he left the house or whether it was still sitting in the little bowl by the front door. He stopped suddenly, causing the man behind him to bump into him as he searched desperately in his jacket for that vital piece of plastic. To his great relief, he had not forgotten it, and he was allowed into the grounds of the very new but very world-renowned research facility.

At the entrance to the sprawling building, he passed another security check by having his retina scanned.

And then he was in the atrium, its calm air-conditioned atmosphere washing over him in soft, gentle waves. Immediately in front of him was a pleasant little waterfall, nestling in its circlet of ferns, but he took no notice. He'd seen it many times before.

He changed into his work overalls in the locker room and spent a few minutes discussing the game with his buddies. They all agreed that yesterday's game had been a travesty of bad refereeing and, as usual, the home team had been robbed.

Then, after taking the lift, he walked down the antiseptic corridors to one of the control rooms where the brains of the organisation were wont to spend many hours staring at computer screens, discussing wriggly lines on printouts and finding errors and misconceptions in the theories of their peers.

The Chief Scientist looked up as Murchison came in, manfully holding his heavy toolbox in one hand. The Chief adjusted his spectacles slightly on his beaked nose as if needing to get a clearer view of this strange phenomenon.

'Ah, Murchison, I was beginning to think you'd decided to take the day off. I've been waiting for you.'

Murchison knew there was no point in protesting that he'd come straight there (except for the brief delay spent discussing the game); Chief Scientist Andrews was notorious for believing that everyone but Chief Scientist Andrews was a lazy, time-waster.

'Still getting spurious readings, Doctor?' Murchison said.

'Why else would I ask you to give up the precious time you waste on trying to answer childish questions in the local rag's crossword? Yes, of course. Do you think you can solve it this time?'

'I'll do my best.' Murchison was already removing the front panel from the recording device. A little spasm of annoyance shot through him as he turned a screw with his rubber-handled screwdriver, and he looked up at Andrews. 'I know I'm only a humble electrician, but I'll do my best.'

Andrews looked completely unabashed and instantly began a conversation with a subordinate.

Murchison worked silently for twenty minutes, testing and retesting the circuits. Then he straightened himself, feeling a slight stab of pain in an arthritic back.

Andrews had left the room, so he spoke to one of the more friendly junior scientists.

'I've sorted it out, Dr Kasim. You'll be able to find those little green men easily enough now.'

Kasim smiled tolerantly. 'I haven't heard that phrase for quite some time, Brian. I don't think you know much of what we do here, do you?'

Murchison looked around. The radio telescope dish was visible through a huge window directly behind glowing banks of instruments, and it effortlessly dominated the landscape. It was

160

now pointing twenty degrees off the vertical.

'No, not really,' he said, 'something to do with Mars or Venus?'

Kasim's eyes twinkled above his expanded smile. 'No, Brian, they're just unimportant balls of rock in our backyard. Figuratively speaking, that is,' he added, noticing the sudden flash of puzzlement in Murchison's expression. 'No, we're interested in things far beyond our neighbourhood. Colossal, vastly distant events—stars exploding, black holes colliding, galaxies pouring out gigantic amounts of energy for reasons we don't yet know. That's why we're here. Ever since Arecibo collapsed, we've lacked a radio telescope of similar resolving power. But now we have the Hawking Telescope, we have more; so much more. Now we'll really get the universe to sit up and take notice.'

Murchison lowered his heavy toolbox to the floor and turned to look at the spidery web of steel that constituted the telescope. 'Do you ever wonder if we're doing the right thing?'

Now it was Kasim's turn to be puzzled. 'Doing the right thing? What do you mean, Brian?'

'Well, who knows what's out there, doc? Could be all sorts of nasties.'

Kasim exploded into helpless laughter. Two other subordinates, who had been half-listening to the conversation, also grinned.

'Brian, Brian, you're priceless. For a start, there's probably nobody out there. This universe doesn't readily support life. And if there were people out there, why would they want to hurt us, instead of joining us in discovering more about this beautiful cosmos we'd both be citizens of?' He chuckled involuntarily. 'Why, Brian, are you thinking they'd come thousands of light-years to eat us or'—and he glanced back at his fellow scientists—'carry off our women to some intergalactic harem?'

One of the others burst into raucous laughter.

Murchison realised that he was making a fool of himself and shrugged. 'Sorry, doc. I'm just a grunt, a dumb working man.'

Kasim reached out briefly to hold the other's shoulder. 'No, sorry, Brian—it's just that your ideas are so damn old-fashioned. I haven't heard anybody say those things since I was a kid. No hard feelings, eh?'

Murchison smiled. 'Sure, doc. No hard feelings.'

***

Well, yes, it's me again.

Look, I know hearing about somebody else's dreams may not be your idea of fun, but I really have to speak to someone, and I'm afraid it's you.

Well, I was in that city again. But I was further into it, if you know what I mean.

I was walking along one of the rather narrow sidewalks, and lots of people were rushing past me. They all looked distinctly worried, not to say unhappy. They all seemed to be carrying the weight of the world on their shoulders. The strange thing is no-one noticed me even though sometimes I just stood there, blocking their way. The really odd thing was sometimes they came up to me and just walked through me as if I wasn't there!

Well, I know what you're thinking.

Of course you weren't there, you idiot—it was a dream!

And I suppose that must be the answer.

I've got a better look at the city now. I mentioned those tall green towers earlier, but most of the buildings are quite low, with rounded outlines, like big, solid bubbles. I'll see if I can go inside one of them next time—if there is a next time.

I remembered to take a good look at the sky, and that seems a bit strange too. It's almost black, but with a peculiar orange-brown tint. Sometimes I can see what look like orange streamers, streaking above the tops of the towers. And another thing, from certain angles, there's a kind of shining glint up there, as if the whole city is under a big glass dome, like a slice of cheese under a cover.

Well, that's all for now.

If I get another dream about the place, I'll tell you some more.

Sorry about that.

***

'I had that dream again, Joan,' Murchison said over his breakfast. Godammit, why did she have to incinerate the bacon!

'Not that very unusual dream about being in a very unusual city. My, that sounds interesting.' She mimed yawning, putting her hand over her open mouth several times.

He looked at her with irritation clearly visible on his face.

Why did she resemble the unmade bed that he had not long quitted?

'It's not what the dream's about, my love,' he said, trying unsuccessfully not to sound irritated, 'it's the fact that I keep having it.'

She raised the index finger of one hand while the other hand manoeuvred a spoon brimming with milky cornflakes closer to her lips.

'Not entirely accurate, my love. You don't have it every night, just on a regular basis. And you've told me that you gradually see more and more of the city.'

The now-empty spoon stopped its descent halfway to the breakfast bowl as an idea occurred to her. 'Why, maybe you'll be able to get a job there—you know, one that's better paid than the one you've already got.'

He scowled. 'Thanks, my love. I'll have you know that being an electrician is an essential job in today's modern world. Absolutely essential.'

'Well, my love' she observed, glancing at the kitchen clock, 'if you don't hurry up and eat that bacon, you'll miss your train and then you'll find out exactly how essential you are at that funny place you tell me you work at.'

He did not miss the train and, on arrival, discovered, somewhat to his surprise, that all the systems were working flawlessly and he had nothing to do but routine maintenance work.

The morning dragged and, as midday finally approached, he found himself stretched out on the floor of one of the smaller laboratories with an inspection hatch open. He was gingerly placing the tip of a probe into the aperture while glancing at the

163

dial on his equipment, when a pair of slim female legs came into view beyond it. Automatically, he looked up and found himself looking into a pleasing oval face, framed in ash-blonde hair so pale it was almost white. Being careful of his back, he struggled to his feet and said, 'Sorry miss, I thought this lab wasn't in use until this afternoon.'

He was rewarded with a beautiful smile. 'You're right, it isn't. I just came back to get a periodical that I'm reading.'

He stared at her, utterly oblivious to the fact that he was staring, until she waved a hand in front of his face and said sweetly, 'Hello, Ground Control to Major Tom. Come in, please.'

For the first time in years he blushed, and finally spluttered, 'Sorry, miss. I haven't seen you before, and you look a bit different from the rest of the crowd here.'

She smiled again. 'Well, I'm not different, and I am one of the team. And it's not "Miss"; it's "Doctor"—Dr Vera Esperanza.'

Murchison decided it was best for his dignity to end the conversation before he dug himself into any more holes, and he backed away slightly. 'Sorry miss, I mean Dr Esperanza. It's just that I thought I knew all the boffins, but I haven't seen you before.'

Her smile faded as if a worrisome thought had just surfaced, and she turned away from him and stared at the radio telescope. From this lab it was seen at a different angle, but it was also closer, and so loomed massively behind the glass, making its interconnecting girders clearly distinguishable and beginning to reveal their true enormity.

'No,' she said, and there was a faint undercurrent of concern or perhaps sadness in her voice, 'no, you wouldn't have seen me. I've only just arrived.' She turned back to him, but this time her smile was forced. 'But I'm here now, and I'm looking forward to helping push forward the boundary of human knowledge.'

Murchison was about to speak when he suddenly realised that Dr Esperanza had the most brilliant green eyes that he had ever seen. They seemed almost to belong to some preternatural creature, one that was human-like but somehow beyond the limits of the mundane world.

'I'm sorry,' he finally managed to utter, 'but you seem to be familiar. Have we met?'

She looked at him for some seconds, then, 'No. I don't think so.'

Feeling thoroughly disconcerted, he merely nodded and, after saying 'Sorry to have disturbed you,' he left, leaving his testing unfinished.

Dr Esperanza looked at his retreating form, and her eyes were very thoughtful.

But as the tumult stirred up by that encounter slowly calmed, Murchison decided that he'd better finish the test before Andrews started checking up on him, which meant he needed to go back to his position on the floor.

He felt oddly reluctant to meet Dr Esperanza again, and self-consciously peered around the doorframe to check that the lab was now empty.

It was, and he managed to complete the testing before clocking-off time. But on the train back to south London, she kept returning to his thoughts.

***

He did not have the dream the following night but woke up with an inexplicable feeling of apprehension hanging over him. Joan noticed his lacklustre mood.

'Look, I know I'm not a celebrity chef, but my bacon's not that bad. The way you're pushing it around the plate, it looks like you think I dug it out of the waste bin.'

He smiled unconvincingly. 'Sorry, love. I don't know why I'm down today. But I think it's something to do with work.'

'What—they found out about your three-hour lunch breaks?'

'Very funny. No, there's something about that place. I've come to the conclusion that I don't like working there.'

Joan slapped a hand down hard on the table. 'Don't start that! Do we really need another spell of you out of work—just when we're getting back on our feet!'

He stood, leaving the cold bacon on the plate. 'I'm not going to do anything silly, Joan. I won't quit until I've got another job lined up.'

She watched him go with lips compressed into a thin line.

At work, his friend Pete also noticed Murchison's mood.

'What's eating you, man?' he enquired as they shared a tea break together. 'Lost the winning lottery ticket?'

Murchison shook his head. 'No, it's this place, Pete.'

'What's wrong with it? The pay's not good, but it's steady work. Nothing too difficult.'

Murchison did not meet the other's stare but seemed to be looking into infinity.

'I can't put it into words, Pete, but there's something wrong with this set-up. What it's trying to do. Something's wrong.'

'Like what?'

'What they're doing. All this probing out into the universe. It's a mistake.'

Pete drained the last of his tea and gave his friend a hard stare. 'You're not making any sense, mate. Are you afraid we're annoying the Martians or something?'

'No, no, of course not. I told you, I can't put it into words. At least not yet.'

Pete shrugged, and then his face lightened. 'Hey, have you seen that new doc that's walking around the place? Quite a looker! I wouldn't mind sending a few exotic particles her way!'

To his surprise, Murchison made no reply, so he picked up his toolbox and returned to his job, giving his morose companion no more thought.

Murchison continued with his work for the rest of the day. He did not encounter Dr Andrews, and, with a peculiar mixture of disappointment and relief, he did not meet Dr Esperanza either.

***

166

Yes, the sky is dark, but every now and again there is a brilliant flash like lightning, but lightning that fills the whole sky, so bright I have to turn away. The flash is so fierce I can see it even if I have my fingers over my eyes, and afterwards, I see these green and blue blobs for a few minutes.

I don't like those flashes. They don't seem right, not normal lightning. And afterwards, there seem to be more of those funny orange streamers for a few minutes.

I've got further into the city, but I haven't learned much more. The people still rush past me in a great hurry, going into buildings, coming out of buildings. And when they come out, they're always looking up at the sky— if it is the sky; I still think we're under some colossal glass dome.

Still, I've got used to them walking right through me. Have you any idea of how disturbing that is? It took about ten goes before I could believe it wasn't going to hurt me.

Well, it looks like I'm stuck with having this damn dream most nights, so I may as well make the best of it. I'm gradually getting closer to one of those tall green towers.

I just wish the people didn't look so bloody miserable!

***

Murchison removed the inspection panel and placed it gently on the floor, trying not to make any noise that would annoy the throng of scientists behind him. He glanced briefly over his shoulder. Yes, all the top brains were there: Andrews, Kasim and, yes, Esperanza.

He dared take another backwards glance, angled this time so he could get a better view of Esperanza. She was sitting on an office chair, the kind that has castors and can turn a full 360^0. Long, shining legs were stretched out in the direction of the window and, by extension, the mighty radio dish beyond it. Like the others in the lower echelon, she was listening intently to Andrews.

He was giving an audio-visual lecture. 'In March 1972, the first Pioneer probe was launched to Jupiter. After its encounter, it carried on into interstellar space carrying this message.' He

167

tapped on a small remote control device, and a large wall-mounted TV flashed into life. A picture appeared on the screen, showing fairly accurate representations of a naked man and woman, next to what seemed to be a very large asterisk. Murchison could make nothing of it and the thought flashed through his puzzled mind: *Has the doc flipped? Is he going to give us a porn show?*

Andrews continued: 'This plaque was designed by Carl Sagan and Frank Drake, both firm believers in the existence of NHIs.'

'NHIs?' one of the lesser attendees queried.

'Non-Human Intelligences,' Andrews responded briskly and returned to pointing at the image. 'They were both eager to allow the NHI civilisation that found the plaque to determine where the message came from, so the schematic on the left shows the position of the Solar system relative to the position of fourteen pulsars and the galactic centre.' He paused and gave an acerbic smile. 'Who can tell me one big problem with this form of interstellar communication?'

There was a momentary silence and then Kasim said, 'The length of time taken by the probe to reach an NHI civilisation.'

Andrews nodded. 'Yes, obviously. The Pioneer probe has still to leave the Oort Cloud despite the inordinate length of time which has passed.' He caught sight of Murchison and said, 'Back to your work please, Murchison. This talk is rather above your pay grade.'

The object of his admonition swore under his breath and returned to examining the spaghetti-like tangle of electrical wires that had been hidden behind the inspection panel.

Andrews resumed: 'So on November 16th 1974, Drake and Sagan tried again, using our illustrious predecessor, the Arecibo Telescope, to send a radio signal. Their target was determined by the dish's fixed orientation, so they were forced to send the message to the globular star cluster Messier Thirteen, which is twenty five thousand light-years away.' He gave another dry smile. 'So our NHI friends have yet to receive the message!'

168

No-one laughed.

Andrews returned to pointing at the screen.

'The message consisted of nearly two thousand binary digits, employing semiprimes so that a bitmap image could be generated.'

Murchison risked another glance, which was sufficient to see Andrews pointing at a strange picture on the screen. It comprised a collection of small black and white squares, one collection of which seemed to be a very basic representation of the human form, so basic that a child might have constructed it. He returned to examining the spaghetti tangle.

'Once again,' Andrews said, 'they were limited by the number of bits they could encode, so the message is very simple, consisting mainly of data on the DNA molecule.

'But it also showed a graphic of the Solar system, indicating which planet sent the message.'

Andrews pressed another key on his remote control, and the image died. He turned so he was facing the entire group of his staff and said, 'That sums up the main attempts at interstellar communication with other intelligences. But I propose to take a giant leap beyond those childish fumblings.'

There was a small susurration of surprised interest from the group.

'Yes,' said Andrews, and he was now beaming, 'I am going to use the Hawking Telescope to send a much more complex message out into space, with a great deal more information about our home planet, our biochemistry, our level of technological civilisation, and'—he fell silent in a dramatic pause—'precise co-ordinates, so that our NHI peers will be able to identify our exact location. And because our telescope, unlike the Arecibo, is fully dirigible, I will send this message to a collection of stars of spectral types K, G and F that are known to host exoplanets.' He gave a self-deprecatory shrug and continued, 'Of course, I will probably no longer be alive when most of the messages arrive but I'm afraid I can't alter the speed of light. But, hopefully, posterity will not forget me.'

169

There was a small burst of applause from the enthralled group, but Murchison, risking another reprimand, saw that Esperanza had not joined in.

Andrews had also noticed.

'I see you appear to be unimpressed with my proposal, Dr Esperanza. Perhaps you could explain to the group why that is.'

Esperanza met his gaze unflinchingly. 'Dr Andrews, I joined this facility because it was stated to be the premier establishment for first-class studies into the major problems of cosmology. This seems to be no more than a comic sideshow and a diversion from real research.'

Andrews was not smiling now. 'Dr Esperanza, I fear you have underestimated the powers of the Hawking Telescope, and I might add, myself. The creation and sending of my messages will occupy less than one percent of the time and energies of this magnificent machine. Does that satisfy you, doctor?'

Esperanza looked down at her interlinked hands for a moment and then, looking up, said, 'I stand corrected on the issue of diversion from more important issues, Dr Andrews, but there is one other consideration.'

'And what might that be, doctor?'

'This telescope is named after the renowned twentieth-century physicist, Stephen Hawking.'

'I think even Mr Murchison over there knows that, doctor.'

'Then perhaps we might consider his warning.'

'His warning? I'm not familiar with that particular message from the great man.'

Esperanza's gaze seemed to take on an intensity hitherto denied to human eyes.

'He reminded us of all the histories of contacts between two cultures, where one is significantly technologically inferior to the other. He used the European contact with Native Americans as an example.'

'And his conclusion?'

'It doesn't end well for the simpler culture.'

***

Here we go again; I'm walking down the narrow sidewalk, with all these worried people passing by me—and through me.

But I'm nearly at the base of one of those tall emerald towers, and this time I'm going to go inside. Maybe I can finally get some answers as to why I'm here and what the hell is going on with all these lightning flashes. I've just realised that before in these dreams there'd been no sound—the lightning flashes had been silent, but now I'm beginning to hear noise; I'm sure that the last time there was a flash I could hear some faint thunder.

Well, I'm now standing outside the entrance to one of those towers. It's immense, and above it is a sign saying something. It's a long way up and my eyes are not too good these days but I think it says "Defense Station #3"; anyway, I'm going in!

The inside is very big and covered with lots of desks, each having a large thing like a computer monitor sticking up from it. On one wall, there are doors that appear to be linked to elevators. I think they're elevator doors because there are displays next to each one which have numbers which keep changing, and every now again, a door opens and people come out and then people go in. Well, I'm not going to try to get in one; they must lead up to the upper floors of this tower, and there's more than enough to see on this floor.

I'm walking up to the nearest desk,, and there are four people sat around it looking at the display on the computer monitor. As usual, they look like they're not having a very good day. The display shows some kind of map, a relief map, I believe they call it. There's a big circle with lots of small rectangles outlined inside it in the bottom right corner. I think it must be a representation of the city I'm in. But the top left has an odd yellow shading over it. And it's not a nice yellow, like a buttercup or the setting sun; it's a bilious unpleasant yellow, like sick.

I lean in, and I'm sure I can hear the faint noise of conversation between these people.

Yes, I can!

But what they're saying doesn't seem to make much sense.

"The Blight," they keep saying, "the Blight is still getting closer."

***

171

Joan looked up from the newspaper.

'Hey, Brian, there's a letter here about that place you work at.'

He had removed the page which held the crossword and did not look up, engrossed as he was in trying to remember the capital of Bolivia.

'Is that right.'

'Yes, some bloke thinks it ought to be shut down, says it's a danger to the world. He...'

Her voice trailed away. 'Hey, it's your letter; you wrote it, you idiot.' She flung the paper at him. 'What did you go and do that for, you numbskull? Do you want to get the sack, just when we're getting ourselves back together?'

He picked up the paper and rearranged the pages into a semblance of order.

'I'm entitled to my opinion.'

'But that place is good for our area; lots of people around here work there. It's not a nuclear power station, for God's sake! What's wrong with it?'

'What I said. It's sending out rays. We don't know what those rays could do to us if we got in the way. Cook us into strips like your bacon, as like as not.'

She glared at him, with lips compressed into a thin line.

'You are going to get yourself into trouble; that's what's going to happen. Rays turning us into bacon! What rubbish!'

But Joan was right: Murchison was in a spot of trouble.

Later that week, he found himself in Andrews' office, and that worthy was holding up the offending letters' page of the newspaper.

'What exactly is the meaning of this, Murchison?'

Murchison found himself staring at his shoes, like a schoolboy in the headmaster's office.

'I wanted the people to know about possible dangers from the telescope,' he finally managed to utter.

Andrews violently slapped the palm of a hand down on his

desk, producing a sharp report which startled Murchison.

'You scientific illiterate! There is absolutely no danger from the telescope. It can produce powerful radiation in the radio and microwave bands but do you really think we're in the business of frying the inhabitants of Uckfield into a crisp? Even if we were such homicidal butchers, we couldn't depress the dish that low, you idiot!'

Murchison tried to meet Andrews' hostile glare. He had had a deep, inchoate conviction building for some time that there was a danger associated with the radio telescope, but he could not bring those fears to the surface; recast them into clear, unchallengeable statements. All he could do was helplessly repeat that somehow there was danger associated with that machine. Terrible, terrible danger.

'I never said anything about frying people,' he said stubbornly, 'maybe it's to do with climate change. Maybe the beams are altering the atmosphere, making it too hot, too cold.' He spread his arms. 'I don't know. It's a possibility.'

Andrews' glare did not soften. 'It is not a possibility. For a start, the dish is mainly a receiver, not a transmitter. We occasionally bounce radio beams off the surface of Venus or Titan, but quite frankly space probes do a far better job.' He leaned forward. 'You have annoyed me, Murchison, annoyed me rather badly. The last thing we need is the poor people of this area thinking that there's a gang of mad scientists here. I can see them now at the gates waving their pitchforks and flambeaux. Your position here is not secure, Murchison; people like you are a dime a dozen, as our transatlantic cousins would say.'

'You can't sack me for my opinions,' Murchison said, straightening his back so he was as tall as he could be.

'No, but I can sack you for a number of things, exempli gratia: being late on the job, the quality of your work.'

'There's nothing wrong with my work.'

'That's for me to decide.' Andrews indicated the office door with a nod of his head. 'Get back to that work. And take this as your final warning.'

At the tea break, Pete looked up from his digestive biscuit and said, 'What's eating you, Brian? I heard Andrews chewed you out.'

'Oh, you heard, did you? Gossip spreads fast by the look of it.'

Pete shook his head. 'Brian, why are you getting mixed up in this kind of rubbish? You've got a good number here, so why mess it up? Just keep your head down and take the folding money at the end of the week.'

Murchison did not reply at once. His gaze was elsewhere, and for reasons he could not explain that gaze was fixed on a mysterious city flanked by tall emerald towers.

***

The city is just as I remembered it; bustling, bustling; lots of people hurrying here and there, strange vehicles hurtling past each other, millimetres apart.

There's a feeling that these people are racing against the clock, against some dread timetable, that their time is limited and they are fast running out of it.

I wish I could help them somehow.

I can hear more of them now, a whirring, buzzing mass of confused sound. I can make out the occasional word here and there.

But some words keep recurring; words like 'Transmitters", 'Nitrogen" and, most often, "Blight." That particular word seems to have some dread import that I don't understand yet. I must admit I'm not enjoying this extended version of this dream at all; it's unsettling. This miasma of fear is getting under my skin.

Now I'm back in the tower and I'm looking at that map again. That yellow discolouration is still there but it's covering a larger amount of the area; it's quite a bit nearer the city.

There's a group of men and women standing in front of the monitor staring at the map. I move in closer until I'm actually part of the group, and I can just make out their speech, or at least parts of it.

'Flamethrowers deployed...effect. En oh two concentration...tolerable

174

level…'

I give up; this disjointed speech is impossible to follow.

What more can I do? Should I try to use one of the elevators?

An odd thought strikes me: if people can walk through me, would the elevator floor go through me as it rises, leaving me permanently stuck on this floor? It would be an amusing thought if these people didn't look so wretched.

I'm at a loss what to do next; it seems I've learned all I can about this weird dream world. I turn to walk back out.

And stop.

One of the group, a woman, has turned her head and is looking at me, staring at me.

She can see me!

Shocked into immobility, I stare back.

She is very beautiful, with fine, delicate features in a face framed by a flow of lustrous hair; hair which is blue on the crown and shades gradually into silver at the tips. But her face, which entrances me, is marred by a sadness, an emotion which I have come to associate with this weird place.

I can make out her eyes, which are a deep blue. The blue of a tropical lagoon; a place far, far away from this dream world which has become more and more like a nightmare.

Her lips are moving, and I half hear, half lip-read the words.

They don't make sense but they are something like: 'Murjaz, it's time to come back. Come back.'

Come back from where?

To where?

***

'I've got to stop Andrews sending that message,' Murchison said.

Joan looked up from her knitting, not sure what her husband had said.

'What—what was that? Who's Andrews?'

'He's the top dog at the observatory,' Murchison said, looking at his wife but not seeing her. Instead, he saw blackness, the cold, inhuman blackness which lies between the far-scattered

175

stars.

She tried to return to her knitting—P2, K8, P2, K12—but found she could no longer concentrate. She placed the unfinished garment on her lap and stared at Murchison.

'What's got into you? What's this message you're rabbiting on about?'

'The one he mustn't send.'

'Yes, I thought I heard you say something like that. What's it got to do with you?'

'I must stop it,' he repeated in a voice without tone or inflection.

Now alarmed, she put the garment on the table and, reaching over, held his hands.

'Brian, what's the matter with you? You've got a good job, a good secure job. Don't put it all at risk now, for God's sake!'

He did not look at her; instead, he saw only the empty, sterile wastes of space, wastes more terrible than any that humankind had ever known.

'I've got to stop him.'

'But why? You know nothing about all that science stuff; you're just an ordinary man. Why get involved with things you don't understand? Why! Tell me why!'

He looked down at his wife's hands which were holding his so tightly that her knuckles had gone white.

'I'm not sure why. Not long ago, the thought came into my mind. I don't know where it came from. I don't know why I started thinking these thoughts. I just have.'

'I think you should see a doctor; I really do—Brian, will you look at me!'

He lifted his head, slowly, tiredly, as if the effort of raising it was a great one.

She looked into his face, opened her mouth to speak and then froze, her loving look metamorphosing into a stare of fear.

'Brian—how long have your eyes been green!'

***

176

Joan insisted on accompanying Murchison while he saw the doctor, but the GP seemed annoyed by the vagueness of the symptoms Joan described.

She took his blood pressure, weighed him, took his height, calculated his BMI and observed that he needed to lose quite a bit of weight. Murchison took it all impassively, not saying anything. The doctor said he should make an appointment to give a blood sample to test for blood glucose, haemoglobin levels and—with a quick look at Joan—testosterone levels.

'Is that all?' the doctor said, 'I think that's your ten minutes.'

'There is one more thing,' Joan said nervously.

'And?'

Joan looked at the silent Murchison and then back at the impatient GP.

'It's his eyes.'

'What about them?'

'They're green.'

'So I saw. A very healthy green. What of it?'

Joan seemed to shrivel slightly under the other woman's gaze.

'They used to be brown.'

The young woman drummed manicured fingers for a few seconds, and then got out an ophthalmoscope, checked the battery, and told Murchison to lean towards her.

She spent a few minutes examining his eyes and then put it away.

Having learned not to expect a response from Murchison, she addressed Joan.

'His eyes are fine except the early stages of a cataract in the left. Are you sure about this colour change?'

'He's my husband!' Joan said indignantly, 'Don't you think I'd notice!'

The doctor gave a wry smile. 'In my experience, married people often fail to notice a great many things about their partners. They're so used to each other that they see what they expect to see.' Noticing Joan's glare, she added, 'When do you think this happened?'

'It must have been in the last few weeks. I'm sure I'd have noticed if it had been any longer ago.'

The doctor made a few notes and said, 'I'll ask the optician to have a look at him, but they're very busy at the moment. I would expect a month or so's wait.' Then she sat up straighter and in a brisk, firm voice said, 'And that really is your ten minutes.'

***

Nothing came of any of the tests. Murchison was not exactly in peak condition, but he was an average man of his age and lifestyle.

But he learned not to discuss his unease about the observatory with his wife again, and she gradually forgot about the whole affair, except that every now and again, in the early morning hours before rising, the change of colour of Murchison's eyes returned to her thoughts.

However, at the workplace, Murchison did try to raise the topic. Pete listened long-sufferingly for a week or so and then finally, one afternoon, lost it with his friend.

Half the tea in Pete's mug jumped out as he brought it down heavily on the worktop.

'For Christ's sake, Brian, drop it, will you! You keep going on and on about some danger in this place, and yet you can't tell me what it is! You're losing it, mate, losing it big time!'

Murchison stared glumly at a half-eaten biscuit.

'I know, Pete, I'm sorry. I don't have the vocabulary, the scientific terms.'

'"Vocabulary"', Pete mocked, 'When's the last time you used a word that big, Brian? Look, I think it's time you and Joan went away somewhere for a holiday, one with sand, sea and you-know-what.'

Murchison nodded whilst giving an embarrassed half-smile.

'Yeah, you're right, Pete. I guess I've been working too hard.'

Pete stared at him for a few seconds and then began chortling uncontrollably.

After that, things were back to normal with Murchison and Pete.

And Murchison almost succeeded in ridding himself of those strange fears and doubts.

Almost, because one day he was passing Andrews' office and the door was open.

Two voices could be heard, one the staccato bark that Andrews used when dealing with someone he regarded as his intellectual inferior, and the distinctly more melodious voice of Vera Esperanza.

'This is ridiculous, Dr Esperanza. I had thought better of you, but it would appear you have forced me to reassess your suitability for this post.'

'But Dr Andrews, science forces us to examine every possibility and not just dismiss them out of hand.'

Murchison stopped, standing just beyond the doorway so he could hear but could not be seen.

'I have considered it and found it to be ridiculous, unworthy of a trained scientist. Dr Esperanza, you appear to have forgotten the vast distances between stars. The idea that there could be physical contact between intelligences in the galaxy belongs to popcorn Hollywood movies where spaceships using ridiculous faster-than-light engines can cross from one star to another in a heartbeat!'

'I have not forgotten the scale of the universe, Dr Andrews, but you may be guilty of anthropomorphic thinking. The time taken to cross between the stars may be far too great for frail creatures like us but there may be others to whom a century or so might indeed be just a heartbeat.'

'And why would they come? What would be worth the titanic expenditure of energy required to reach us? To steal our water? To extract the Earth's core for iron? Perhaps you are hoping that they will come to steal our women.'

There was a long silence, then, 'I will forgive you that highly offensive remark, Dr Andrews, and I can say only this: To try to predict what would be the truly alien needs and drives of an NHI civilisation is futile by definition of the word "alien." And I will bid you good day.'

Murchison realised that it was time to pretend he was simply passing by Andrews' office and began to move but collided with Dr Esperanza as she shot out of that office.

She began to expostulate but stopped when she saw who it was, and gave him a smile that caused a momentary flutter in his heart.

They walked down the corridor together.

'I'm sorry about that, doctor,' Murchison said, all the time realising how much he had enjoyed that brief moment of close physical contact with this alluring woman.

'That's OK—Brian, isn't it?'

He looked up at her, for she was slightly taller than he, and found himself drowning in the gaze of bright green eyes.

'Yes,' he said, and then found himself stuttering slightly as he tried to continue, 'I—I couldn't help overhearing your conversation with Dr Andrews.'

Her eyebrows arched. 'I wouldn't have thought that was of much interest to an electrician.'

'No, no, I'm sorry—I was listening in, I'm afraid. And I agree—there is danger in Dr Andrews' idea.'

Esperanza stopped and stared at him. An odd silence developed.

And then she said: 'Have we met somewhere before?'

***

I'm looking at this woman, this gorgeous woman. I'd like to get to know her, but the strange thing is she's reacting as if she knows me. I can't understand much of what she's saying; everything's too quiet and she's speaking very quickly and with an unusual accent.

I'm sure I heard her say "Come back" as if I belonged here, which I obviously don't.

I've tried speaking to her, asking who she is, where I am, but she doesn't seem to be able to hear me.

And then there was an awful blue-white flash from directly above, sending everything in the room into black and white patterns.

And then I woke up.

***

Murchison knew the time had come.

He was standing in the observation room, which looked out onto the vast curved undersurface of the radio-telescope dish. It loomed above him, vast and cold; uninterested, unaffected by human emotions and problems, concerned only with catching the faint wisps of information which were the fading remnants of colossal events in distant space.

In the exact centre of the dish rose a mighty antenna, which was partially visible to Murchison beyond the great curve of the bowl—a transmitter which would soon be sending Andrews' message out into the far reaches of the galaxy.

It was a cold, drear January day, and the sky was covered in a horizon-spanning mass of undifferentiated, featureless grey and black cloud. In the distance beyond the perimeter fence of the observatory, Murchison could see the skeletal shapes of leafless trees tossing in the otherwise unseen winds. He opened the door which led out onto the platform from which the inspection ladder ascended. Immediately the strong wind tried to tear the door from his grasp and slam it shut. The howling of that wind was like that of a huge beast watching him, perhaps warning him not to attempt the ascent.

He adjusted the heavy load of his backpack, so it rested squarely on his shoulders; he didn't want it pulling him off centre as he climbed. It had more than enough tools in it for his act of sabotage. He would put the antenna out of action for a long time, during which he would be able to tell his story about the dangers

181

of Andrews' mad scheme to the police, the press, the media—everyone, anyone who would listen.

They would shut down the observatory for good. Perhaps he would have to spend a short time in prison for damaging property, but that would be a small price to pay for the salvation of humanity.

In time, the true story would come out, unearthed by investigative journalists, and his efforts would be recognised and applauded for their heroism.

He stepped out onto the platform and was immediately knocked to one side by the force of the gale. He held onto the railings to steady himself and, as he grew used to the wind's power, he moved to the ladder.

Holding the rungs, he tilted his head back to look at the grey underside of the radio dish which almost blended into a sky of almost the same dull shade of grey. It seemed an awfully long way up.

He made another adjustment of his backpack, which had slipped somewhat, and began his ascent. As he moved clear of the platform's safety railing, the wind redoubled its power, clutching him, pawing at him like some invisible animal. He pressed himself closer to the rungs and moved on.

At one stage, when he had ascended perhaps ten metres, he made a mistake and looked down. He saw that a group of three men had noticed him and were pointing and gesticulating. No doubt they were shouting as well, but even if the wind had not been roaring around him, he would have been too high up to hear them.

He returned his gaze to the underside of the radio dish. Already he could see the rectangular outline of the inspection hatch. All he would have to do was open it and step out onto the curved upper surface. He would then slide down to the central antenna and disable it.

Just then, a booming, amplified human voice crashed around him. Someone was using a powerfully amplified PA system.

'MURCHISON! I DON'T KNOW WHAT YOU'RE DOING BUT GET DOWN! GET DOWN!'

So he had been caught. Never mind, he was too near his goal now to be stopped. He would make sure that the damage he would do could not be rectified in less than several days.

That would be enough for him to tell his story.

He was nearly at the hatch now. He was reaching up to release it when the backpack suddenly shifted under a particularly vicious blast of wind. He tried to bring it back as it pulled him to one side, tried, lost his grip on the ladder and began his fall.

It was unlikely that any human being could have survived a fall from such a height.

And Murchison did not.

***

My eyes gradually open, fighting eyelids that seem determined to stay shut.

There is light; terrible, bright light that seems to be angle-grinding strips of tissue from my retinas.

'He's back,' I hear someone say, 'Look like he's OK.'

I realise that I'm lying on my back, and I try to sit up, but my body seems unable to comply. My muscles feel as if they've been replaced by immobile replicas, cast from concrete.

But there are arms around me, gently pulling and supporting, helping me into a sitting position.

'There you are, Murjaz; it's over. You did your best, there's nothing to reproach yourself with.'

I look around. There are four people around me, two on each side, all of them wearing very plain grey coveralls of exactly the same design. I can now see that there are wires, or thin cables, attached to me. I am only wearing trunks, for modesty, I guess. One young woman is deftly removing flat electrode terminals from my head.

When she has finished, for some reason, I touch my scalp and discover I've been shaved so closely that I can't even feel stubble.

Warmth is beginning to flood into me, and I feel my muscles relaxing, becoming obedient. I am lying on an extremely soft, padded couch in a small room which, now that my eyes have adjusted, I realise is only softly lit.

I say the classic words which everybody is supposed to say at times like these: 'Who are you? Where am I?'

An old man with enormous bushy white eyebrows comes into view.

'It's alright, Murjaz, you're suffering from disconnection amnesia. It will gradually fade over the next forty-eight hours and you'll get all your memories back.' He tries to smile but fails. 'We've not lost one yet.'

I am now able to turn, so my feet are over the side of the couch. I am helped to stand by two men, who, having released me, stay extremely close.

'You haven't answered my questions,' I say. My mouth feels like it's been coated in sandpaper. As if in answer to my thoughts, I am immediately given a glass of a pale purple liquid. I drink it. It is slightly sweet and warming.

The old man appears to be in charge.

'I see you can't wait for your memories to return, Murjaz, so I will attempt to give you the answers that you need. But first, you must shower and then have a proper meal. Then we will speak.'

I am shown where to go for the former, and not long afterwards, I am sitting at a table laden with fruit and what I take to be some type of textured vegetable protein. The old man is watching me from the other side, with what I trust is a kindly expression.

I finish the last of my drink and fix him with my stare.

'Now talk,' I say.

He tries to smile and does better than the first attempt—but in all honesty, it's not much better.

'Do you remember anything of what you've been doing?' he says.

184

'Not really. I remember that I was with people who were dressed peculiarly and had an odd way of talking. I had something important to do—something vital.' And then it hit me. 'And I didn't do it. I failed.'

My stern gaze has become pitiable, I'm sure.

He nods kindly. 'You did fail, but you are not the first. I hope you will be the last, but it's very difficult to be certain.'

'What was I supposed to do?'

He does not answer at once and appears to be gathering his thoughts. And then: 'Have you heard of a man called Andrews?'

I think. I get the feeling that I have heard of this man, and somewhere in my subconscious there are recollections of him. I also do not answer immediately, but search in the basement of my mind.

'Yes. He had a telescope. A big telescope. But you couldn't look through it. It was like a big metal bowl.'

He nods in encouragement. 'Yes. It's starting to come back. Now be patient, for I am going to tell you a long story of what has happened and where you have been.'

I fold my arms and prepare to listen.

'Now there is one thing we must make clear: Andrews was not a bad man—far from it. He was a very clever man and was, in many ways, admirable. He had a clear vision, and he pursued that vision. He was in charge of what we call a radio telescope, an instrument that uses invisible parts of the electromagnetic spectrum to visualise events far out in space, in this galaxy and far, far beyond.

'But apart from pure research, he had a great dream: to create an interstellar community, communicating by radio waves and sharing knowledge, discoveries, helping each other learn more and more about this universe.

'And so he sent out a message using the power of his radio telescope to a large number of the closer stars that have a spectral type not too dissimilar to our sun. It contained many clever ways of determining our exact position in space, even accounting for stellar drift during the time it would take for the message to arrive

185

at its various destinations. It also provided many items of information about Earth and its life-forms, in particular the biochemistry of the human race.

'Andrews did not see the results of his pet project, although he garnered many awards for his pure research work. But two hundred and twenty years after he sent his message, three enormous vessels arrived in the Solar system and took up geosynchronous orbits around Earth.

'They hit us with a tremendous electromagnetic pulse that destroyed all our communications and eliminated all our AI systems. All over the world, power failed. Every aircraft fell out of the sky.

'The orbiting vessels disgorged smaller ones which landed all over the world, but mainly in populated areas. For a long time, they did nothing but make copies of themselves. We attacked them, of course, but our offensive weapons were very limited in the early days after the electromagnetic pulse. High explosives, for instance, had no effect upon them.

'Then, after about twenty years, humanity had managed to regroup, using systems and machines that had been underground at the beginning of the attack. Of course, we had tried to communicate using every part of the EM spectrum but they—whoever they are—ignored us.'

'Whoever they are?' I interrupt, 'we've not seen them?'

'No, we have not. We believe that what has arrived in our system are simply automatic machines. The intelligences behind those devices have not yet arrived. They are waiting for their machines to finish their work.'

'And that is?'

'To exoform Earth, to make it suitable for whatever beings have decided to do this to us.'

'Exoform. That's a big project, I imagine.'

'It is. It's been going on for just over a hundred years, and it will probably be another two hundred before they finish. From what they're doing, we can deduce that the directing intelligences have a more nitrogen-heavy biochemistry than we do, as one of

186

the procedures they are employing is to fuse atmospheric nitrogen and oxygen together to form various oxides of nitrogen.'

I suddenly remember that I know something about that: vast bursts of energy in the atmosphere which produce long, curling trails of orange vapour.

I finally find the strength to ask the question that I am afraid to ask.

'And we can't stop them?'

'No. From time to time we manage to knock out one of their ground devices but the original ones simply manufacture replacements from the surrounding materials. The air is already too heavy in nitrogen oxides for us to breathe.'

I lean back in my chair and close my eyes.

Only a short while ago, I was blissfully unconscious and now I am sitting next to someone who is telling me that the end of the world is nigh. It's too much.

My companion senses this and says, 'I think that's enough for now, Murjaz; it's best you take it easy for the rest of the day and get a good night's sleep.'

My eyes open. 'But you still haven't told me my role in all this. Where I've been and what I've been doing.'

'Well,' he says, 'you haven't actually been anywhere. But that's enough from me. Someone will meet you tomorrow and tell you all that has been happening to you and why.'

'And he will be able to answer all my questions?'

'Yes, and all the questions you haven't asked. She will tell you everything.'

***

I have not slept well; many thoughts kept circling around in my mind, and often I found myself looking at the faintly glowing numerals of the clock on the wall. So now I feel as if I haven't slept at all—except I know I must have.

A young man brings me a simple breakfast. He says nothing

to me, and I can't think of anything to say to him. As I begin to eat I realise that the breakfast is even simpler than it appeared at first glance; it merely comprises strips of vegetable protein and a drink of some insipid fruit juice. But I finish it, for I feel completely drained as if I have recently undergone some physical ordeal. One thing is certain: I wanted a better breakfast. These people must be living a very straightened life here in this city.

My door opens, and the elderly man enters without knocking. Clearly manners are no longer important in this society. But he has a companion, a tall, beautiful woman with unusual hair. It is blue at the crown and gradually shades into silver at the tips. It is most striking.

But her appearance does more than stimulate my drowsy senses; suddenly I am electrified as a memory bursts into my consciousness. A name comes to me, a strange, musical name which somehow I know does not belong in this city.

'Vera,' I say, feeling that it is somehow someone else speaking, that an unseen man has taken control of my vocal cords, 'Vera Esperanza!'

The elderly man looks back and forth between us and, fixing on me, says, 'Murjaz, this is the person of whom I spoke yesterday. She has much to teach you, so I will leave you two together.' And he leaves.

I feel as if I am going mad. Why did I say that strange name? Who is this woman?

She comes up to me and points to the nearby couch.

'Come,' she says in a melodious voice, a voice that soothes and refreshes me, 'sit down and we will talk.'

I am led like a little child to the couch and we sit together. I realise that I am staring at her in wide-eyed amazement, but I cannot stop doing it.

I say again *Vera Esperanza*, but even as I say it, another memory arises: a picture of the woman whom I am naming. And I see great similarities between the faces of my memory and my new companion, but they are not the same. Mesmerizingly similar—but not the same.

As if to confirm my conclusion, she takes my hand and raises it softly to her soft lips.

'No,' she whispers, 'not Vera. My name is Viña.'

'I knew a woman like you,' I stammer, 'somewhere, some time, but your eyes are different. Hers were bright green.'

She nods. 'Of course. That is a minor side-effect of the process; we don't know why. All transferees have that characteristic.'

Transferees? I don't know that word.

'Viña, it's a nice name, but who are you? Do I know you?'

She smiles, a gentle, wistful smile. 'Yes, Murjaz, you do know me. I am your wife.'

I stare at her. Is she mad? Am I going mad?

But she continues to smile at me, and the nature of the smile changes, becoming warm, loving.

She lowers my hand from her lips. 'Soon, my darling, soon you will remember it all—how we met, how we fell in love, how we have loved. Soon.'

Then she looks over her shoulder, and her smile vanishes.

'But there is something I must show you, something that I do not wish to see and something that you will wish never to see again. But it will help you remember so we must both endure it.'

She leads me out of the room and on to a huge concourse full of people and their intermingled conversations. Everywhere there are people, sitting in front of terminals, poring over printouts.

I know this place—it is the ground floor of one of the emerald towers of my dream city.

So my city is not a dream.

She takes me to one of the elevators that I saw in my sleep, and we are sent hurtling upwards; the doors open and I am led into a vast room that terminates in a gigantic picture window.

'Come Murjaz. This is one of the faces of the enemy.'

I walk slowly, reluctantly towards the window. Gradually what lies beyond becomes apparent.

And I stop; unwilling to go any further.

But Viña urges me on until I am standing just before the window.

And I see horror.

The city ends in great ramparts on which at regular intervals stand some type of antenna. A faint bluish glow is visible between the antennas.

And beyond is a crawling, writhing mass of bilious yellow slime, like living vomit; vomit with its own volition; its own foul hunger.

Embedded in it I see the shells of buildings, with the yellow pestilence dripping from their eaves. Here and there are skeletal trees covered in this necrotic suppuration.

There is a small gap between the wavefront of the crawling matter, and the wall of the city and I see vehicles similar to those I envisioned within its ramparts in my dreams but bigger, more military-looking. From time to time, they shoot great fountains of raging fire onto the creeping wavefront, which stops its fluid motion; it blackens, crisps and then is whirled away by the wind.

'What is it?' I finally manage to whisper.

'We call it the Blight,' Viña replies unemotionally, 'their machines started extruding it eighty years ago. Strictly speaking, it does not destroy any organic matter it comes into contact with but—changes it. The ratio of elements within is altered; some increase their proportion, some decrease their proportion. We believe that the result is a kind of protoplasm, to use an old-fashioned term, the same material which comprises the unseen intelligences.'

'Can it not be stopped, destroyed?'

'Not by chemical means. Simple fire will destroy it, as you have just seen, but our sources of hydrocarbons are gradually being lost to us as the Blight advances. Earth is slowly being wrapped in a yellow shroud.'

I look up at the sky. The combination of nitrogen oxides and its natural blue have made it a sick green, the colour of poison.

'You have domed this city?'

190

'Yes. We shelter under a dome of the strongest, most inert, glass that we have been able to manufacture to keep out the poisoned air. We also have screens of microwave radiation, but everything we do depends on energy and that is running out too.'

Suddenly, staring at this endless vista of slowly churning vomit makes me feel sick too.

Viña notices and gently pulls me away from the window.

'Come,' she says, 'we'll go to my room.' She corrects herself. 'Our room.'

We go up another level, and her room—our room—does not have an outward-facing window. Instead, it shows a cityscape, and I am looking out over the small rounded buildings, which are the main type of structure the city holds. In the distance another emerald tower is visible, framed against a sky of a very different green.

There is a feeling of memories coming back, as if a dam is slowly crumbling.

I walk to a table on which sits a large book. I open it up, and there is a bookmark within, holding a place in a work called The Tempest by someone called Shakespeare.

'I recall reading this,' I say wonderingly, 'but I didn't finish it.'

'There may still be time,' my wife says. 'Come and sit with me.'

When we are sitting together, she runs her soft hand along my cheek. 'Murjaz, how I have missed you. But your body has not left this city. How strange it has been.'

I hold the hand that has been caressing me. 'It is time you told me everything. Where have I been but not been? And why?'

She looks deep into my eyes and I steel myself. I feel that what is coming is something I will not wish to hear.

'Murjaz, we cannot defeat this invader. For a hundred years we have fought it, and we have achieved nothing. This city, and few like it in other parts of the world, are all that remains of humanity. Every organism that lived on the land and did not escape the Blight has been absorbed into it, cats, dogs, men, women, children. It is unstoppable.'

I lower my head. 'Then this is the end.' But then I look up. 'But that doesn't explain what happened to me. Now I really must know.'

She nods her agreement. 'Of course. We cannot defeat the Blight. But what if we could stop the NHI invasion from ever happening?'

I feel a pulse of excitement. 'Time travel? But that has been shown to be impossible.'

'Sending physical objects is impossible, but we can send a portion of consciousness back into the period just prior to Andrews sending his message and somehow prevent that message from being sent.'

'And I was one of those consciousnesses. I lay on that couch while a portion of my mind was sent back into—into—' I hunt for an image, a name. It comes to me.

'Murchison! I was Murchison! I remember!' Then I stand, looking down at her. I feel anger.

'But he died. You made me kill him.'

She stands next to me, holding me.

'No, no, that was not our intention. We can only send mentalities back where there is a DNA link, and the chances of someone with a link also being involved with the radio-telescope are minimal so we have to use what we can find. Murchison was available and he was linked to you, so we used him as a vessel for your will, your volition. But he was too lowly in the organisation; he could not convince Andrews not to send the message. And he died trying to sabotage the telescope. That was never part of our plan.'

I sit back down, and she joins me. I start to speak, trying to unravel the puzzle by my own efforts.

'So the pool of possible individuals is very small. So the chances of stopping the message being sent is very small.' I feel my eyes become moist. 'So it is all for nothing. The whole of biological development on this planet has been for nothing, just because one man was too naïve, too trusting.'

192

Viña holds both my hands. 'We have one last chance.'

'And?'

'We have identified another individual who was working on the project just before the message was sent. And this individual is much higher in the organisation and might be able to dissuade Andrews, without resorting to crude sabotage.'

Suddenly it all becomes clear. A tremendous wave of remembrance bursts over me, and I groan, holding my head, overwhelmed by a deluge of sights and sounds.

And when I resurface, I look at Viña. 'Vera Esperanza. She's the last chance!'

'Yes. She is the last chance.'

A terrible foreboding weighs down on me as I say the next words, words I do not wish to utter, but must.

'And it's you who will be going back. Your will, your volition will be implanted.'

She smiles sadly.

'Yes. We are not able to be as precise as we would like with our temporal placements. It is possible that I will be there as part of Esperanza at the same time as you were part of Murchison.'

I remember Esperanza's green eyes, and I feel myself give a ragged kind of smile.

'You were, my love, you were. You were—will be—the Vera Esperanza I met. Or rather a part of her; trying like I did, to prevent that appalling mistake.'

Suddenly I don't want to talk about this existential disaster anymore. I just want to spend time with my wife.

'When are you leaving?'

'Tomorrow night.'

'Then we have one night of loving to make up for our separation.' I stop. 'How will we know if you have succeeded, without having to wait for you to return?'

And then a terrible, terrible thought turns my entrails to water.

'But can you come back if this city is no longer here?'

Another smile. 'We must hope that we get the chance to

find out.

'But in the meantime, stand by the window from time to time and think of me, your wife, your lover. It may be that the two realities will be in superposition for a nanosecond and you will see the Blight disappear before you forget there ever was a Blight, and instead of this last fortress, you find yourself looking out over vibrant green fields from a home in a city very different from this one.'

She has been gone three days now.

On each day, I have stood for a while at the great window looking at the advancing Blight.

And I wait.

NO END TO TOMORROW

Eternity has been given to me without limit;
Behold! I am heir to Eternity.
  - **The Egyptian Book Of The Dead**

'So you want to be immortal, Mr Johannison?'

The man on the other side of the desk (hatchet-faced; thin, backward swept hair; small squared-off glasses) leaned back onto the soft plastic of his chair, baring a smile as thin as his face.

'Can you tell me why?'

Johannison smiled uncertainly. 'Well—uh—well, why does anybody want to be immortal?'

'Ah!' The thin man was leaning forward again, an index finger cleaving the inadequately ventilated air. 'But why do YOU want to be immortal?'

Johannison rubbed his large, open-pored nose. 'Don't want to die, I s'pose.'

The inquisitor smiled once more; if anything even more thinly than previously.

'Pardon my persistence, Mr Johannison, but you seem to be dodging the question. I could now rephrase my original query as "Why do you not want to die?"'

With a shrug, Johannison replied, 'Like life, I s'pose.'

'Ah!' The man made some rapid notations on a paper pad before him with a pen that leaked and squeaked at the same time. After about a minute of this, the inquisitor's sparse cranial covering moved out of sight as he lifted his lined face from close scrutiny of the pad.

'Good, good. I can tell you, Mr Johannison., that you may fit all our requirements.'

He paused to flash a yellow smile.

Johannison responded with a nervous smile.

Christ! How had he gotten into all this!

As the inquisitor bent over his scribbles once again,

195

Johannison drew a deep breath and thought:

Let's see; it was three days ago (or was it four); anyway, it was some time about then…

***

Johannison put down his dog-eared copy of *Tales From Beyond The Veil,* muttered something and directed a vitriolic glance out of the window. He took up the magazine again, discovered he had lost his page, and thrust it into the rack with a second mutter.

'Martha!'

He waited, his stare resting aggressively on the kitchen door.

No-one emerged, the only sound from that direction being the radio, tuned, as always, to Station KZBX—"*Your local, neighbourly station!*"—blaring out the latest smash-hit.

'Martha!'

The radio was cut off with the suddenness of a slap, and a thin, haggard-looking woman thrust her head into a restricted view around the fractionally opened door.

'Whadyawant?'

Johannison pointed at the window.

'Point A: Shut those kids up; Point B: Turn that radio off— or at least' (and he assumed a pleading expression) 'turn it down a decibel or five.'

More of Martha's head appeared around the door.

'And what's it to you, Fatso? I'm doing the washing-up. And I need something to take my mind off you while I'm working. The kids have been in school all week; they need something to keep them from flipping. And you just sit there—you out-of-work slob—sitting down—reading!'

Her voice rose to a shriek many times louder than the radio, 'Reading!'

Johannison opened his mouth to retaliate, but a memory of the many wearisome arguments which had been played out in this small house flashed through his mind.

Instead, in tones dripping with reproach, he replied, 'I'm not staying here to be screeched at.'

'So who's stopping you, Chunky?'

Martha's head and shoulders disappeared, and a second later the radio erupted into life once more, its bass-line almost shaking the ornaments off the wall shelves.

Since no-one was actually stopping him—Johannison went.

***

Madame O'Hara was a great favourite of Johannison, partly because she was so corpulent that he looked positively undernourished beside her, but mainly because she shared (with eight others) his *Interest In Life*. Of course, he wanted to write The Great American Novel in addition to communing with the other side, but maybe its denizens could help him with that as well. A Creative Writing Group can only take you so far. But he always felt a little ill at ease with O'Hara because she was an *Active*, while he was only a *Passive*.

As he stared at her across the grey darkness of the room, he knew she was about to become Active once again.

She gave a small twitch that started at her eyelids, then shivered its way down until it was eclipsed by the tabletop. At the moment of eclipse, the ballpoint pen that was held loosely between her fleshy fingers began racing across a sheet of paper. After about a minute of this, a second twitch emerged from below the tabletop and travelled back up her body to end at her eyelids.

Lights snapped on all over the room. A tall, thin woman leapt up as if stung and snatched up the paper.

'Oh, do let me see what you've written, Madame!'

Madame O'Hara waved a tolerant hand. 'You may, Marcella.'

Johannison, peering over Marcella's bony shoulder, glimpsed the message: "*Wret tyu mm ngh*" repeated a great many times. Rashly, he whispered to the woman: 'What does it mean?'

'What does it mean!' she gasped in horrified tones, 'What does it mean? Why—can't you see? Can't you SEE?'

Johannison was saved from further discomfiture by the perfumed approach of Madame O'Hara herself. The paper was wafted away from both of them as she breathed forth a *Hello darlings* and then eagerly began to peruse the writings.

Her face fell slightly, but she disguised the emotion with a yawn.

'Oh dear, the spirits are cryptic today. No doubt this message is of vital importance to someone, somewhere, but I don't know HOW they expect me to pass it on if they REFUSE to write in English instead of Spirit. Oh well, maybe next time.'

She was about to depart, but a timid hand restrained her.

'Yes?' she enquired as her eyebrows arched to show her displeasure at being touched.

Johannison let his hand drop and, with a nervous smile, said, 'Ah…it's about *the Other Side*, Madame. I wonder if you could spare me some of your valuable time. Oh, I understand that your time is very valuable…but I was wondering…'

It looked very much to Johannison as if Madame O'Hara was thinking, *Jeez, How do I get rid of this fat creep?*

But he was used to that, so he ploughed on.

'…you see, Madame, I get these dreams; you know, sometimes I think I dream of the life to come, you know, when I'm in Spirit, but I keep forgetting and …'

'I'm so sorry,' Madame O'Hara interrupted, looking directly at him for the first time, 'but I really do have to go. I have an appointment with a Magnetic Faith Healer. Perhaps next time?'

'Sure,' said Johannison mechanically, wondering if she knew that this was the tenth time that they had had this exact conversation. 'Sure.'

He turned away, momentarily conscious of the many wasted days that he had spent on this quest, and, perhaps, of the transience of life itself.

He did not notice that the newest member of the Spirit Circle, a person who hardly ever spoke, was following him down

198

the stairs, or that he continued to follow him across the road to where Johannison got into his old 2034 Impala and drove discontentedly away.

The silent man then made a swift and short phone call.

***

'Huh?' Johannison grunted on pulling the folder from its brown envelope. The title hit him like an uppercut.

DO YOU WANT TO BE IMMORTAL?

it demanded in vast blue and green capitals.

DO YOU EVER GET FRUSTRATED AT THE SHORTNESS OF LIFE

ON THIS EARTH? WOULD YOU LIKE TO SEE THE WONDERS OF THE

FABULOUS WORLD OF TOMORROW?

WELL, NOW YOU *CAN*! YES, THE WHOLE WORLD CAN OPEN

UP BEFORE YOU. NOW YOU CAN LEARN TO *LIVE*!

JUST FILL IN THE SIMPLE QUESTIONNAIRE ENCLOSED WITHIN AND *MAIL IT*

RIGHT AWAY!!!!

Johannison upended the folder, and a collection of sheets fluttered out, one landing in his Korn Kracklies.

Hurriedly wiping milk from its glossy surface with a nearby tea towel, he glanced at the fine print. He twisted his head to see whether Martha was in sight and, finding she was not, he turned to the luridly-coloured folder. His Kracklies streamed away into a cool, flavourless mush as he thumbed his way through.

After a few minutes of intense reading had passed, Martha flashed through the doorway, glanced at the table and snapped, 'What's the big idea, Chubby? Celebrating Ramadan?' and then snatched the breakfast bowl up with an incredible feat of legerdemain and vanished into the kitchen after an expert U-turn.

Johannison twisted around and yelled: 'Hey, Martha, come and look at this!'

She re-entered. 'What is it? You got another chin?'

'No—this.'

She glanced through it, spending a lot less time on the wording than he had. Then she sniffed and said, 'What you want I should do? Turn somersaults for joy?'

'Let's have a sane, rational, intelligent, unbiased opinion.'

'It stinks. Now get back to your Humpty Dumpty impersonation and let me get on with the household chores, willya.'

She vanished.

***

'Fred?'

'Mmmm?'

'You busy, Fred?'

Fred sighed and rotated his lean body so that his eyes met Johannison's.

'No, I'm not busy, Hanny boy. Speak up, what's on that big mind of yours?' Johannison briefly glanced at the occupants of the Pool Room before replying. He saw old men with bald heads, fat men with cropped, white moustaches, big brawny men with tattooed torsos padded out with gristle.

What did they know of the mysteries of the World Beyond; of rainy evenings when knockings came from beneath the table, and Madame O'Hara smiled knowingly?

He turned back to Fred.

'Fred...Fred, would you like to be—uhh—immortal?'

Fred's bushy eyebrows lifted in surprise.

'Why, I guess I would if I could be. But who's gonna give it to me?' The end of his marijuana cigar glowed briefly orange. 'You Hanny?'

'No, not me. But Fred—why would you want to become immortal?'

200

Fred chuckled and looked down at the floor for a moment.

'Hanny, you always were a one…Look, who wants to become a mound of fertiliser one day? You? Now look, buddy, we all know there ain't no Hereafter; all you got is right here. And if you can make it last a little longer, well, there's a whole lot of women in the world; it'll take a helluva time to ball all of them, know what I mean? I mean…Hell! I gotta shoot. Hang around, Hanny boy!'

Fred turned and leaned over the green baize. He shot and chuckled as he watched the ball do exactly what he wanted it to. A peevish voice off to Johannison's right said, 'You lucky bastard!'

'That's the way!' Fred said, grinning, and turned back to Johannison, who was looking around again.

Bored eyes above smouldering reefers gazed disinterestedly into his for a few seconds.

Someone yawned.

Fans whined.

Someone laughed.

CLICK! Went the shining coloured balls as they ricocheted off each other.

'Could you spare me a few moments, Fred?' Johannison finally said, surprised to hear a note of pleading in his voice.

Fred was focused on chalking his cue. 'I'm sparing one right now.'

'No, I mean somewhere private.'

The peevish voice came again, sounding even more peevish this time. 'C'mon. Fred shoot!'

Fred ignored the owner of the voice.

'You in trouble, Hanny?'

'No, Fred, no!'

Fred threw his cigar butt away in a streak of red. 'Then why all the secrecy?'

Before Johannison had time to reply, the owner of the peevish voice rounded the table and planted himself between Fred and Johannison. 'Look, bud, are you gonna play pool? No?

Then stop bothering Fred; he's got a game to finish.' He turned to Fred and the two men began to walk away. 'C'mon, Fred, we got the…'

Johannison looked down at the folder in his hands and walked out into the sweet-smelling sunlight.

***

A man can take only so much indecision, and then self-disgust will force him into action—any action. Johannison reached this point that night as he looked at those glossy sheets with their tantalising promises. A cat was howling outside. A thin drizzle was falling. He reached out and signed his name…

…And so, three days later (or was it four?) he was here, sitting at this desk with this skeletal quizmaster firing meaningless questions at him. It wasn't what he had expected. He hadn't expected dancing girls and dark-skinned genies offering him magic potions, but neither had he expected to be taken for an airplane ride, driven down dirt roads all through the night and finally dumped outside a place that appeared to be a run-down bean-canning factory. Now he was underground somewhere, and outside the door to the room he was currently occupying was a humming madhouse filled with ultra-scientific apparatus. None of it had any recognisable function—at least as far as his knowledge of ultra-scientific apparatus went. He had entered the building at ground level through a large, dry and dusty, room, occupied by what seemed to be the aged, dry and dusty, staff of the so-called "Michigan Farm-Fresh Food Co." He had a feeling that they were not as senile as they looked—no-one possibly could be. He toyed with the idea that they were simply actors—but someone was beckoning him…

The *someone* was an old, withered twig of a man whose face seemed composed entirely of deeply incised lines and wrinkles. His eyes were little slits enclosed by folds of ash-coloured skin, but his crowning glory (if that is the correct phrase) was an absolutely bald scalp. It was so ceramically bald, it caught highlights from the strip lighting above him. He gave Johannison a swift, X-Ray glance and turned immediately to Johannison's interrogator.

'What did the Controller say?' he demanded in the crisp tones of those accustomed to the pleasures of strict authority.

The inquisitor replied in a hushed mumble, in which Johannison caught the phrase: 'His Beta's are farther ahead than we thought.'

The bald man subjected Johannison to another momentary scrutiny and said, apparently to the interrogator although he was looking at Johannison, 'Then we must proceed at once.' He spun on his heel, nodded to someone, then looked back at Johannison and snapped, 'Follow.'

***

After the interview with the hatchet-faced man with squared-off glasses, he was taken to a variety of rooms filled with mysterious machines. And then there were lights and whirring noises coming from the deep entrails of those machines, none of which bore any resemblance to anything he'd ever seen before. There were clicks and buzzes, and multicoloured lights blinking on and off in unpredictable patterns.

There were fine gold sensors that had attached themselves to his skull and glaring indigo lights on the end of extendable metal arms; lights that looked like eyes as they stared deep into his own.

His feeble protests had gone unheeded in the gabbling rush of cybernetic frenzy. The realisation slowly formed in his shining brain: Something was radically wrong.

He wanted to go home, but these white-coated jailers had dangled the promise of eternal youth before him while unseen forces pawed at his mind.

Then one day, he awoke from what must have been a drugged sleep to see that he was next to a large window and beyond which the sun was peering over distant hills and milk-white clouds were drifting across a furnace-bright sky. It was the first time he had seen the sky in what seemed like aeons.

On a small plastic table at his side there was a breakfast of bacon, eggs, sauté potatoes and orange juice, which he attacked with the vigour of a starving man. It must have been twenty minutes later, during which the plate had become completely empty, that the door to his room slid back without any warning, and the bald man walked in.

He was smiling, although his face showed that he found that rather hard to do.

'Good morning, Mr. ... ahh—Johannison. I trust that you had a restful night?'

Johannison nodded dumbly; warily content to await future developments. The bald man, unconvincing smile frozen on his face, sat at the bedside on a small folding chair.

'Now, Mr—ahh—Johannison, you must be wondering what this rather hectic week that you have just spent was all about. I do so hope'—and here he leaned in uncomfortably close to Johannison, 'that you were not in any way—ahh—put out by your recent experiences. You see, Mr Johannison, we are not fakers. This is not some kind of scam. We are not kidnappers hoping to extort some vast sum from your charming wife. We really have discovered the way to obtain immortality. A gift of immortality that will not require you to leave this earthly realm.'

He rose from the chair, walked to the window and looked out at the young sun, his back to Johannison.

'Immortality, Mr Johannison, can you see what a double-edged sword that would be to humanity; overpopulated, warring humanity? Oh yes, you could immortalise scientists, artists, humanitarians working for the good of the human race, but what if people like Hitler or Stalin could have gotten hold of our treatments? You take my point? So we had to be sure of you, Mr Johannison, find out what makes you tick, so to speak. Now we know we can trust you and, more importantly, that the human race can trust you.'

He turned from the window,

'Yesterday we made our decision. Today, Mr Johannison, you will become the Earth's First Immortal. Johannison! A name that will ring down the centuries; greater than Caesar, greater than Alexander, Shakespeare, Einstein, Gagarin! The First Immortal!'

***

The First Immortal!

That mystic phrase echoed around Johannison's brain all that morning. He felt like a child on Christmas Eve and, to his amazement, a bit of Shakespeare came back from that Creative Writing course he had done quite a few years ago:

> *...so tedious is this day*
> *As is the night before someone festival*
> *To an impatient child that hath new robes*
> *And may not wear them...*

Yeah, how right that old guy was!

He was on a metal catwalk that bridged a ferroconcrete cavern and leaned over the railing, his eyes numbed by the welter of equipment below: huge cylinders, throbbing pumps, serpentine pipes that wound in all directions, guard with machine-gun...

What!

But a technician pushed him on.

The catwalk passed over a vast metal sphere into which all the piping he had seen earlier appeared to enter or exit. His question about its purpose received a gruff and vague reply about it being some special line of research.

At last, they descended a metal staircase and stood for a while on the cold, unyielding concrete floor until the bald man appeared and propelled Johannison on his way.

A small group of middle-aged men looked up from their instruments as Johannison approached. It might have been his imagination, but he thought he detected a distinct nervousness in their manner, a continuing alternation of swapping technical jargon with the bald man and then casting strange glances at himself.

Finally, they seemed ready. With an engaging smile, one of the men said, 'Would you step this way please?'

Johannison followed and found himself next to two people, a man and a woman, both unsmiling and both dressed in medical-type white coats.

'Roll up your sleeve, please Mr Johannison,' the man said briskly and authoritatively.

Johannison suddenly felt nervous.

'Why do I need to do that?' he said, and was surprised to find that his mouth was suddenly dry.

'It's a relaxant to prepare you for the next test,' the woman said. He saw that she was trying to give a reassuring smile but failing miserably.

Johannison was instantly seized with a sense of foreboding; a desire to turn and run—run fast as he could, out of this strange place, back to Martha and her sneering ways, back to the noisy kids outside the window,

But he did not.

He meekly rolled up his sleeve and the woman placed the cold nozzle of a hypodermic gun against the flesh.

There was no pain, merely a brief touch of something that would have been sharp had it pressed further in.

But it did not.

And then he was instantly unconscious.

***

Darkness. Silence.

A shroud of nothingness.

Johannison tried to open his eyelids, but he saw no light. Indeed he could not even feel his eyelids responding to the pull of his muscles, and he felt a strange feeling of airiness as if he were a disembodied spirit. He tried to move his legs, but it was like trying to wag his coccyx. Nothing happened.

206

Memories slipped into his mind like blood oozing through a bandage: the men; the woman; the hypodermic gun…slowly it all came back to him, and with it came a feeling of intense fear. Those people were using him for something, something at which he could not even guess.

He wanted to be home, with Martha…Martha! Surely she would alert the police, surely they would find him here?

Suddenly a voice came. It was a strange unnatural voice that had a quality, some form of unnatural timbre, that a voice had never before possessed.

'Johannison, can you hear me? If you can, don't try to speak; just think your reply.'

Johannison did not react for some time, so perplexed was he by this strange situation, but finally, he concentrated on thinking a coherent reply. To his further puzzlement, the voice returned.

'Good, good. Now I want you to relax, Johannison; nothing can hurt you now so bear with me for a little while, for I am going to treat you to an update on current affairs.

'Two years ago in the Guangzhou Centre For Advanced Studies a certain physicist concluded his research into what we term in the West: *Null Spacetime*. I won't bore you with the details, but Null Spacetime can be produced in the lab by juggling with the famous Hartmann Micro/Macrocosm Hypothesis, and its chief glory is that it permits acceleration of matter far beyond the accepted value of c. To put it in vulgar parlance, the Chinese now have what the fantasy writers have long termed a "faster-than-light drive."

'We believe that they now have a colony on the second planet of the nearby star Tau Ceti and possibly on one in the Beta Hydri system as well.

'The remnants of what used to be called the Western Democracies do not have this drive, nor is it likely to possess it in the significant future since the leader of the Chinese team was one of those men of genius who occur once in a lifetime. And we believe he has since been executed to prevent any possibility of defection.' The voice paused. 'Do you see what this means, Johannison?'

He did not reply. Little of the speech had been absorbed, but he had at least established the speaker's identity. It was the bald man, the one who had held out such glowing promises of immortality.

Finally, he asked, 'Where does immortality fit into all this?'

'In a moment, Mr Johannison, but as you did not answer my question, I will answer it for you.

'It means that the Chinese have the means of obtaining impregnable strongholds where they can mine, farm, experiment, *breed* until our feeble democracies are dust specks beside the most powerful tyrant in history. Do you understand this?'

'Yes.'

'Good. But I have another side of the coin to show you. For some decades, work has been going on in the United States into what we term "Paraphysics." Of late, it has received tremendous support from the Government and funding in the form of millions of your tax dollars. I'm sorry—did I say "millions"?—I meant billions of dollars. These dollars have been sunk into this research, with as yet little to show for them. But a few results have indeed emerged lately, and one of them appears to suggest that the human mind is capable of—ah—"spatial distortion." But only under very unusual conditions. However, when it does happen it's as if the mind wants to go somewhere, and instead of letting the body take it there, IT takes the body. The paraphysicists, of which you have no doubt guessed I am one, believe that given time we can develop, using no vastly energy-demanding machines, an—ah—star drive more efficient than that of the Chinese.

'But we haven't got time. We need to compress the research work of millennia into a few centuries, and for this we require a mind for unlimited study. A potentially immortal mind.

'But it goes deeper than that. We also require a mind which has its paraphysical powers closer to the surface, so to speak. We have found that people who dabble in, or at least show a great interest in, psychic phenomena, have this type of mind. After much study of you at your seances, we have selected you.'

Fear was now surging through Johannison, but he desperately strove to keep control.

'But why this rigmarole about immortality, the brochure, the advertising?'

'We could have just asked you to volunteer, but as the experiment is somewhat demanding, it is unlikely that you would have acquiesced. We could have just kidnapped you, but the Chinese are as aware of our activities as we are of theirs and would have assassinated you to keep you out of our hands. The "Bean Canning" subterfuge is just one of the ways we attempt to keep ourselves below their radar. Madame O'Hara, for instance, is a Sinoagent, and we believe Martha may be one as well. It is not likely you would have lived much longer if we had not "harvested" you. A fool-advertising gimmick that only a fool would take seriously and the fool who answered it would, and did, pass right under their noses.'

There was a long silence. It seemed that aeons passed away.

'And so here we are. We, and my successors, will study you for many centuries; and after us will come the other schools of the new psychology which will be built upon our research. Whether you will still be sane by then is an open question, and we are genuinely sorry that this has had to be done. And, of course, we are a branch of the Government, so no police or agents will ever release you, but then you will not be the first martyr to give his all for his country.'

'Wait! Wait!' Johannison screamed soundlessly, 'What do you mean centuries? I'll be dead!'

'No, you will not,' the unemotional voice continued, 'We are men and women of our word. You have asked for immortality, and you have it. Of course, immortality is a very hard thing to obtain. Your body picks up poisons from the air you breathe, from the water you drink. Even food is a slow poison from oxidative stress. Every movement of your muscles generates free radicals that strain your resources; every breath of wind tears at

209

you with pollutants. Cholesterol accumulates, neurons die, mutations combine, your heart deteriorates; there are cancers and many, many other forms of degeneration. Even your own cells contain radioactive atoms that weaken you from within, while gamma and cosmic radiations from without penetrate your innermost tissues. So we have done the only thing that could give a potential immortality, at the very least.

'We have stripped your brain from your body and placed it in a tank of nutrient fluid—the large sphere that you may have seen. It will shield you from any environmental danger; any form of radiation. All poisons that you generate will be immediately sucked harmlessly into the solution, and your nutrients will diffuse through your cell walls. The fluid will slow down neuron death to an infinitesimal rate.' The voice paused as if searching to find the next words. 'Of course, this is necessary for the survival of your country and...'

But Johannison was no longer listening. To his surprise, the first wave of horror had already passed, and he was thinking—hard!

There had to be a way out—there just had to be!

Maybe it would take him centuries, but perhaps—just perhaps—there were powers of an unfettered mind that they had not yet imagined.

One day his mind would take him somewhere; somewhere beyond their reach or that of the Chinese they feared so much.

A great calmness came over the brain that floated in its lightless tank.

He would find it: he had plenty of time.

After all, there would be no end to tomorrow.

DISAPPEARING ACT

The room was hot and drugarette smoke hung in bluish wraiths in the air. The representatives of the multinational companies sipped their iced drinks between drags on their spliffs and studied Burrows as he opened the cabinet; most of them with expressions of bored indifference.

'I don't claim this is magic, gentlemen,' he said with a confident smile, 'I can't even claim I discovered the phenomenon through late nights at the lab, poring over sheets of complex mathematics. It was an accident pure and simple, but occasionally that's how things happen in science: look at the discovery of the microwave background or finding penicillin. Sometimes it's just one guy being in the right place at the right time—and this time I was that guy.'

The expressions of the people in his audience did not change; one or two glanced at their watches. Burrows' satisfied smile did not waver: he was sure of his spiel, confident in his performance.

'I'd been working on generating a stable electromagnetic shield; one that occupied a precise location in space and thus could form a barrier against energetic particles. I'd opened the door to the generator and was holding a coffee mug, and as I bent to look inside, I fumbled and my mug fell into it. Fortunately, I'd drunk most of the coffee!' He looked back at the assembled business people at this point; some of them took the hint and smiled; weakly.

Here's the money shot, Burrows thought, scanning the audience so he could see every detail of their coming reaction.

'And the mug just vanished. Vanished before my eyes. No puff of smoke. Just vanished.'

There was a slight ripple of laughter from some of the visitors; the kind of laughter that people might make when not quite sure if the speaker intended to be funny. Most just sat stony-faced. Burrows was not worried; he'd soon make them sit up and beg.

He turned back to the two and a half metre structure behind him. It was slightly longer than it was tall and was a dull matte grey as if it were made of low-grade steel.

Which it was not.

He slapped the cabinet with a sweaty palm which left the misty mark of his hand on its smooth surface for a few moments.

'This cabinet, ladies and gentlemen, will remove any object placed in it.'

Back to the assembled high-fliers.

Nothing.

He smiled tolerantly.

'Do any of you have some small object that you do not mind losing if I place it in the cabinet?'

The attendees looked around at each other for a few seconds, clearly not wanting to be the first to get involved in this charade. Eventually, an extremely smartly dressed woman straightened her long legs and came towards him.

'Here,' she said, giving Burrows the same stare as she would have given to a hobo begging for a handout, 'The Wall Street Journal is particularly inane today. You're welcome to it.'

Burrows took the paper and had started giving his thanks when she abruptly turned her back and returned to her seat.

He gave a slight shrug and placed the item in the cabinet. After a few more minutes, a pen had joined it, along with a withered rose and an empty drugarette packet. He had to hand an expensive watch back to its owner, explaining that it was far too valuable to lose; all the time thinking: *It probably isn't that valuable to the likes of you, is it?*

Then he addressed the meeting again.

'The new versions only operate when the door is closed, but as you can see, this cabinet has one that is completely transparent, so there can be no doubt as to what is happening. I wouldn't dare to waste the time of such important people like yourselves with cheap fairground tricks, I assure you.'

The stares he received indicated to him that he had not

212

convinced them.

Very well.

'Watch the inside of the cabinet very carefully,' he finally said and closed the door. There was a soft metallic click as the door met the door-surround.

Instantly there was a swirling purplish glow inside the structure, and the objects inside seemed to flicker for an instant.

And then they were gone.

There was a susurration of reluctant surprise from some of the attendees.

Burrows looked at them, and his face bore an expression that indicated that he was now completely in control; if they didn't believe him at this precise moment—they soon would.

But a stern-faced man at the front met his gaze and said, 'An amusing little trick. At least you didn't charge an entrance fee. But I've seen a lot better. I'll ask my secretary to send you my bill for a wasted journey.'

Burrows grinned. They didn't all know it yet, but he had them now.

'It's no trick, sir. You can X-Ray the cabinet, take it apart, look for hidden compartments, holes in the floor, tricks with mirrors. You'll find none. It makes things disappear—plain and simple.'

'Well, I'm going to disappear,' the man replied and stood up. He glanced around, obviously expecting that others would be joining him, but everyone else remained seated.

Burrows saw him hesitate for a moment but, unable to lose face, he gave his goodbyes and left.

Burrows addressed the meeting again.

'The potential of my invention is vast. Think of all the things we have in the world that we'd be better off without. Take simple litter in the streets. Gone. No more landfills.

'Think of all the plastic pollution in the seas. Gone.

'The company that licences my invention will be the nearest thing to a money tree this world has ever seen. Oh, you can walk out now if you want, but you'll be kicking yourselves for the rest of your lives. Your unemployed lives, that is, after your CEOs have fired you.'

A few of the delegates stood up, but instead of walking out, came to examine the cabinet.

Eventually, all of them were. Burrows noticed one individual who seemed to be on the point of climbing into the device. He took in the man's appearance: lanky, bespectacled, and with a sparse growth of white whiskers that he presumably regarded as a beard and identified him as Stepford: one of his off-the-shelf tame scientists. He wagged a finger at him and Stepford moved away.

Soon Burrows found himself in conversation with a Korean magnate who drew him to a corner of the room while the others were still clustered around the device.

'We'll test one, Burrows, and I mean test it. But if we find it's not a trick, you'll be a very rich man.'

'It's not a trick. You can have this very machine as I've got far better ones in the pipeline. But when you're testing it, give it an hourly rest period or it'll break down. And make sure no-one's inside when you close the door because they won't be coming back.'

The magnate gave a nod of understanding, but there was something in his expression that chilled Burrows, especially when he said: 'Precisely. That's what we're hoping.'

***

And, of course, it was no trick.

Burrows licensed his invention and became the very rich man that the magnate had prophesied.

It was not entirely clear what was the full range of uses that his company had put the cabinets to; there were rumours that certain people who were no longer to be seen in the public life of various countries had been given the opportunity to study a Disposal Cabinet (as they came to be known) from the inside after the door had closed—but nothing was ever proved.

214

One very important use of the Disposal Cabinets was finally solving the problem of nuclear waste. For decades, fission reactors had been producing large quantities of waste that were both toxic and violently radioactive. As the climate change disasters had accelerated, nations had been forced to return to using that form of atomic power. Wind and solar had proved insufficient to maintain an industrial society and fusion power remained a perpetually retreating pipe-dream.

So it was back to fission power and back to the huge amounts of waste that no-one knew what to do with.

Except now they did.

Burrows easily managed to scale up the Disposal Cabinets so that they could handle tonnes of the dreadful stuff, and their deadly radiation did not affect their working in the slightest. Soon every country in the world had their reactors and the associated Disposal Cabinets.

Atomic waste went in, spitting gamma rays and charged particles.

And nothing came out.

The world was saved.

**

Burrows walked through the great cathedral-like building where the Disposal Cabinets were produced in an endless stream to be sent all over the world; each one depositing a large sum of money into his bank account before it waved goodbye.

But now the building was silent: this production line was being stripped down in readiness for an upgrade to increase production. It seemed odd to be in this place and not have the ears assailed by the endless clanking, whirrings and hummings of the busy machines.

But there was a sound; a very quiet sound.

It was a man muttering to himself.

Burrows rounded the shoulder of a bulky machine and saw Stepford standing in front of an open Disposal Cabinet. He was wearing some kind of backpack from which a power lead descended into a long hand-held device which Stepford was moving around just inside the cabinet, touching the walls at regular intervals. From time to time, he looked down at a dial on the top of this probe and, each time, he muttered something which Burrows could not catch at his distance.

Finally overcoming his surprise, he strode up to the other and tapped him on the shoulder. Stepford started; obviously he had been too engrossed to realise he was not alone.

'What exactly are you doing?' Burrows snapped, 'This facility is off-limits at the moment while the upgrade is being prepared.'

Stepford turned and looked down at his superior. 'Burrows, have you ever wondered where these things go?'

'Yes, but it's impossible to find out. It's some kind of quantum tunnelling, but I'm sure you're aware it is impossible to determine all the parameters in a single measurement without causing the collapse of the wavefunction.'

'I am indeed,' Stepford replied coolly, 'I have written several papers suggesting solutions to various problems raised by that situation. But I have a theory which would account for the properties of this device.'

'I too have various theories,' Burrows said, his hackles rising, 'You may have forgotten that it was I who invented the Disposal Cabinet.'

'A serendipitous invention, I believe. And just what are these theories?'

Against his will, Burrows found himself drawn into a discussion with Stepford, instead of disciplining him.

'Well, it seems to me that there must be some kind of spatial warp which sends the object to a different location. I suspect it must be a very long way away; otherwise, we'd have seen some sign of them. Maybe another galaxy.'

Stepford turned away and looked into the shining interior of the cabinet. 'No, it's not that at all. The energies required would be too great. It's not that at all.'

216

Burrows was suddenly angry. 'I hope you're not trying to belittle my work on this thing! I am regarded all around the world as one of humanity's greatest benefactors. There's a statue of me in Pyongyang that's twenty metres tall! Twenty metres!'

Stepford did not reply directly and seemed to be talking to himself as he said, 'One more measurement, and I'll have it. Just one more.'

And then, to Burrows' horror, he stepped up into the cabinet and began running the tip of his probe along the walls and ceiling.

'Get out, you idiot!' Burrows yelled, 'I don't want your greasy fingers all over that machine! That one's going to Saudi!'

Stepford ignored him and continued his measurements, regularly looking down at the numbers that danced on the display of his machine.

Now incandescent with fury, Burrows jumped inside and seized the other's nearer arm. Stepford staggered slightly under the intrusion, and the tip of his probe was crushed against the wall, snapping off its thin point.

There was a bright blue flash and a sudden throb of activated machinery.

Burrows spun around in time to see the door closing.

There was a shimmering purplish glow.

***

Burrows groaned and opened his eyes.

He slowly rose to his feet, looking anxiously around.

He appeared to be standing in a vast grey desert, or maybe some arid plain, given that he had found the ground to be a hard, impenetrable solid.

There were no apparent features, except in one direction he could see that a slice of the land had split open and a jagged slab had been thrust up. Beyond that there seemed to be a huge mountainous wall, but it was lost in grey obscurity due to distance, and he could not quite understand what he was seeing.

217

He heard a nearby noise and looked down to see Stepford struggling to his feet.

The scientist had a strange expression; it seemed to be satisfaction.

He pulled him upright, snarling, 'Look what you've done, you moron! We're in another galaxy by the look of it! We'll never get back!'

Stepford did not look too alarmed and, extricating himself from Burrows' grip, he looked around, taking in the drab, featureless landscape.

'Interesting, very interesting,' he said, apparently to himself as he adjusted his spectacles, 'It looks like I was right.'

Burrows found himself pleading. 'Look, if you know where we are, perhaps you can think of a way back. Can you!'

Stepford was looking over his superior's shoulder.

'Let's walk that way for a while. I think I need one more little piece of evidence.'

Burrows stared at him for a moment and then fell in behind the scientist, who had walked off without waiting for a response.

They walked for perhaps twenty minutes, and then Burrows became aware that there was something odd about the ground in front of them. Stepford had marched on ahead, and it took a few seconds to catch up with him. He grabbed an arm.

'Wait, damn you, wait! I...'

Stepford turned. 'I dislike people who don't finish their sentences.'

Burrows pulled Stepford's arm and pointed at the slab that some unknown force had thrust up. 'I thought I saw something move behind that piece of ground.'

Stepford glanced disinterestedly in the direction indicated.

'I doubt it. There's not likely to be life here.'

'What, on an alien planet? How can you possibly know?'

'This is not an alien planet. Walk a little further and I'll show you.'

Despairingly Burrows followed and then suddenly stopped, recoiling.

218

They were on the edge of a cliff—but what a cliff!

The cliff edge was an almost perfect right angle, and it fell away, revealing a vast chasm whose bottom was clothed in impenetrable darkness. The cliff was gigantic, titanic, mind-rendingly unimaginable.

Burrows backed away from it like a frightened beast, his eyes wide and staring.

'That cliff,' he managed to whisper, although his mouth was sandpaper dry, 'it must be twenty miles high!'

'No,' Stepford reproved; gently, understandingly, 'only a few centimetres.'

'What!'

Stepford turned to stare down at Burrows.

'We're not standing on the edge of a tremendous cliff but the edge of the cabinet. This grey desert is the floor. Your machine doesn't send things anywhere. They stay right where they're put. It shrinks them to microscopic size.'

'What—impossible! You can't shrink people down like that and keep them as functioning human beings!'

'Not by throwing away matter, no,' Stepford said, and there was a hint of puzzlement in his voice, 'somehow it must miniaturise the atoms themselves. I wonder how.'

Burrows was about to utter another objection when his peripheral vision caught a movement.

He turned and, in amazement, saw something come from behind the upthrust slab.

It was unearthly and shapeless, with quivering vacuoles in its substance and with cilia that formed a vibrating collar about its edge.

'Run!' screamed Burrows, and the two men began to flee before the advancing monstrosity. But it was strangely difficult to move; it was as if the air was thicker than normal.

'You're wrong, you bastard!' Burrows panted, 'that creature is not from this earth!'

'I don't understand,' Stepford said, 'my calculations must have been right! I…'

But there was no more time to speculate.

The creature had caught up with them, and with a gentle sucking noise, the bacterium absorbed them through its cell wall.

DATE OF EXPIRATION

The ship, a two-kilometre bluish cube, materialised not far above the UN Building in Greater New York on that sunny afternoon late in the hectic year of 2047. A spacetime warp (although none of the astounded spectators was able to identify it as such) shot out like an unrolling chameleon tongue to terminate in phosphorescent mystery in one of the decaying streets which surrounded the great monolith. Delegates turned their heads in horrified bewilderment; generals reached for their personal radiophones in order to put NorthAm forces onto High Alert; cabbies darted back into their hover-taxis, and the hitherto somewhat bored tourists gulped in goldfish fashion (or turned and ran—depending on their assessment of the situation).

A minute passed, maybe two; perhaps three: no-one was counting; and then down that shimmering ramp of kaleidoscopic light came two entities; not quite walking; not quite gliding or crawling, but some unpleasant amalgamation of all three. They reached the end of their bizarre ramp and "flowed" off onto the chipped tarmac of the senescent street, becoming somehow suddenly more clearly defined and distinct than they had been on their first appearance. Cabman Art J. Schwartz (married; two kids; knocking off one of the waitresses at the local Drug-AX speakeasy) was the person closest to the two creatures when they left the ramp and thus was humanity's first member to get a close-up view of these new-style tourists—not that he wanted to; he was too terrified to move.

They were over two metres tall and covered in rainbow-coloured scales. They stood on two thick legs, possessed both a pair of pincered arms and a pair of constantly writhing tentacles; the whole unpleasant structure being topped by a pear-shaped, three-eyed head. The nearer creature's trinocular gaze bored into Art, who was wondering if God was still interested in saving his soul after all these years of boozing, drugging and fornicating, and then a thin, dry prairie-wind of a voice told him: 'We have come for payment.'

'Payment?' croaked Art, in a voice several octaves higher than normal.

That gaze seemed to become even more penetrant, demanding.

'Yes. Your payment of oxygen—all the oxygen in your atmosphere.'

Art was never sure later whether it was at this point that he had started running; all that he could remember was that he came to his senses two city blocks away.

***

'They can't do this!' the Vice-President of the North American Federation gasped weakly, 'How the hell could they take away Christ-knows how many gazillion tonnes of oxygen from the air?'

Zimmerman was his scientific adviser, a fat, balding, bespectacled gentleman with a taste for garish sweatshirts. He stopped scratching at a pimple on one of the folds of fat that comprised his neck and replied. 'It's actually about 1.2 trillion tonnes, I believe. And yes—they can do it. They've given us the details of how they plan to take it. It all depends upon the paramagnetic properties of the Oh-Two molecule, and you just need a magnetic field flux of several quadrillion teslas...'

The Vice-President looked harassed.

'OK, OK. I believe you, but stick to English in future—now what's all this crap about payment? Payment for what, for Chrissake?'

'It seems.' Zimmerman began, picking his words with great care, 'that this race first visited Earth some two hundred thousand years ago when our ancestors were still chasing mammoths and hitting each other on the heads with clubs, and made an—uhh—business deal.'

The Vice-President made a strangulated sound.

'The deal,' continued Zimmerman hurriedly, 'was that these

222

creatures would give those cavemen the ability to develop a technological civilisation in return for all the oxygen in our atmosphere; the payment to be collected at a much later date, which—which unfortunately for us—turns out to be now.'

'But this—this "contract"—can't possibly be valid—it just can't be!'

'They seem to think so.'

The Vice-President put his hands on either side of his face and pushed the loose flesh slowly up until his eyes were mere slits of ash-grey.

'Then humanity is doomed; we'll all perish. Suffocated.'

'Not necessarily,' Zimmerman said, with that lack of emotion which the Vice-President hated so much. 'They can give us a reduction process by which we can liberate oxygen from the planet's silicate crust while they're making away with the original supply.'

The Vice-President shook his head. 'I don't believe it; it sounds too pat.'

'Well,' Zimmerman said, 'I made a holorecording of their interview with me in which they outlined the finer points of the situation—as they see it.'

He motioned to a man at the rear of the room, and the lights died abruptly; there was a slight humming noise, and then at the other end of the room, a moving hologram blossomed into full-colour life. It showed Zimmerman and one of the eldritch visitors. The Vice-President winced slightly.

Zimmerman's 3D duplicate was saying. 'Do you mean to say that our present civilisation, all our achievements, all our science are entirely due to your interference?'

A tentacle waved briefly like a lank of seaweed in an undersea surge.

'Of course. Such creatures as you could not possibly have reached this level of technology unaided; your nervous systems are far too primitive.'

'Yes, yes.' Zimmerman's avatar was pressing a mauve handkerchief to its shiny brow. 'But this business of a transaction: we are not bound by the—ahh—"deals" made by long-dead savages!'

'Of course you are.' The isosceles triangle of glowing eyes seemed to shine more brilliantly for a second. 'If your grandparents were to bestow a fortune on you, you would not question their right to present you with riches you have not earned, so why would you deny the right of your more distant progenitors to place this debt upon you?'

'But it's immoral! Damnit, it's immoral!'

The image of the alien debt-collector turned slightly as if to end the quibbling, its many-coloured scales flashing with a strange iridescence, but it turned back and spoke again.

'You speak like the poorly-trained ape that you are. Our morality is far beyond your understanding and is amenable to quantitative treatment. "Good" is what increases the quantity of pleasure in our species; "Evil" is that which decreases it. Obtaining your oxygen is pleasurable to our species; therefore it is good. Therefore we will take it.'

'But why do you need it?'

'The root-mean-square of atomic oxygen in our atmosphere is one-fifth of the escape velocity and thus is being lost to space. Two hundred thousand years ago the situation on our world was dangerous, now it is existential.'

'But this process you described of making oxygen from silicates—why don't you do that?'

'Our crust is non-silicate, being composed of the fluorides of aluminium and silicon. It contains no oxygen.'

'Oh. But why all this rigmarole about a legal transaction; why not just come and take it?'

The voice that answered would have been almost angry if it had been human, but as it was not, its tones merely sounded sharper.

'We are at present being monitored by one of the more powerful civilisations which lie nearer to the Galactic centre. It is merely temporary, but they have certain ideas about animal welfare which we must, temporarily, conform to.'

Zimmerman's image sighed. So did the real Zimmerman, and he motioned tiredly at the unseen cameraman, and the hologram vanished instantly to be replaced by the pale, sad, green walls of the Vice-President's private quarters.

There was a long, slow silence; a silence that hung like a thick invisible smoke that refused to dissipate; a silence that then seemed to cling to the men like cold treacle.

Zimmerman stared helplessly at the Vice-President; waiting for him to come up with some ingenious solution, some magic words which would dispel the danger; some brilliant escape from the trap.

The empty minutes passed, and the Vice-President remained like an Egyptian carving of a brooding minor god; motionless and seemingly lacking the promise of motion. Then he stirred.

Zimmerman leaned forward so that he would be able to hear every syllable of the magical solution.

'We will refuse to pay,' the Vice-President whispered.

***

The refusal was delivered the next day at the General Assembly of the UN.

The Debt Collectors stood like statues of beings from some obscene, pagan pantheon; only their restless tentacles showed life, twitching at irregular intervals, otherwise they were as immobile as monitor lizards under the noonday blaze.

The Secretary-General was exceedingly nervous. It was plain that he was having visions of death-rays incinerating him where he stood; or hordes of invading Hunter-Killer robots tearing him into bloody shreds. Nevertheless, he did not falter but pressed on with the declaration that could spell the doom of humanity. When he finished, silence fell with the weight of a landslide; every eye was fixed on the creatures.

'We have shown you how to make oxygen,' one said.

'You can find other worlds with our type of air,' the

Secretary-General replied, 'ones without intelligent life.'

'Oxygen-bearing planets depend on life to bring them into being,' the second said, 'and life is very rare.'

'But Earth is not unique,' the Secretary-General said, 'you yourselves are the proof of that.'

'The oxygen tension on our home is down to 100 mm,' the first said, 'By the time we find another world like yours, it may well have fallen below the minimum necessary to sustain life. By not honouring your contract you may well be condemning us to extinction.'

'We are not responsible for transactions made by ignorant savages,' the Secretary-General said with a convincing air of finality.

'Very well,' the second said, with equal finality, 'we will leave you.'

Their shapes blurred for an instant as if seen through a heat-haze, and then they were gone.

Passers-by reported that the weird cube ship disappeared at about the same time.

A pandemonium composed of equal amounts of joy and relief broke out in the chamber as if a threatening thundercloud had dissipated into a calm and beautiful blue sky.

***

The air-conditioning sucked away the blue wreaths of drugarette smoke in an unending susurration.

Through the aromatic fog, strip lights gleamed on balding heads, while the drugarette butts waxed and waned like tiny, bloody moons.

The President was old, but he felt older than his seventy-seven years; responsibility weighed on him with the mass of a neutron star.

'There's no reply then?' he snapped.

'None, sir,' a harassed senator answered, 'the entire West Coast has gone silent. Internet, radio, TV, laser link—all silent.

Every satellite has gone off the air. There's not a plane in the sky.'

The President turned slowly, as if the slightest motion caused him pain. Another senator stirred uneasily under his bloodshot gaze.

'All the fusion reactors have gone off-line,' the second senator eventually said, 'the last station on Baffin Island ceased power at 13:00 hours. The entire Grid is going down.'

The President nodded briefly, as if he had been expecting that.

'OK, OK,' he said, in a voice that was hardly above whisper, 'Get back to your homes while the ground vehicles still work.'

The gloomy room slowly emptied until only the President and his Second-in-Command were left. In the silence that ensued only the faint whine of the air-conditioning unit was audible.

And then it stopped.

'Well,' the President said, 'They were telling the truth, and they obviously believe that a deal's a deal.'

'What in God's name is going on?' the Vice-President demanded in what he had intended to be a firm voice.

The Leader of the North American Federation—the most powerful man in the world—smiled grimly in the smoky gloom.

'Don't you get it? We ratted on the deal. It's like any kind of financial contract. If you don't pay your dues, the goods are confiscated.'

The Vice-President ground his last drugarette into an ashtray.

'You mean—God, you mean our civilisation; the entire modern world! But how can they do it?—How!'

The President shrugged.

'Does the dog know where the light goes when his master flips a switch in the kitchen? I don't know how they're doing it—but doing it, they are!'

'But where will it stop, how far will it go?' the Vice-President said slowly, fearfully.

'Obviously, they will return us to where our ancestors were

227

when they accepted the contract.'

The Vice-President stiffened. 'You mean—back to the caves?'

'Exactly.' The President stood up and turned his face away from the other man. 'MRI scanners, genetic stabilisers, cars, trains, elevators, light, heat; one by one, they'll all fail. The newest, most complex will go first. But they'll all fail. Then we'll start forgetting how things used to work. Eventually we'll forget how to use a plough; plant a seed.'

'But we'll all die—in our billions!' the other cried, in near hysteria.

'Not all of us,' the President reproved gently, 'some will survive. The hard ones, the ruthless ones, the born-survivors will pull through. Somewhere. Eventually.'

'But to what? Endless barbarity!'

'Perhaps,' mused the President, 'but after all, we were shown the way, once; perhaps some memories will survive. Maybe we can do the long climb back up by ourselves this time. Perhaps.'

There was another long silence. The air in the room became oppressive with the failure of the air-conditioning.

When the pallid light suddenly snapped off, the two weary men slowly rose to their feet. The President reached out in the semi-darkness and grasped the other's shoulder.

'Come on,' he said, 'let's go outside. Somehow we've got to turn our over-civilised minds to the task of rediscovering how to do things.'

'Like what?'

The President's smile was hardly visible in the hot gloom.

'Like how to make an axe out of flint.'

ANGEL AND DEMON

Ever since Kowalski's guerrillas had taken over the village, we knew we were living on borrowed time.

Every week we would assemble in what used to be our village hall and go through the sadistic ritual that he enjoyed so much. One by one, each of us would draw a card from the dog-eared pack that he placed before us. Each person would, with drawn features, turn the card over and stare at it, knowing that what he saw would mean life or death. Any standard card would mean another wretched few weeks of life, but one card ensured certain doom.

In typical savagery, Kowalski had chosen the Joker as the emissary of death. If when you turned over the greasy, dog-eared card, you were confronted by the smiling face of that purveyor of innocent fun you knew that you probably had only seven days to live.

You were forced to wear that torn and tattered purple T-Shirt which many unfortunate villagers had worn before you and were thus marked for execution by Kowalski's thugs.

You had only one chance of life: on the sixth day, the one before your execution, you had to present Kowalski and his goons with a gift of some kind. If he approved of it, you could remove the tattered T-Shirt and receive the gift of another seven days of miserable existence.

Many villagers had tried to escape the firing squads by offering ever more elaborate gifts, but only one had actually been permitted to remove that dread item of clothing. And of course, a few weeks later he had turned over the Joker again and had not escaped the second time.

There were not many of us left in the village now; a few had tried to escape across the marshes but had always been caught and had been shot on the spot. So, no-one else tried and with bitter resignation they awaited their fate.

I'm not entirely sure why the guerrilla band hated us so

much. They were all from the slums and disease-ridden alleys of the big cities and had nothing but contempt for us simple peasants. They treated us as if we were just some kind of pitiful apes—not human at all, and every one of them despised our country-ways and knowledge. 'There's only one thing a man needs to know,' Kowalski had said to me once as he rammed the muzzle of a submachine gun into my belly, 'and that's how to handle one of these!'

And so, my time was nearly up. I had taken my gift late on the previous evening of the penultimate day of my period of freedom. It had been a gift of our simple foodstuffs: some wormy apples; some emaciated pears; some mushrooms; some eggs and a few thin, pale slices of bacon. 'For your breakfast,' I had said to the bored-looking killers that made up Kowalski's band of hired guns. One had looked at one of the apples, thrown it in my face and kicked me out. I could hear them bellowing with laughter as I limped away.

And now was the last day: the day that would almost certainly bring my execution.

I stood before the desk, which still bore the basket that I had used to deliver my gifts. I could see there was half an apple and one thin mushroom left inside it.

I looked Kowalski in the eye, wondering if I should speak first. He stared back.

Finally, I plucked up courage and asked: 'Did you enjoy my gifts, sir?'

He stared silently for a while and then said: 'It was filthy muck not fit for pigs.'

'But you did eat it, sir?' I asked in a pleading voice.

'Oh yes, we all ate it,' he rasped, 'Seeing as there's little else in this backward crap hole.'

'And?' I said, looking around at my would-be executioners, 'Do I ...?'

'Live?' Kowalski snapped, and shared amused glances with his gang, 'after giving us that pile of manure! What do you think!'

My shoulders slumped for a moment, but then I

straightened myself, and looked around the room at his gang of murderers.

'I had hoped that you would enjoy my simple offerings, but it seems that some of you may have upset stomachs. A few of your gallant men look a little queasy.'

And that was true: quite a few of the men were looking distinctly unwell and were shuffling awkwardly as if they wanted to leave the room.

Kowalski's grin disappeared instantly, and he stared ferociously at me. 'How do you know that?'

I returned his stare, this time my spine was straight and my gaze firm.

'And how do you feel, sir? Is your stomach churning, is your brow slick with sweat? No need to answer, my lord, I can see it is from here. I think you may be ill, sir.'

Kowalski was now thoroughly alert. 'What have you done?' he roared.

I smiled. 'You mocked our country ways, sir, but if you had known a bit more of the ways of nature instead of bullets and guns, you would have been able to distinguish between the common Field Mushroom and the Destroying Angel. They are easily confused, but the latter is, of course, invariably fatal. I believe all of you have about three hours to live. The last hour is quite painful, I regret to inform you.'

I don't quite know how I got out of the village hall; perhaps everyone was too stunned to react quickly.

I will head for the marshes and try to get away from that murderous band, but it is unlikely that I will make it. They know as well as I which are the only safe ways across those treacherous bogs.

But my life is not that important.

Kowalski and his thugs may be demons in human form, but I have achieved justice: I have visited the Destroying Angel upon them.

RETAIL PURSUIT

John stared angrily at the shopkeeper. His arms were tied behind his back, and he tried the bonds once again and felt them slightly loosen. The shopkeeper was clearly not that adept at tying knots. Still, it was too soon to make his move. He'd have to wait for the moment.

Ignoring the other man's threats, which he'd heard several times already, he looked around at the shop again.

All the shelves were overflowing with unsold items: toy trains, plastic machine guns, cowboy outfits, construction kits for building a plastic miniature of a WWII bomber, partly assembled doll's houses…It just went on and on. And in the corner was one of those huge teddy-bears; the kind that is almost the size of an adult human.

John didn't like that teddy-bear: there was something about its expression, an expression a simple toy just shouldn't have…

The shopkeeper was speaking again. 'Now, be reasonable sir. We've all got to make a living. Just buy something and I'll let you go.'

John looked up at the man: he was well past middle-age, corpulent and seemed permanently out of breath. Every sentence ended in a wheeze.

If it came to violence, John was sure he'd come out on top.

'Look,' the man said, 'I'll tell you again: ever since the pandemic, it's the law—if you walk into a shop you must buy something before you leave. I'm within my rights to keep you here until you do.'

'And, I'll tell you again,' John replied, giving the string around his wrists another twist, 'I only came in here to ask the way to the bus stop. This is a toy shop. I don't want any toys. I don't need any toys. I'm thirty seven, and a well-respected Shakespearian scholar, specialising in the tragedies—I haven't played with toys for over eighteen months.' And then he added the final rebuff, 'And I don't have any grandchildren. And even if I did, they'd be too intelligent to be interested in the kind of tat you have in this place!'

That hurt: John could see that he had hit home.

'So that's the way you want to play it,' the shopkeeper said, in a tone which revealed barely-suppressed anger, 'well, we'll see about that. Modern toys have changed a bit since the pandemic. You obviously don't know that. Here, try this.' And he picked a large doll off the shelf and held it in front of John's face.

John looked at the doll. And to his horrified surprise, the doll's head rotated so it was face on to him and its eyelids flickered open, revealing china-blue eyes.

'Hello, mister,' the doll said, 'I like you. Are you going to buy me?'

John was too shocked to speak for a minute or two and then he said, 'No, I'm not.'

The doll's face contorted and a little hand struck him across the face. 'Bad man!' the doll shrieked.

The shop keeper replaced the doll and looked at John.

'Changed your mind yet?' he asked, with a note of satisfaction in his voice.

'No,' John said, 'I do not want to buy a toy. I don't agree with this crazy law. I do not want a toy. I will not buy a toy, do you hear me!'

The man disappeared behind a block of shelves and came back with a plastic model of a Tyrannosaurus rex. It was about 4 feet high and seemed quite heavy by the way he was carrying it.

He dumped it in John's lap and John stared at it. It's head was unpleasantly realistic and it had an open mouth, revealing dagger-like teeth. So he was not surprised when its eyes opened and its jaws moved. 'Hello human,' it said, in a hissing, snake-like voice, 'do you want to buy me?'

John found the creature's reptilian gaze distinctly alarming but he held to his principles.

'No,' he said firmly, 'I do not want to buy you.'

The T. rex bent forward and bit him on the shoulder. It was quite painful.

233

The shopkeeper took it off John's lap and shook his head. 'People like you,' he said, 'just free-loaders. Not doing their bit to help the country get back on its feet. Well, there's a way of dealing with your sort of parasite.'

He placed the plastic dinosaur on the table next to John and disappeared into the back of the shop. John could hear him rummaging around back there.

It's now or never! John thought.

He gave his bound hands another twist and felt the string slide down one hand. One more twist and he was free of the chair. He leapt to his feet.

Just in time: the shopkeeper reappeared and in his hands was what looked like a plastic battle-axe. At least, John hoped it was plastic.

John never found out: one kick sent the man and his weapon, real or otherwise, flying.

John spun around, triumphant.

To find the doorway blocked by the large teddy bear. The fluffy toy was not much smaller than John. Its eyelids rose, revealing bright red eyes; eyes that were almost demonic.

'Buy me,' it said, in what could only be described as a threatening growl, 'buy me.'

John had to act fast. Acting instinctively he reached for the plastic T. rex and flung it at the bear. As it hit the bear he heard the little dinosaur say, 'Buy me!'

Taking advantage of the bear's confusion, John smashed the door open and ran out onto the pavement.

But it was exit: pursued by a bear.

MRS LANCELOT'S REVENGE

Mrs Lancelot (or "Gwen" to her friends) looked up as she heard the heavy iron-studded door creak open. She put on her best "Where The Hell Have You Been?" expression as he shuffled in, trying to avoid her gaze. Well, he might succeed in avoiding her gaze, but that wasn't going to stop her.

'So where the Hell have you been, Lance?' she said, rising from her needlework and walking towards him.

He sat down heavily, looking flustered, and ran a hand over his sweaty brow.

'Oh, you know,' he said in a weak voice she could hardly hear, 'Holy Grail stuff again.'

'Holy Grail Stuff again,' she repeated, in somewhat mocking tones, 'Do you ever think about lending a hand around here?'

She walked back to the sink, demonstrating with a quick wave of the hand that it was overflowing with unwashed crockery, greasy pots and scummy pans. 'Are these supposed to clean themselves? Ever since you upset the house-elves, I've had to do all the dishwashing myself. A little bit of help now and then isn't much to ask, is it?'

Using a serving spoon, she banged a particularly large vessel that was full of vegetable peelings. Like everything else in the kitchen, including her, it was covered in a film of sticky grease that hid its underlying colour. Perhaps it had been silvery; perhaps not. 'Look at this—it should have been emptied days ago!'

He winced slightly at the accusatory voice from across the kitchen.

'It's not easy out there, Gwen,' he said, still avoiding her gaze. 'There are all sorts of dangers when one is out questing. There are manticores, mandrakes, gryphons, wyverns, basilisks, anthropophagi…'

She held up a plump hand, palm towards him. 'Dragons. Don't forget the dragons. There're always dragons .'

He looked relieved. Perhaps she was taking an interest in his work after all.

'Yes,' he said, finally daring to cast a glance in her direction, 'Dragons. Yes, of course; there were dragons, dragons everywhere one looked!'

'What colour were they?'

He looked confused. 'What colour? Is that important?'

'Just answer the question, Lance.'

'Well...' he said slowly, his forehead corrugating slightly as he thought back to the details of his latest quest. 'There were...' A long pause. 'There were ... black ones with long, sharp teeth. And purple ones with horns. And...and...'

'Any red ones?' she asked sweetly. She had now sat back on her rude but sturdy three-legged stool. It needed to be sturdy as it failed to fully encompass her ample bottom. 'Any red ones?'

Lancelot raised his head fully and stared at her as she sat opposite, a worrying smile playing on her lips. It looked a bit...sardonic. That meant there was danger.

But where?

Was this a trap?

'Red ones, hmm, red ones,' he said slowly as if weighing each word on his tongue before letting it free into the malodorous kitchen. 'Red ones...'

She raised a thick eyebrow. 'Yes, Lance?'

He thought rapidly, lowering his gaze and staring at his delicate, aristocratic hands.

Definitely a trap. But what was the right answer?

Oh, this was terrible. He'd rather fight the Three-Headed Giant of Eriador again then go through this kind of interrogation!

'Red ones,' he said, raising his head again. 'Yes. There were red ones. Terrible, terrible beasts. As tall as the tallest tower in Camelot; teeth like rapiers. And the fire they breathed out! You should...'

The plump palm had been raised again. He stopped. Obviously, he'd guessed wrong.

'How strange,' she said, in a voice which dripped honey. (Poisoned honey, that is.)

'The last time you came back, you told me that you'd driven all the red dragons out of Arthur's realm. Sent them packing to Ireland I believe were your exact words.'

He groaned inwardly. That was right! He had made that boast on his previous return to explain why he'd been away so long! By the sacred Table Round, he was getting forgetful in his old age!

But she hadn't finished. 'In fact, Sir Lancelot, I have it on good authority that you've been spending several days boozing at a disreputable tavern in Lyonnesse; that is why you've been away so long, isn't it?'

He stood up slowly, his head bowed. There was no longer any point in subterfuge. His ageing memory had tripped him up.

Only one thing to do now. Take it on the chin and help around the house until she forgave him; as she always did.

He crossed to her and held her tightly. He tried to kiss her, but she turned her head at the last moment.

'Well, Sir Lancelot,' she said in a voice as hard and sharp as Excalibur itself, 'I may forgive you eventually, but you have to prove yourself worthy.'

'Anything, my dearest heart.'

She removed herself from his grasp and indicated the overflowing sink and the utensils around it. 'Start by tidying this place up. And throw those vegetable peelings onto the midden— they're stinking the place out. But remember to bring the pot back—you're stupid enough to throw that away as well.'

He meekly obeyed.

One week of this and then I'll be free to go Questing again! were his thoughts as he picked up the pot which contained the vegetable peelings. It was surprisingly heavy.

As she watched him stagger out of the hut under the unusual weight of the pot, Mrs Lancelot allowed herself a small smile of triumph.

Poor Lance! She thought, if only he knew I'd been digging

in the garden last year and under a large turnip had found the Holy Grail itself; just where Joseph of Arimathea had buried it for safekeeping all those centuries ago!

While he'd been out fighting giants and witches, the Grail had been sitting in the kitchen all the time!

Should she tell him?

She thought about that long and hard.

Only after he'd been especially Good and Noble.

Well, she thought, *I won't be telling him for a long time!*

THE DYING VILLAGE

Richard Jones stared worriedly at Donato Toma. There was something wrong here. A creeping disquiet was beginning to stir deep in his mind.

Toma was still smiling.

'We are glad Signor Jones, that you have come to live here in Roccasicura. We are in urgent need of fresh blood here.'

Jones gave a weak smile.

'Thank you, Mr Toma. You have a very nice village. It's—it's …'

'Yes,' Toma inquired, leaning forward slightly.

'It's very…' Jones' thoughts swirled as he tried to think of a suitable compliment. 'It's very sunny,' he finally said, rather weakly.

Toma smiled. 'Si, you come from cold, grey Inglaterra, no? It always rains there, so I have heard. But the sun, you can have too much of it you know. It is bad for the skin.'

Jones grinned weakly. 'I suppose so, but we don't really have that problem in Macclesfield.'

An awkward silence fell. Jones finally broke it by asking 'What kind of job skills are you actually looking for, Mr Toma? Your advert just said that you need more people, new blood, but didn't mention any qualifications.'

Toma's expression saddened somewhat.

'We have a big problem, Mr Jones, a problem found throughout our beautiful region of Molise. We have sun, we have scenery, but fewer and fewer people. Soon Macchiagodena and Roccasicura will be empty of people. Only ghosts will live here, Mr Jones, and they don't enjoy our favourite ruby-red drink. We will be finished. That's why we need more people.'

'I understand that' Jones said with a touch of eagerness. At last this conversation was starting to make sense. 'We have exactly the same problem in the countryside up in Lancashire. People moving out of old areas. Looking for excitement.

Looking for the bright lights.'

Toma nodded. 'Si, we in Roccasicura like excitement but perhaps not so much the bright lights.'

Jones relaxed. This was going to be OK after all. If all they needed were people, he was quite prepared to lounge around the bars, quaffing the vino rosso that Toma had mentioned. But there was still the problem of his suitability for employment. What could he offer this dying village?

Then, at last he had it.

'I'm not very good with my hands, Mr Toma. But I did work in the library in Bolton. I'm very good at sorting books by the Dewey Decimal System. Do you have a library here?'

But Toma was no longer listening. He had crossed to the window and had parted some of the slats of the Venetian blinds. Over the soft hills of southern Italy the last rays of the sun had already winked out, leaving a clear sky of rapidly deepening blue.

'Belissima,' he said in a soft, breathy voice, apparently to the landscape itself.

'Mr Toma,' Jones said, experiencing the odd feeling that he was interrupting something, 'Did you hear what I said? About Bolton, I mean. What would you like me to do?'

Toma turned back to his visitor. There was now no illumination in the room, except that from the darkening sky.

'Do?' he enquired in a tone which held an odd mixture of puzzlement and amusement. 'Do? Why nothing. Except die of course.'

Jones' brow furrowed. 'Dye? But I don't have any experience of that. I'm not at all familiar with the textile industry.'

'Pardon, Mr Jones,' Toma said and Jones was alarmed to see that his smile had become quite wolfish. 'Your English language. She is such a difficult way of speaking. I said *die* not *dye*.

'Ah – here they are.'

He had turned to the door as he had uttered that last sentence, and gave a look of pleasure as it opened and three figures came in.

Jones leapt to his feet. The light was now poor in the room

240

but there was something odd about those three figures. They were smiling broadly but—but they appeared to have fangs!

'Mr Toma, I …' He turned to his interviewer and then stopped, unable to move.

Toma was there in the gathering gloom and was also smiling broadly. Being much closer to him, Jones had no doubt about his possession of a pair of very sharp-looking fangs.

'You see, Mr Jones,' Toma said with the hint of a throaty chuckle, 'we don't need engineers, or computer programmers, or financial advisers, or' and he gave a real chuckle 'librarians. I told you right at the beginning exactly what we need in Roccasicura. Fresh blood.'

Jones screamed.

But not for long.